LOST IN FRANCE

In the Sarthe region of France, a battered, disorientated young woman is left on the Dubuis family's doorstep, her identity a mystery — even to herself. Five years after being taken in by the Dubuis family, Marie-Anne has fallen in love with a local farmer, but officialdom threatens the security he offers. Meanwhile, in England, another woman has also found the man of her dreams and a new family. Both couples are planning for their futures when an old photograph sets off a ripple of events which will enmesh all four. Can they emerge from the tangled web of past tragedy to live happily?

GILLIAN OGILVIE

LOST IN FRANCE

Complete and Unabridged

ULVERSCROFT
Leicester

First published in Great Britain in 2006 by
Red'n'Ritten Limited
West Sussex

First Large Print Edition
published 2007
by arrangement with
Red'n'Ritten Limited
West Sussex

British Library CIP Data

Ogilvie, Gillian
    Lost in France.—Large print ed.—
    Ulverscroft large print series: romantic suspense
    1. Romantic suspense novels
    2. Large type books
    I. Title
    823.9'2 [F]

    ISBN 978–1–84782–024–2

Published by
F. A. Thorpe (Publishing)
Anstey, Leicestershire

Set by Words & Graphics Ltd.
Anstey, Leicestershire
Printed and bound in Great Britain by
T. J. International Ltd., Padstow, Cornwall

This book is printed on acid-free paper

With thanks
to Alick,
for his constant support
and belief in me over the years.

1

The woman stood inches from his car bumper, sodden hair plastered like seaweed across her face; soaked clothes dragged at her slumped body. He cursed, his hands gripping the steering wheel in frustration. He could neither drive over her to escape nor leave her to die in the savagery of the storm. She looked at him through curtains of rain. There was no light in her eyes. Films where zombies moved trance-like about the screen flashed through his mind. He was getting fanciful. This damned storm was to blame. With a further profanity he forced the door open against the wind, staggered round the bonnet, grasped her shoulders and bundled her into the passenger seat. In those few seconds his expensive suit was soaked.

After squelching back to his own side, he set off. This was a total disaster! If only he hadn't taken this wretched short cut he'd have been home free. There would have been no problem.

In the dashboard lights the woman's face was chalky-white. Spiky lashes lay fanned on pale cheeks. With the car's movement her head lolled on the back of the seat. How could he get rid of her? Ahead there was a fork in the road. He slowed the car and peered around. No signpost. He scrabbled on the floor under his unwelcome passenger's feet to find the roadmap he'd consulted earlier. The river was here. There was the fork. Or, in the dark, had he already passed that one and was *this* his fork? He turned left.

The road rose and twisted. Soon he had climbed out of the river valley and was totally lost. His powerful headlights illuminated only silvered shards of rain. Should he retrace his path? At that moment a light twinkled in the distance. He needed to ask directions, but not before he had dealt with the woman. There must be no awkward questions. What then? His unease grew as he studied her. The last thing he needed was a dead body on his hands. The obscuring, wind-tossed trees caused the light in the distance to flicker. Hedges on the narrow road were broken only by barred gates. The car crawled along as he sought his target. There! No! Yes! With only sidelights to guide him, he steered into an open yard. The glass fanlight above the door of a substantial building glowed softly. No other light showed. Silently as possible, he turned the vehicle. The roar of the wind and the drumming rain should deaden the engine's expensive purr.

With a grimace of discomfort he eased out of his seat and leaned into the weather. Awkwardly he half lifted the semi-conscious woman and lurched with her across the yard. He propped her against the door while he felt for the bell. In panic his fingers ran over the surface. No bellpush! No knocker! He rapped his knuckles on a wrought-iron pull set into the wall beside him. He yanked it down hard three times.

A clamour loud enough to wake anyone within kilometres rang out in the depths of the silent house. He propped the woman securely in the angle of the wall, and dived back into the car. With darkened headlights, the vehicle rolled quietly out of the yard. Light showed in the rear view mirror. Good, someone was home; they could deal with her. He retraced his tracks to the right road. The shocking weather was no alibi; he shouldn't have been in this part of the country. The powerful car regained the fork in the road and roared off into the night.

★   ★   ★

Monsieur L'Inspecteur Henri Mercier finished reading the file on his desk and patted it with satisfaction. What devastation it listed!

Lorries flung across roads like cardboard boxes, trees and roofs torn from their moorings. Three people had died on the roads and two in their own homes. The men of his new command, with the Fire Brigade, had worked round the clock. After seven difficult weeks, order had been restored.

As the waters receded, the carcasses of dead animals were buried and the bodies of two unfortunate women, swept away in the torrent, had been returned to their grieving families.

The third body had never been found. A shoe had been retrieved downstream from where a woman had entered the river, and a part of a torn skirt had been found tangled in a weir many kilometres away on the other side of the town. In six months or a year, some fisherman might make a grisly catch. A relative had identified the clothing; at this stage there was nothing more to be done. The commanding inspector, Antoine Grosmenil, had since retired and handed over to Henri, the new arrival, who was now in charge.

He made space on the shelf behind him to push in the fat file. A sheet of paper, stuck to the back of it, fell to the floor. He picked it up. On a routine Report Sheet were notes from the Gendarmerie in Maréchal les Deux Chapeaux, a village high in the hinterland of the Sarthe valley, about twenty kilometres from Sablé. A young woman, possibly the victim of an attack, had been dumped on a farm doorstep. There were no follow-up notes indicating further action. He snorted. The Report was dated in the previous month. No doubt this domestic mystery had been cleared up by his predecessor, but no conclusion was entered. He wiped away the sticky residue, which had attached the paper to the file, reached for the telephone and dialled.

'Allô?'

'Bonjour, Madame. Voici Henri Mercier, Inspector of Police at Sablé. Have I the honour to speak with Madame Dubuis?'

'I am Madame Dubuis, but perhaps you wish to speak with my mother-in-law?'

Henri didn't care which woman he spoke to as long as she could answer his questions. 'I have here a report concerning the arrival of a young woman at your farm.'

'Ah! Yes. My husband's mother made the report, sir. I will fetch her immediately.'

Before he could prevent it, the receiver was laid down. He heard footsteps, the slam of a door, then silence. Monsieur L'Inspecteur was not accustomed to fume at the end of an untended telephone.

At last he heard sounds of life returning.

'Allô? Who is this?'

5

The voice was full of authority. Henri's temptation to berate the speaker for wasting his time died instantly. Here was a force to be respected. 'Henri Mercier, Madame, Inspector of Police at Sablé.'

'How can we help you, M'sieur?'

'You reported the arrival of a young woman . . .'

'Mon Dieu! That was over a month ago!'

Henri found himself apologising. 'The storm, Madame — no communications — and I, Madame, was not then in command. I trust the matter is resolved?'

'But no! The poor child was ill. When she regained consciousness, it was weeks before her voice returned.'

Henri was unwilling to listen to a recital of medical details. 'I am sure, Madame, your care was much appreciated. But now she has recovered you will have made arrangements to restore her to her family, n'est-çe pas?'

'If, young man, you had the good manners not to interrupt, you would have learned that is impossible. The child has no memory.'

Henri's heart sank. He had now embroiled himself in a routine matter, more suitably dealt with by a junior officer. 'Madame Dubuis, I shall do myself the honour to visit you this afternoon.'

At fourteen thirty hours Henri's driver leapt from his seat and hurried around the official car, which stood before the farmhouse. He opened the rear door and Henri emerged: his immaculate uniform, with knife-sharp trouser creases and gleaming belt and buttons, proclaimed his high rank and authority. Courtyard gravel crunched beneath shining shoes; the effect was all he could have wished. He would teach this old woman to call him 'young man' in that tone of voice.

The front door opened. Framed in the aperture stood a figure of equal authority to his own. Dressed all in black, a double row of jet beads at her throat and pure white hair dressed high on her head, Madame Dubuis took in the glory of Monsieur L'Inspecteur. As two combatants their gazes locked. Some silent recognition passed between them before Madame Dubuis stepped back and graciously invited Henri to enter.

M'sieur L'Inspecteur politely declined the offered refreshment. 'Merci, Madame, but we are here on business. We must solve the problem of this young person.'

'As to that, it is no problem. She is a good little thing and gains strength rapidly. I hoped she would tell us her name and how we could help her, but, alas, there is no recollection, none whatsoever.'

Henri was sceptical. He had questioned the officer who recorded the report. The young woman had arrived at the height of the storm. It was impossible she could have walked far. His own theory was a tiff with the boyfriend, which got out of hand. She either jumped out of the car and strode off in a temper, or he pushed her out meaning only to cool her down. No doubt, on his return to the spot, he had been horrified to find her gone. Now, having caused so much fuss, they were both too frightened to tell the truth; but he would get it out of her.

'If I might interview the young person?'

'Certainly. This way.'

★ ★ ★

The slight figure was almost smothered by the bed's goosedown quilt. Large, fearful eyes looked into Henri's stern face.

'Please, M'sieur, can you help me?'

Henri relaxed. He would use kindness with this one. 'I think, Mademoiselle, we must help each other. You will tell me everything, no matter how small, and I shall find your people.'

Doubt and hope warred in her eyes. Hope

won. There was a shy smile. 'Thank you, M'sieur. You are kind. But I am afraid I can tell you nothing. I don't even know my name. I have tried so often, but when I do my head hurts.' One hand crept up to the scar above her ear. 'When that happens, I feel so sick, and frightened.'

Henri gently patted the small hand, which lay on the covers. 'Do not be afraid, Mademoiselle. Mme Dubuis is here to care for you. We shall soon have you home again. I have with me a photographer. With your permission, Madame?'

Soon the police photographer was ready.

'Remember, Raoul,' said Henri, 'the young lady is not a criminal. She may smile if she wishes and she will need no number.'

The photographer sniggered. Madame Dubuis greeted this pleasantry with a small laugh. She approved of the inspector's attempts to relax her young visitor.

'Indeed, my dear. Show us your pretty smile. I'm sure anyone who has seen it will know you at once and hasten to be reunited with you.

'Now, Mademoiselle, just the fingerprints. It won't hurt a bit, and Raoul will clean off every trace of ink with his little bottle of spirit. Isn't that so, Raoul?'

'Certainly, M'sieur L'Inspecteur!'

The picture was reproduced in the national press all across France.

DO YOU KNOW THIS WOMAN?

Antoine Grosmenil scrutinized the photograph. As Inspector of Police in Sablé until his retirement, he had prided himself on knowing all the faces he saw on a regular basis. He shook his head. This young woman was not a local. He would stake his pension on it. He frowned in concentration, casting his mind back to the time of the storm. Death and destruction. Such sorrow! When there is no body to bury, grieving is held at bay by foolish hope. But miracles seldom happen and the river yields up only the dead. For a moment he had thought — hoped even — but it was quite impossible. His knowledge of the distance and geography involved, not to mention the ferocity of that fearful night, extinguished the tiny flicker of excitement he had momentarily felt on reading the details. No. This young daughter of France had her own sorrows to bear.

★ ★ ★

Time passed. It appeared no one knew the attractive young woman. She was not wanted for any crime. Interpol was uninterested in her. Henri consulted Madame Dubuis. 'I confess, Madame, I do not know what is to be done. Police resources have been exhausted. We shall not close the file, but what is to happen to her? I suppose we should place her with the Sisters of Mercy?'

'Amongst their geriatrics and mentally unstable? Certainly not! Some years ago, the good God took to himself my granddaughter . . . a sweet girl. The farm has been empty of young laughter ever since. This child shall stay with us. She can help on the farm as our Angélique did. Who knows, perhaps one day something will restore her memory.'

2

It was five years later that Marie-Anne Dubuis slipped her feet out of her wooden sabots and wriggled her bare toes in the hot dust of the courtyard. 'Chuk, chuk, chuk,' she called to the hens as she broadcast their food with a sweep of her arm. From all directions they ran towards her with stiff-legged gait, heads thrust forward, their beady eyes swivelling to seek out the elusive grain. Marie-Anne smiled. Today was a good day. Her dough had risen without problem. The kitchen was tidied and washed down. Now the hens were fed, she had only to gather in the washing before she could get away to the fields. She raised her face to the mid-morning sun, eyes closed, and let the heat soak into her body. Yes, life was good. She could still hear the dance tune played on the radio that morning. With her flat basket on one arm, her free hand caught up her skirt and she danced around the yard to the melody in her head.

★   ★   ★

In the angle of the wall the man stood in the shadows watching her. Cloth cap pulled low over his brown hair, on his tanned face a fan of faint lines radiated from eyes screwed up to gaze through bright sunlight. He took in the simple blue dress covered by a large white apron. She had not yet hidden her hair from the heat of the day and the sun put honey lights into the straight brown fall as it swung around her head. As she danced there in her bare feet, she looked like a child. The blunt features of his normally sober expression softened into a smile of amused affection. How often in the last four years had he watched her like this, or as she crouched beside his small son, heads together, sharing some entrancing pleasure? Her childlike wonder in everyday miracles was, for him, one of her greatest charms.

Some slight movement caught her attention for she stopped short, whirled to face him, eyes wide. Her hand flew to her throat in alarm.

'Maurice! Oh! How you startled me.'

'Forgive me.' He advanced with outstretched hand. 'I didn't want to interrupt your enjoyment.'

She blushed and disclaimed, but he felt her tremble as they shook hands and exchanged the traditional kiss of welcome on each cheek.

He frowned, puzzled at her obvious fear. But she recovered immediately, and spoke briskly. 'It's a good thing you did. I've wasted too much time already. What are you doing here? There's nothing wrong is there? Claude?' she asked with a sudden anxious frown.

'No. Nothing at all. Claude is, as always, fighting fit and very annoyed with me, because I insist he does his holiday tasks before he can help with the harvest.'

'I sympathise with him,' she declared. 'This is the last day.'

'Here, yes. But we have our own fields to gather in. La Lavendière is ready first, then ourselves next door at Les Rosiers, and so on down to the village.'

'What a strict Papa you are. He's only five years old.'

'I know and you'd spoil him rotten between you, you and his grandmother, if I permitted it.'

At the thought of Madame La Salle, the small indomitable woman who was Maurice Boucher's mother-in-law, Marie-Anne pulled a wry face. Try as she might she'd never been able to make friends with little Claude's grandmother. The older woman seemed to disapprove of everything and everybody except her adored grandson and, occasionally, her son-in-law. Only when she looked at the small boy, whose mother had died so soon after his birth, did her lined face relax its habitual grim expression, and the iron trap of a mouth soften into a smile.

'So why are you here?' queried Marie-Anne as she returned the grain basket to the fodder shed, and slipped her feet back into her clogs.

'I finished early, so I've come to help.'

'Your help is expected in the fields,' she mocked.

'Yes, but not yet. So I thought I'd come and help you carry the hampers.'

'Maurice, you're an angel!' She accepted eagerly. 'And for that you shall have an ice cold beer while I pack them. First I have to get the washing in. Come on. You can hold the basket.'

She hurried across the dusty yard, into the cool dimness of the old milking shed. A wonderful smell greeted them. Not sweet sun-dried hay and the warm smell of patient beasts awaiting attention, but a subtle mixture of perfumes. Maurice sniffed in pleasure, but Marie-Anne would not linger. She crossed the concrete floor to the far wall, opened a door and disappeared into the sunlight.

Maurice followed and emerged into a large garden, enclosed by high stone walls, where the strength of the scents was stronger — almost overpowering. The hot sun drew fragrance from every leaf and petal of lavender and rose, while on the path his boots bruised the invading chamomile and creeping golden thyme to release their pungent odours.

By a cunning arrangement of pulleys the lines of washing were suspended from metal supports and hoisted high above the beds of herbs. Breezes blew the mingled perfumes over and through the laundry, to scent the linen with a sweet subtle fragrance dominated by strong lavender.

That was my first conscious memory, thought Marie-Anne as she lowered the lines of washing: a soft bed on a bright morning; watching the sun make rainbows through the prisms hung from the dressing-table candle-sticks. Surrounded by that wonderful fragrance I felt cosy and secure when I heard Grand-mère's voice. She swallowed the lump in her throat and deftly folded the linen to place it in the waiting basket held by a patient Maurice.

'Marie-Anne?' he asked quietly. He was so sensitive to her moods; he'd quickly noticed her distress.

'It's all right.' She shook her head, with a watery smile. 'I was just thinking of Grand-mère. I still miss her so much. I know it's been two years since she died, but I *need* her, Maurice.' Her voice held such a wealth of longing he could only nod.

'I know,' he said softly. 'I know. You were very special to her, too.'

'She was so good to me. We were happy together. Why did she have to die?' she exclaimed with passion. 'She had never been ill, never! We didn't even say goodbye. She just didn't wake up that morning.' Marie-Anne dashed the back of her hand across her eyes to brush away the tears Grandmère would not have wished her to shed.

'I gather the doctor said something about her heart just giving out. She was a good age you know.'

'I know. But we had so much to do — the business! That's something I want to talk to you about, Maurice. But not now. Come, we must hurry.' She led the way back to the farmhouse.

Once Maurice was settled at the scrubbed table with the promised bottle of chilled beer, Marie-Anne bustled about. First, she sprinkled the dry linen with lavender water then rolled it tightly in preparation for ironing. Next, she filled the big wicker hampers with her newly baked bread, still fragrant and warm from the oven, rounds of cheese, thick slices of home-cured ham, jars of juicy fat pickles and a slab of freshly-churned butter. Large thermoses full of cold beer and cider completed the load.

17

They left the retired sheepdog, Merlin, to guard the empty house and set off for the distant fields where friends and neighbours had gathered to help with the harvest.

'You wanted to talk to me about the business?' queried Maurice as they walked companionably side by side along the rutted lanes carrying their heavy baskets.

'Yes. You know Grandmère knew just about everything about herbs and flowers?'

He smiled at her grandiose claim.

'Well, she did! Practically! Anyway, enough to make up her oils and pot-pourri. I know I can never hope to be as good as she was — her mother-in-law taught her over the years from the time she came here as a bride. Grandmère passed it on to me every day for nearly three years before she died. She said I was doing well.'

'So?' prompted her friend.

'So, I wondered if perhaps I could carry on with the expansion on my own. Before she died we had such great plans. Her agent in Paris, who buys her dried herbs and petals in bulk, uses them to produce all sorts of fancy gifts. His profits are enormous compared to ours. We thought we could produce the finished article ourselves. You don't look a bit surprised?' she concluded.

'I'm not. In fact, at her request, I had already carried out a commission for Madame Dubuis.'

'You?'

'Yes. I'm not totally useless you know.'

'I didn't know you knew anything about aromatherapy and perfume?'

'I don't really. Or at least I didn't. I know a great deal more now, though.'

'How?'

'Via the Internet.'

'Yes! You have a computer haven't you? And the Internet is that thing they're always talking about on the television? Do you surf?' she finished with a laugh.

'For your grandmother I did. And managed to make up quite an interesting file of material for her consideration.'

'What kind of material?'

'Suppliers of fancy goods, agents, comparative prices etc. etc. But then she died before I could give it to her.'

'Please. Will you give it to me? It could help me to get going myself.'

'Are you sure you want to?'

In time, he had hoped, she might consider a very different future.

'Of course.'

'Why?'

'Why not? It's what Grandmère and I wanted to do. And I would like to have my own money. Marie-Thérèse and Jean-Yves see I never lack for anything. If I need new clothes or shoes, or want to go to the cinema, the money is there as soon as I ask for it, but . . . '

'But it's the asking?'

'You do understand, don't you? I know the work I do is appreciated and helpful, but I should like to contribute more — something of my own.' She looked wistful as she spoke of a subject so dear to her heart.

'And you feel you'll be here always?'

'Why not?'

'You might want to travel? Or perhaps, one day, you might have a home of your own?'

She was silent. There was no way she would ever want to leave this valley and the people in it, the only home she had ever known, but she understood Maurice's delicate allusion. She was well aware the young farmer regarded her with more than the usual friendship displayed between neighbours, as she had explained to her confidante before she died. 'Grandmère, I am truly fond of Maurice and I adore little Claude. Should I consider it? Marriage with Maurice would be so safe, give me security and status. I don't look for a grand passion, but I do prefer

Maurice to any other man I know.'

Grandmère had laughed. 'There are so many then? Let me see. We have Cousin Jean-Yves, but he's married; Maurice, and, of course, Monsieur le Curé. Then there is old Pierre in the butcher's shop and the other tradesmen and neighbours you meet in the village and after Mass on Sundays?'

'You can mock me, Grandmère, but life with Maurice would be comfortable and predictable from seed-time to harvest. We'd have the setbacks and triumphs, which go with farming. Perhaps we'd have a sister or brother for Claude. I love him already as much as if he were my own. I long for a child, Grandmère. When Claude winds his plump little arms around my neck, and presses his cheek to mine, his warm breath tickles my ear as he whispers his secrets. He smells so lovely! Sometimes I have to stop myself clutching him too tightly in case I frighten him. When my arms are empty they ache to hold a child of my own.'

Grandmère had looked sad and a little troubled, hesitated a moment and then patted her hand in empathy.

The force of these emotions surprised Marie-Anne, but perhaps most women felt so strongly maternal? She didn't know. She had no friends her own age with whom to discuss such things. When she'd broached the subject to Marie-Thérèse the older woman had turned the talk to other matters. Marie-Anne hadn't liked to persist and open old wounds. She knew Marie-Thérèse's motherly heart had broken when Angélique, her only daughter, died of meningitis in her late teens. Sylvestre, the son of the house, was doing well in Canada and showed no inclination to come home. The farm had been in his family for seven generations, but, so far, nothing moved the young man to return. This, too, was a source of sorrow to Thérèse and her husband.

★ ★ ★

'Penny for them?'

Marie-Anne realised she must have walked for some considerable time in silence, lost in her own thoughts. 'Oh, no, my friend! They're worth much more than that,' she laughed.

'You looked so sad,' Maurice said quietly. 'Grandmère wouldn't want you to grieve so, you know.'

'I know, and I try to be positive, but sometimes the future seems so dark and frightening. I'm always . . . '

'Marie-Anne! You mustn't be afraid. Let me . . . '

'Halloooo!' A hail broke into his urgent speech. In the fields ahead, hunger and thirst had sharpened the eyes of the watching workers.

Marie-Anne gave a sigh of relief. Before she let Maurice put into words what his eyes told her so clearly every time they met, she must make up her mind how she would answer him.

★   ★   ★

In the days that followed she had little time for introspection. Harvest Home at La Lavendière involved her in much cooking and serving. This was a rare occasion for farming neighbours to meet and relax. Wine and gossip flowed in equal proportions. The brief respite from rural toil was enjoyed to the full.

True to his promise, Maurice brought the business material he had collected for Grandmère.

'Maurice, thank you. You're so good to me,' her voice fell away. Her cottage industry success would be the last thing Maurice Boucher would wish for. She had no time to think about that now. The Dubuis family were next involved with the harvest at Les Rosiers, the adjacent farm.

★   ★   ★

Maurice's farm was lower down the hill than La Lavendière, nearer the village. The house nestled in a hollow sheltered from the prevailing wind, a sunny spot with glorious views across the valley.

'Heavens! They've nearly as many flowers as we have,' exclaimed Marie-Thérèse as she took in the riot of roses, which covered every inch of the mellow brickwork and softened the stark functional lines of the farmhouse. 'One would never miss the scent of flowers here,' she continued with a sly glance at Marie-Anne.

Life could be very pleasant for Marie-Anne as mistress of Les Rosiers, were it not for its present ruler, Mme La Salle! Maurice's mother-in-law was certainly an obstacle to household harmony. Convention dictated Maurice's new wife would be mistress in her own home. His mother-in-law should stand aside for the bride. However, since the tragic death of her own daughter, the day after Claude's birth, Mme La Salle had run Les Rosiers.

Would she be prepared to give up her place now? And for someone she disliked?

These questions whirled around in Marie-Anne's head and gave her no peace. She went about her duties on the farm with a distracted air not unnoticed by her cousins.

'Leave it, Mother,' advised Jean-Yves in answer to his wife's concern for the younger woman. 'She'll come to you in her own good time. You know what it's all about?'

'Of course! Do you think I have no eyes in my head? Am I the one who is so stupid? Jean-Yves, it would be the perfect answer! Don't you think I should give her a little nudge? It would break my heart to lose her, but she wouldn't be so very far away.'

'Leave it. You may do more harm than good. Patience, ma vieille, patience!'

★ ★ ★

Despite her full day's toil, sleep eluded Marie-Anne on those hot summer nights. She took out the printed pages Maurice had given her, to study afresh the ideas she had discussed so eagerly with Grandmère. Hot tears filled her eyes and ran down her cheeks; focussing on the closely typed text was impossible. Instead she sat and thought back to Grandmère's words of wisdom and sighed; they had had such wonderful plans . . .

'We have an untapped workforce here, Marie-Anne. On farms up and down the valley women sit each evening with their knitting needles or lace pillows while they chat and listen to the radio. Some have television. I suppose that's progress. But idle hands have not come to the Sarthe with it, Dieu soit beni! A cottage industry where housewives and their daughters could earn extra money using their traditional skills is a possibility.'

Grandmère's eyes shone as she outlined her plans. 'The women can make dainty containers, pillows and sachets of all shapes and sizes, from material or fine knitting. They can decorate them with their own lace and some pretty silk ribbons. We can get those from the markets in Sablé. Filled with our pot-pourri, we can sell them ourselves for the full price,' she said with the true Frenchwoman's satisfaction in a bargain. 'We'll be able to afford decent payment for our workers and still make a healthy profit. And everyone will be satisfied.'

'Except Monsieur Crockard,' smiled Marie-Anne.

'If he hadn't cheated us in the first place I would never have thought of setting up our own marketing business,' Grandmère snorted with a toss of her head . . .

In Grandmère's passionate enthusiasm Marie-Anne had 'seen' the young girl who had helped the Maquis during the perils of the German Occupation.

★ ★ ★

And what bitter sweet memories Marie-Anne held in her heart of Grandmère's death and funeral . . .

When the doctor had departed, after confirming that Grandmère was dead, Thérèse and Mme Lepâtre, their neighbour, laid out the body with great reverence. Loving hands brushed the beautiful white hair for the last time. Finally Marie-Anne had been permitted to enter the room. Grandmère lay peacefully at rest on her bed, hands folded on her breast, her fingers entwined through the beads of her rosary, where it would stay until her funeral.

'Do not be afraid, little one,' said Thérèse softly.

Marie-Anne shook her head. Afraid of Grandmère? What an idea! She approached the bed and gently kissed the forehead, surprised at the chill of the skin, the solidity of the flesh. This was the only sign that the beloved figure lying there would never smile at her again, never stroke her hair with that tender work-worn hand, nor rest an old soft cheek against her firm warm flesh. As Marie-Anne knelt and prayed for the soul of her dearest friend she gently fingered the rosary beads she'd seen in daily use.

Then came the day of Grandmère's funeral.

The grand old lady had died at the age of eighty-five. Arriving at the farm as a young bride, she had lived a long time in the Sarthe and, for many folk around, hers had been the hands that welcomed them into this world.

Not only every villager from Maréchal-les-Deux Chapeaux and the local farming community was there that day, but Marie-Anne recognised shopkeepers and several inhabitants from Sablé-sur-Sarthe, the nearest town. Many people unknown to her also came to pay their last respects.

She stood with Marie-Thérèse and Jean-Yves at the head of the bier and acknowledged the respectful nods of greeting and quiet words of commiseration from the mourners as they filed past. So great was the crowd the line spread back around the gravestones and through the cemetery gates into the street, making a slow-moving black snake whose uniform colour was interrupted here and there by the brighter hues worn by younger people who no longer followed sombre past traditions.

The wooden-handled whisk dipped into holy water, moved through the sign of the Cross over the waiting coffin and was handed to the next in line. Thus all those who had come to honour Grandmère bade her farewell. Marie-Anne wondered what stories they could tell of Grandmère's long life? As she fought for control she looked up into the vastness of a cloudless blue sky. A perfect day! Perfect for life. Oh, Grandmère! Why did you have to leave us? Now I'm so alone.

She stood in the churchyard and clutched Grandmère's rosary beads until they dug into her flesh. 'Yes, child. Grandmère would have wanted you to have them,' Thérèse had said when Marie-Anne had protested.

To blink back the tears she concentrated fiercely on the blue dome overhead. A tiny movement caught her eye. As she focused on it she heard the first notes of the skylark's song. The small bird fluttered so high above them she could barely keep track of its position, but the wonderful rich sound grew louder and louder.

The beautiful liquid notes trilled on and on. Involuntarily, Marie-Anne smiled. Her heart lifted as she recognised the heavenly music, which fell like a benediction upon them all from the throbbing throat of the brave little messenger.

'Thank you, Grandmère,' she whispered. 'I will try and be happy . . . '

★   ★   ★

The call of the nightingale in the pear tree outside her window brought Marie-Anne back to the present. She sighed and looked once more at the papers in her hand.

'Oh, Grandmère,' she thought in despair. 'You commanded respect far and wide. Whatever idea you proposed would have been received with interest and considered seriously. But will the women listen to me? How will they regard such a novel idea put to them by a stranger?'

* * *

Marie-Anne left her room and went down into the old milking parlour where bundles of herbs hung up to dry. She had continued to gather, mix and store them even after Grandmère's death; and she still supplied the agent in Paris. She'd learned her lessons well. It comforted her to perform the same chores they'd done together. While her fingers were busy, her heart spoke to the old woman of her hopes and fears. Here where they'd worked together she felt Grandmère's spirit guide and soothe her.

Smiling to herself, the young woman felt an inner peace as she recalled her lessons:

'Always distil the pure essential oil of the

lavender. It has great value. Its properties for calming and repair are unbelievable. You've seen the small brown bottle in the cupboard by the cooking range? That's lavender oil. Use it directly onto burns and scalds. It promotes rapid healing and prevents scarring. For a soothing effect and to promote healthful sleep, put the oil in a burner. There are numerous other uses for it, too.'

She had listened to Grandmère and followed her instructions, but was content to sell the rest of her harvest in its dried form just as before, until now.

The prices quoted in Maurice's material surprised and delighted her. Grandmère had been right. She could pay her home-workers well and still earn a living for herself if she sold direct to the retailers. She'd need to send out exploratory letters to 'test the waters'.

★   ★   ★

This brought her full circle to Maurice and his useful computer. Again Marie-Anne sighed. How could she presume on his friendship to produce her letters while she still kept him at arm's length? So far she'd managed not to be alone with him since their walk to the fields; she was only putting off the inevitable.

* * *

'What do you think of Maurice?'

The question was tossed over Marie-Anne's shoulder as she stood by the old stone sink.

'Maurice?' responded Marie-Thérèse a trifle too airily, from her seat at the big kitchen table on which vegetables were piled. 'Maurice is a very fine young man. Why do you ask?'

'Come on, Thérèse! You know very well why I ask. The next time we are alone together he's going to ask me to marry him. What should I say?'

'Why are you asking me? Your heart should tell you the answer to that question.'

'It isn't as simple as that, and you know it.'

'Yes,' agreed the older woman. 'You're right. It's not simple at all.'

'Of course I shall have to tell him before he gets an opportunity to ask me to marry him. There'll no doubt be all sorts of paper complications, and I have to give him the chance to change his mind.'

'He wouldn't do that!'

'He might.'

'Never! He adores you. But you? Do you love him? Do you want to be his wife?'

'Thérèse, wouldn't it be wonderfully simple

to be Madame Boucher of Les Rosiers?' asked Marie-Anne. 'Settled with my own place in the order of things here in the valley. Yes, of course, I love Maurice. I love him dearly, but not with a grand passion. Perhaps that'll come when he kisses me properly.' Her hands fell idle at the basin in the sink. Her unseeing eyes gazed out of the window as she spoke.

At the table Marie-Thérèse continued to pare and chop vegetables for the soup while she listened to Marie-Anne's spoken thoughts.

'When I think of us being married, I try to imagine what it must be like to have no privacy, to share my bedroom and even my bed with someone else. Maurice has a good strong body. I'm sure it would be pleasant to be held in his arms, but . . . When I think farther, I feel so strange — not fearful exactly — let's face it, living on a farm there are no mysteries about the coming together of the sexes. But I feel almost — well — guilty! Is that normal, Thérèse?' She paused a moment in thought, then went on with a grin. 'Do you think it's a throwback to the teachings of the Sisters? Perhaps they taught me that it was a sin to indulge in impure thoughts.' She shook her head. 'It's just not knowing if the love I have for Maurice will be enough to make him happy.'

'And you? Would you be happy with this love?'

'I think so. Yes! My life would be very fulfilling. I would care for Maurice and Claude. Then I've always longed for a child of my own. Sometimes the yearning is so strong I feel there's a part of me missing, a void I need to fill. Yes. Marriage with Maurice would make me happy,' she said with certainty. 'Don't take any notice of me, Thérèse. Just the normal jitters of a virgin contemplating the biggest change in her life I expect.' She plunged her arms anew into the basin and started to make up for lost time.

'My goodness, these onions are strong.' Marie-Thérèse wiped her eyes on her apron. 'I must go and rinse my face.' As she passed behind Marie-Anne she laid her arm along the girl's shoulders and gave her a fierce hug before she hurried out of the kitchen to weep unseen.

★ ★ ★

'You should have told her then,' said Jean-Yves that night from the depths of the huge feather bed they had shared for so many years. 'You've put it off for so long, always said the time wasn't right and now, when the

34

moment is thrust upon you, you do nothing!' Jean-Yves was as near being cross with his wife as he ever remembered.

'Don't scold me, Papa. I know I should have done it then. She has a right. And it must be done now, before anyone else can hurt her with the information.'

'We're the only ones left who know the truth, now that Mother's gone.'

'Yes,' said Marie-Thérèse doubtfully. 'At least I hope so!'

3

It was a golden autumn day, with a tang of wood smoke in the air. The sun lingered on. The unbroken powder blue of the sky hinted at possible night frost to come; the garden basked in the mid-day heat and winter seemed far away. Lower temperatures had lessened the overpowering effect of the massed herbs, but Maurice's boots still bruised the invading thyme, which deadened his footsteps. He walked up to the old wooden bench where Marie-Anne was lost in thought, studying the notes he had made for her project. Heat reflected off the old lichened wall behind her made this the warmest spot in the garden. Unaware of his approach, she sat bathed in sunshine. Absorbed in her calculations, she absent-mindedly twiddled the stub of a pencil between her fingers. He took in her trim figure and the gloss of health in her hair, and smiled in amusement. Once again he'd caught her with bare feet, as natural as a child.

As his shadow fell across her page she looked up, startled. 'Maurice! You're like a cat, you walk so quietly.'

'I'm sorry. Truly I didn't mean to make you jump. You were so engrossed in your work you wouldn't have heard an elephant.'

She grimaced ruefully. 'You're probably right.'

'Why the great sigh? Problems?'

'You know when Grandmère and I talked about our new venture it didn't seem that difficult. Perhaps I'm just stupid; everything is so complicated. I'll probably need to employ an accountant and I don't think we earn enough to pay one.'

'You're not stupid, just unused to the ways of commerce. You're right. It is complicated. There are so many new rules and regulations, which Grandmère never had to deal with.' He sat beside her and caught her hand in his. 'Marie-Anne, I hate to see you look so depressed. I didn't mean to speak yet, but please will you . . . ?'

She leaned forward and placed a finger on his lips. 'Hush, Maurice. I think I know what you're going to say; and I will listen if you still want me to, after you've heard what I must tell you.'

He smiled in satisfaction. 'There's no need. I'm pretty sure I know what you're going to say.'

She frowned, puzzled. 'I don't think you

can,' she began doubtfully. 'I want to tell you about my relationship with Jean-Yves and Marie-Thérèse.'

'Now it's my turn to stop *you*,' he said and traced the sweet curve of her lips with his fingertip. 'I do know — all about it.'

'But how?' she frowned.

'Claudette's mother, my belle-mère. You know how thick she and Grandmère used to be. I think Grandmère must have told her, early on you know, and she reminded me about it. There was an appeal for information, apparently, though most folks have forgotten, if they ever knew. Life was chaotic at that time and then, because the Dubuis took you on as a sort of cousin, folks just accepted you as one of their family. Most people probably never think about it, but Mémère told me again — it must be six months ago.'

'Yes. That'd be right! Just about the time you started showing an interest in me!'

He chuckled. 'That may be the first time you and she noticed it, but I assure you the interest had been there much longer. You never knew Claudette, my wife, and I wish I could say you'd have liked her, but she wasn't an easy person to get to know. Temperamentally she was as unlike you as could be. Volatile was her middle name. No, please let me tell you about her,' he begged as she would have interrupted him. 'I really feel I want to explain how it was. My father was killed in a tractor accident in one of our top fields where the fall is so steep. He and my mother were devoted and though she tried, for my sake, to carry on with her old routine, her heart wasn't in it. When she caught a very bad dose of 'la grippe' she had no resistance or will to fight. She died in just a few days . . . I was stunned. It made me face up to my responsibilities.'

He paused recalling the past.

'I suppose I was ripe for marriage. To return each evening to an empty kitchen soon makes a man long for companionship and — yes, you mocking one — someone to cook him a decent meal.

'Be that as it may, about seven years ago, when I was asked to help set up the Farmers' Co-operative, I travelled regularly to Angers for meetings. The first time I stayed overnight, Claudette shared my table in the dining room at the pension. We got talking. I'm sure I bored her to tears with my problems,' he said ruefully. 'But she was very sympathetic and I began to look forward to my regular visits to town. Truth to tell, I was flattered by her interest in a country bumpkin like me. She was so glamorous. Her hair was the palest gold — just like Claude's — but curly. Paris, with its bright lights, shops and theatres was her home. She spoke of it with passion. It was all strange to me, but I was dazzled and, by this time, totally besotted. I was amazed and grateful, when she agreed to be my wife.'

He sighed for the eager young man of his early youth, and continued with his tale. 'We had a quiet wedding at the Mairie with only her mother and a couple of friends of mine as witnesses. Neither of us had any close family and I didn't want to overwhelm her with a bunch of distant cousins. After the wedding Madame La Salle disappeared, presumably back to Paris. I didn't see her again until Claudette was so ill during her pregnancy. She wasn't an interfering mother-in-law.'

'She's certainly changed then!' Marie-Anne couldn't help herself. Along with the rest of the community, she had suffered the jibes and unwelcome advice from the harsh old woman. 'Sorry, Maurice. Go on.'

'I realised my mistake almost immediately we returned home from a short honeymoon in Nantes. I don't mean I didn't still care for her, but I knew I should never have married her; never have expected her to adapt to the rigours of farm life in a small rural community. Like a hothouse bloom left out in the frosts of winter, first she drooped and then she shrivelled. In the beginning the local women were friendly. They tried to show her our ways — especially Grandmère and Marie-Thérèse — but she wasn't interested and so, when she rejected their overtures, criticism and hostility crept in. Claudette didn't care. She became more and more disillusioned. She raged at me and wept bitter tears of regret. She felt trapped. I knew I'd been at fault and tried to make it up to her. We often visited Angers to shop or go to the cinema, to the detriment of the farm, I confess. Tasks got postponed and the place started to look run down — it doesn't take long. Still I could do nothing right.'

He shook his head in remembered helplessness. 'Then, almost overnight, she changed. So sweetly she begged me to forgive her and promised to try harder to fit in. She drove around the countryside to acquaint herself with the area. Occasionally she went all the way to Angers and once, even Le Mans — she hadn't meant to go so far and had to telephone me to let me know where she was. By this time it was dark, so she suggested it might be wiser for her to stay there and drive back in daylight. I agreed. I was just so relieved to see her happy again. It was about that time we found she was pregnant. I was overjoyed and did so hope it would cheer her up; but she hadn't wanted a child. She rejected the idea and had a hard time of it. Finally she asked if her mother might come to help her. Of course I said 'Yes' and Mme La Salle has been here ever since. Truly I don't know how I would've coped without her when Claudette died. She has cared for little Claude since his birth.'

He looked at Marie-Anne with a troubled frown. 'Of course you would be mistress of Les Rosiers, but, if you could bear it, I believe it would be only right to offer her a home with us. She has no other family and nowhere else to go. Besides it would break her heart to leave Claude and he does love his Mémère.'

'I realise that Maurice. But she seems to hate me. I don't know if we could survive under the same roof.'

'I understand how you feel. Perhaps she'd consider living in one of the cottages? Then she wouldn't be under your feet. She'd still be able to see Claude every day. Perhaps it's not you she dislikes, but the thought that I'll send her away when I remarry.'

Marie-Anne was sceptical. She remembered the hostility in the older woman's hard eyes from the very first day they'd met. It had always puzzled her. There had been no thought then of a marriage between herself and Maurice, yet still Mme La Salle had seemed to resent Marie-Anne's very existence.

Suddenly Maurice started to laugh. Marie-Anne looked at him, eyebrows raised in interrogation.

'Oh! Marie-Anne, chérie,' he gasped between chuckles. 'Here we are discussing our future living arrangements and I haven't even asked you!'

Marie-Anne smiled in response to his mirth.

'Dear Marie-Anne, if you only knew how many hours I've agonised over the right words to persuade you; how I've imagined so many romantic settings for the great moment; the torments of doubt I've endured.' He stopped to draw breath, composed himself, and became serious for a moment. 'My dearest, am I jumping the gun, taking too much for granted? Does our conversation really mean what I think; what I hope?'

Marie-Anne nodded in answer. 'I suppose it must, don't you? But I do feel I have been deprived of those romantic moments and flowery phrases you mentioned,' she said, only half teasing, for every girl loves the treasured memory of the moment when her future husband asks the most important question of their lives. Perhaps Maurice sensed this, for he took her two small hands in his, studied them, then turned them over and gently kissed each of the work-roughened fingertips. He raised his eyes to hers and said solemnly, 'Marie-Anne, ma bien-aimée, will you do me the honour to be my wife and make me the happiest man on earth?'

At the ardent look of love in his brown eyes Marie-Anne blushed and lowered her own. 'Thank you, Maurice,' she whispered. She was suddenly shy of this man she had known for nearly five years. 'I will try to be a good wife. And at least Claude likes me,' she concluded.

With a shout of laughter Maurice turned her face up to his. For a moment Marie-Anne's eyes widened as she realised he was about to kiss her. Maurice hesitated. Then she reassured him with a smile and he bent his head to embrace her lips. At first the kiss was tentative. Maurice was being very careful. The last thing he wanted to do was hurry her, or frighten her with a too passionate embrace. He was sure she was totally inexperienced. As he felt her respond, his grasp tightened, his kisses became more demanding. When Marie-Anne at last struggled to break free he released her immediately and apologised if he had hurt her.

'No, no, you didn't hurt me.' She put a hand to her head where pain sliced through her skull. 'I think I must have sat out here too long. I feel as though I've a touch of sunstroke.'

'Just so long as it's not my kisses making you feel unwell,' he joked and got to his feet. He pulled her up beside him.

Arms entwined, they strolled back to the farmhouse to tell the happy news to Jean-Yves and Marie-Thérèse. Maurice was embraced, congratulated, and welcomed to the family. Marie-Anne was amazed when Jean-Yves conjured up a dusty bottle of champagne. Some months before, Marie-Thérèse's romantic heart and devout wish for the young woman's welfare had prompted her to hide one in the depths of the cool marble-slabbed larder — just in case.

⋆　⋆　⋆

A farm is busy all year round; they discussed the possibility of a very early Spring wedding. The winter-planted cereals would be well up and in his absence neighbours would care for Maurice's beasts. The young farmer was a popular and respected member of the local community, and could always call upon assistance, knowing it would be willingly given. The honeymooners would return before calving and lambing began. Before the plans could go any further, Mme La Salle had to be told. Marie-Anne dreaded it. Even Maurice had misgivings about his mother-in-law's reception of the joyous news. In his own happiness he could spare compassion for the lonely, embittered old woman. She lived in his house, tended to his daily needs, but rarely exchanged more than a cursory word with him. Meals appeared, clothes were washed and ironed, the house was as clean and tidy as anyone could wish, but, were it not for his son, Maurice would have asked her to leave long ago. Only the child made the house into a home; only he could make his grandmother smile and unbend to any degree.

When Maurice finally screwed himself up to make his announcement her initial reaction was an anticlimax. She regarded him steadfastly with her black boot-button eyes, pursed her lips and turned back to her cooking pots.

Claude, on the other hand, gave the news a rapturous welcome. 'Papa, Papa!' he shrieked. 'Does that mean Marie-Anne will live with us — always?' His eyes shone at his father's reassurance. 'She can share my room, Papa. There's plenty of space for another bed and then she can tell me stories when I wake up early.'

His father smiled, but noticed, at the edge of his vision, the old woman's back stiffen at these innocent words.

'No doubt your father would like to put her in your sainted mother's room; give her everything that belonged to my darling, everything!' Mme La Salle spat out her venom. 'She's bewitched him. He can't see through her plots and cunning traps, but I can. Oh, yes! I can!'

As Maurice opened his mouth to refute her angry words, the old woman whirled round and rushed out of the kitchen.

Claude stared after her in amazement. 'What's the matter with Mémère, Papa?'

'I'm not sure, my son. Don't let it bother you. She'll soon be better.'

Uneasily he wondered if his words were true. She had given up everything to care for him and the boy for the last five years. Would the old lady accept the new regime or would he be forced to ask her to leave?

★　★　★

Eager to hear the outcome of his ordeal, Marie-Anne was unhappy and yet not surprised at Mme La Salle's outburst. 'I suppose it's only natural she should feel that I'm a usurper,' she said sadly. 'To lose a daughter must be terrible, and an only child at that.'

'True, but it's been five years. She must've realised long before this that it would be only natural if I married again. It'll be so much better for Claude to have a younger person in the house — and that's not the reason I asked you,' he added laughing.

'Fortunately for you, I believe you.' Marie-Anne gave a humorous shake of her head. 'What are we going to do?'

'Time is supposed to be a great healer. Perhaps we must give her a while to get used to the idea,' he offered, with a helpless shrug of the shoulders. 'Then I'll try and talk to her calmly and explain she's not being turned out. She will always have a home at Les Rosiers near Claude.'

No more was said on the subject, but, for the next few days, it was not far from Marie-Anne's mind. Could she really live with that hard-faced old woman? Small, yet ramrod straight, the eternally black-clad figure of Madame La Salle haunted her every waking moment. Would the older woman agree to occupy one of the farm cottages? At least that would be an improvement on having her in the same house. At last Marie-Anne decided she could bear the suspense no longer. She would screw up her courage and speak with Maurice's belle-mère.

The following day she raced through her normal chores. She popped two freshly baked gingerbread men into a basket, and walked along the rutted lanes to the narrow footpath across the fields to Les Rosiers. Claude would be at school so the two women would be undisturbed.

The last of the roses still clung to the walls of the farmhouse. The old building looked like a faded beauty in the tattered remains of her glory. Drifts of fallen petals covered the ground along the path, and lay like a discarded shawl at her feet. Marie-Anne waited for her knock to be answered, and looked round at the neat borders on either side. Why had she instinctively approached the front door of the farmhouse? One always visited neighbours through their kitchen doors.

Farms are messy places and the formal entrance was usually reserved for funerals, the visits of M. le Curé or other dignitaries, and strangers. Into which category would her hostess put her? The young woman smiled to herself. So it was a pleasant face, which greeted Mme La Salle as she shot the bolts and pulled open the heavy carved door.

She gave no acknowledgement, but stood in confrontation and waited for her visitor to speak.

'Bonjour Madame,' smiled Marie-Anne, determined to reach out in friendship to this difficult old woman. Silence and the unnerving stare of hard black eyes answered her. 'May I come in and speak with you? There are things we must discuss so we might agree on future arrangements.'

With narrowed eyes the older woman waited a moment longer, pursed her lips and grudgingly stood aside to allow Marie-Anne to pass in front of her into the dim hallway. Mme La Salle closed the front door behind her visitor, and made as if to enter the formal salon. At this stage Marie-Anne took charge and walked determinedly across the highly polished hall into the large kitchen. Here everything was spotless and regimentally tidy. Light streamed through unshuttered windows to strike sharp rays from shining glass and gleaming metal. Although warmth from the big range dispelled the chill of autumn, the room could have been a museum. Nowhere was there the wonderful embracing welcome of the lived-in kitchen at La

Lavendière. Determined not to be intimidated, Marie-Anne placed her basket on the scrubbed table-top and turned to say her piece.

'Mme La Salle, I know Maurice has told you of our intention to marry, but perhaps he hasn't explained very well. As Claude's Grandmère, there will, of course, always be a place for you at Les Rosiers. No-one would want to deprive him of his beloved 'Mémère',' she smiled. 'It might be a little awkward were we to try and share the house as we're not related; but I know there is a vacant cottage on the farm, which Maurice would be very willing to fix up to your wishes.'

Marie-Anne ploughed on through the speech she had been rehearsing for the past three days. 'That way you could see Claude every day and still retain your independence. I know it must be hard to think of change when you have been mistress here for so long, but these things happen every day, don't they? It's customary.'

'Never!'

Marie-Anne jumped as the old woman barked out the single word with such vehemence.

'Never! You will never be mistress here, my fine lady. With your airs and graces, you've trapped that dolt into offering you marriage.

Well, you may fool him and all the world but I know you for what you are.'

'I don't understand. I certainly haven't trapped anyone.'

'Don't play the innocent with me. You really have done well for yourself,' sneered Mme La Salle. 'Whether the Dubuis really believe this milk and water Miss and your big innocent look I neither know nor care. I suppose you're an extra pair of hands while Sylvestre is in Canada. But how they have the stomach to put someone like you in Angèlique's place I don't know.'

'Someone like me?' Marie-Anne's bewilderment was plain.

'Putain!'

'Oh!' Marie-Anne gasped in horror of the disgusting name hurled at her. Her reaction provoked a grim satisfaction in Mme La Salle.

'The truth hurts, does it? You and the truth are such strangers it needed me to introduce you.'

The older woman gave a mirthless cackle and Marie-Anne watched with horrid fascination as the hostility in the black eyes turned to hate. Flecks of spittle gathered in the corners of Mme La Salle's mouth and flew from her engorged face as her voice gradually rose into a shriek. 'Thought you'd come and take my darling's place did you? It should have been you. You should have died, not her. My angel! My precious one! She should have waited. She could have had anyone, anyone! Why did she choose him? But there, she could never see she only harmed herself with her tantrums. She was my princess, so beautiful, so delicate,' she crooned. 'Why did she throw herself away on that clod?'

The woman rocked from side to side in grief. Her wild eyes were glazed, words tumbled out of her mouth, their sense jumbled as she looked into the past. 'All Paris was at her feet, but she saw only him. He should have left his wife. How could he not prefer my darling? He broke her heart. But she had her pride, her dreadful pride. She said she'd be married within the year and she was. But what a price to pay! And then *he* came crawling back.

'I knew it would end in disaster. I warned her. I warned her, but she wouldn't listen. She wanted him again. She believed his sweet words, his lying promises. A mistake he called it, but what about her? And then a baby on the way! The bumpkin's baby. She never wanted it. *He* didn't want it either, but I did. I promised to care for it when they'd gone.' At this point Mme La Salle became aware once again of Marie-Anne. 'You shan't have him. You shan't have my boy. I know all about you and I shall tell the bumpkin.'

Marie-Anne was stunned by the incoherent ravings. Mme La Salle seemed insane, but this last threat held no fears for her. 'Don't bother yourself, Madame,' replied Marie-Anne tartly. 'Maurice knows about me and it makes no difference to him.'

'Knows about you does he? I think not! Perhaps you told him you were no kin to the Dubuis. Maybe you told him you lost your memory, but what about the rest? What about the child? Harlot! Trollop! We don't want you here. You and your bribes. Get out!' She stepped towards Marie-Anne and dashed the basket with the gingerbread men to the floor. 'Get out! Get out!' She looked so wild; there was such menace in her advance that Marie-Anne gave ground until she reached the outside wall. With her hand behind her, she groped for the knob, flung open the door and ran into the middle of the courtyard. As she came to a halt she heard the door slam and the great bolts clang across, barring her return. Shaken, she set off for home.

4

'Honestly, Marie-Thérèse, I think she's mad. Should we contact Maurice and warn him? And then there's Claude! What shall we do?'

Marie-Thérèse dried soapy hands on her spotless white apron and sank into the comfort of her familiar rocking chair before trembling legs let her down altogether. The dreaded moment had come. For five years she had expected it and still she was unprepared.

'Child,' she began hesitantly, 'calm yourself. One thing we can be sure of, Madame La Salle would never harm Claude.'

'You didn't see her, Thérèse. She was like a woman possessed. I really felt frightened. I think she's capable of anything. And she was raving. The things she called me. Why does she hate me so? What have I ever done to her?'

'I believe it's enough that you survived.'

'Survived?'

'Yes. You lived and her daughter, Claudette, died — the same night.'

'But that's not my fault! Her death has nothing to do with me — I didn't realise it was the same night?'

'Yes. You came to us in the night, so ill in that dreadful weather, and Claudette gave birth to Claude. She'd been out earlier in the storm and was exhausted. Her system couldn't cope with all the exertion. Mme La Salle had always encouraged her to be indolent so she had no stamina. How she ever had the strength to walk back to Les Rosiers's door was a miracle. They found the truck with an empty petrol tank, two kilometres out of Maréchal on the Paris road.'

The allusion to Paris struck a chord in Marie-Anne's memory.

'Mme la Salle mentioned someone from Paris. It sounded as though Claudette had been in love with him. It was all so muddled. Do you know who he was?'

Marie-Thérèse shifted uneasily in her chair and wouldn't meet Marie-Anne's enquiring eyes. She began to pleat the hem of her apron between her fingers and spoke diffidently, with bent head. 'A few months before she died there was some talk. Claudette had been seen with a stranger. One woman from the village swore she saw them in Le Mans and again another passed them on the road in a car with a Paris number plate. I didn't want to believe ill of the girl. She'd made herself unpopular enough. It could all have been idle gossip and mistaken identity, but she certainly married Maurice quickly enough once they'd met.' She sniffed indignantly. 'Seems she didn't need much leisure to repent it either.'

'What do you mean?'

'She was never cut out to be a farmer's wife. Like I say, Madame La Salle encouraged her to be lazy. Waited on her daughter hand and foot she did, and not just because she was pregnant. It'd always been like that, Grandmère said. The mother wanted so much for the daughter to have everything she'd lacked. The clothes she wore! Here in the country! Complete Paris fashions. Ridiculous!' Marie-Thérèse snorted.

'Claudette was the child of Mme La Salle's middle age, after she'd given up hope of a family. It's plain the mother is of country stock and just as well, as it turned out, but she raised the girl in Paris, to be an ornamental doll. Claudette's marriage to Maurice was a bitter disappointment to her mother. Madame la Salle had planned on a doting, wealthy husband for her darling. The mother knew what hard work farming could be and tried to dissuade the girl until the last minute — even on her wedding morning, Grandmère said. But Claudette was stubborn.'

'Proud,' murmured Marie-Anne remembering.

'Yes. Proud and stubborn. A bad combination.'

'I still don't understand why she should call me all those names.'

'It could have been something Grandmère said.'

'Grandmère?' repeated Marie-Anne astonished. 'Grandmère would never have said anything bad about me. And why? Why should you think that?'

Marie-Thérèse floundered through a jumble of facts she couldn't think how to present to the distressed young woman in front of her.

'Marie-Thérèse, please! Please tell me.'

With a deep sigh the older woman took Marie-Anne by the hand and drew her down to the chair beside her. 'How much do you remember of your arrival here at La Lavendière, ma chère?'

'Nothing. You know that. My first memories are of Grandmère's voice, the smell of lavender, and sunlight shining through the prisms on the candlesticks. It threw rainbows all around the room. My head hurt, but Grandmère told me not to worry and I fell asleep.'

'Yes, my child, but you had been with us then three weeks and it was another four before you spoke.'

Marie-Anne's eyes widened as she took in these details. Then she frowned. 'Why?'

Marie-Thérèse raised her shoulders in a typical Gallic shrug, head thrust forward and palms uplifted. 'Who can say? You had been so ill. The doctor came and recommended rest and tranquillity. You'd had cuts and bruises and a bang on the head. 'A severe shock to the system,' he said, 'but no need of medicine.' So we nursed you, Grandmère and I, and eventually you came back to your senses.'

'But with no memory,' whispered Marie-Anne.

Marie-Thérèse nodded and lovingly patted the hand she now held in a comforting grasp. 'Alas, yes, child. You know, for we have told you, how it came about. Jean-Yves found you on the doorstep, soaked and exhausted and brought you in. However,' here she hesitated and gathered her courage, 'there is something more, which we have never discussed. Grandmère was going to tell you, but kept waiting for the right moment. Then, we were all so happy together we gradually thought of it less and less, and then she died so suddenly.'

Marie-Anne swallowed hard. She sensed she wasn't going to like what was coming. A dull pain throbbed in her skull in that same place where she suffered her recurring headaches — headaches, which had eased over the years until, now, they only came when she was distressed.

'Go on, Marie-Thérèse.'

'While Jean-Yves went out into the storm to fetch the doctor, Grandmère and I looked after you. He was gone a long time. The doctor was away from home. Jean-Yves followed him from place to place before he caught up with him. While he was gone, you lost the child you carried.' Her trembling voice sank to a whisper. 'He was so tiny. A perfect little boy, but we could do nothing. You couldn't have been more than three or four months gone. I'm so sorry, so very sorry, my dear.'

Pain crashed through Marie-Anne's head. She stared in disbelief at Marie-Thérèse. With detached fascination she watched the fat tears roll down her old friend's cheeks, run along the jawbone and gather on the trembling chin before they splashed onto the whitened knuckles of Thérèse's clenched hands.

'A baby? Me? A baby?' The thought was so completely alien to her she could only repeat the words in disbelieving whispers. She got up and paced the floor. She'd always hoped she would one day have a family. When little

Claude's hot breath tickled her ear as he confided his innocent secrets she never wanted to let him go. Waves of longing for a child of her own would sweep over her. She'd thought this was probably normal, but she'd had no one to ask.

Because of Marie-Thérèse's lost daughter, Marie-Anne had felt it might be too painful to question her on motherly love. But that she, Marie-Anne, had carried a child? She, who had never known a man? A gurgle of hysteria bubbled up in her throat — a second virgin birth? Hardly!

'Tell me again how it was. How did I come to stay with you?'

★   ★   ★

With misted eyes Marie-Thérèse looked back to that dreadful night. Disturbed by the imperious clamour of the jangling bell, Jean-Yves muttered grumpily as he heaved himself from the depths of the feather mattress. Shuffling bare feet into his old worn slippers he dragged his dressing-gown around him as he stomped angrily downstairs. The hall light lit up the white skin of his scalp where his greying hair stood up in tufts. The pale forehead, protected from the elements by his customary beret, contrasted sharply with the deep mahogany tan of his face. She heard the thud as he shot back, first the top, then the second of the great bolts, which held the massive front door closed. Her straining ears heard only Jean-Yves's amazed questions. 'What's going on? What on earth?' She couldn't catch the agonised plea from the white-faced figure that confronted his startled gaze.

'Aidez-moi,' the woman whispered as she fell forward into his arms.

'Maman, come quickly, vite, vite.' The urgency in her husband's voice propelled Marie-Thérèse from the warmth of her bed. She levered her comfortable bulk upright and in no time she was taking the weight of the young woman's body in her strong peasant's arms while Jean-Yves closed the door against the wildness of the night.

Roused by the disturbance Grandmère Dubuis appeared at the top of the staircase. She had thrown a warm fringed shawl around her shoulders. Her night-time plait of pure white hair lay on her breast. Taking in the scene at a glance, she commanded them to bring the stranger upstairs, put the large farm kettle on to boil, seek hot water bottles and fresh linen, and fetch the doctor without delay. Trained always to obey her, they scuttled about to good purpose. By the time

Jean-Yves had scrambled into his clothes and braved the storm to find the doctor, the prospective patient was already stripped, dried and between warm, sweet-smelling sheets.

Birth held no terrors or mystery for Grandmère. She had been acting as midwife to the women of the valley for more years than she cared to remember. Countrywomen looked upon childbirth as normal and, despite medical advances and modern arrangements, an undertaking to be endured better in the comfort of their own homes. They preferred Grandmère's ministrations to visiting the gleaming hospital far away from their loved ones. Yet, despite the many births she had attended, Grandmère was always profoundly distressed at the loss of a baby. She helped the unknown young woman with as much tenderness as if she had been her own daughter. When at last she held the silent child in her hands, she made the sign of the Cross and said a quiet prayer. Wrapping the minute body in clean linen she laid him aside to attend to the mother.

For many hours the two women nursed their patient. Grandmère feared the onset of pneumonia and kept the hot bottles constantly refilled. As time passed the stranger became fretful, struggling and whimpering, trying to fling off the clothes covering her feverish body. It was with relief that Grandmère passed responsibility to the doctor.

Jean-Yves had trekked from patient to patient before catching up with him. The storm had brought down the telephone lines for miles around. Doctor le Brun was exhausted.

Rapidly he examined the sufferer. When he had finished here he had still to get to Les Rosiers where Claudette Boucher had gone into labour. Mme La Salle, her mother, was adamant that the doctor should attend immediately. The message she had sent had sounded like an order, but Doctor le Brun was too used to the fears of relatives to take offence.

'You have, as always, done well, Madame,' he complimented Grandmère.

'She is young and strong, which is well considering the cuts and bruises she has received. There is one particular blow to the head, which may cause a concussion, but the skull is not fractured and her life is in no danger, thanks to your prompt actions. I shall leave a mild sedative solution to aid her rest; she needs nothing more. Sad that the child is lost, but she is young enough to have another one to gladden your old age.'

Marie-Thérèse gasped with pain as she felt the sharp kick delivered by Grandmère's slipper-shod foot — thank goodness she hadn't been wearing clogs! 'What was that for?' she demanded as soon as the doctor had been shown out by Jean-Yves.

'I'm sorry, my child. I was afraid you were about to say too much to the good doctor.'

'Too much?'

'Yes,' replied the older woman decisively. 'These hours while we have watched over her I have realised this young woman may be in trouble. Think about it. How did she get here in this condition? Someone has given her a mighty blow to the head. With that wound and all the cuts and bruises she couldn't have come far. Yet she is a stranger to us — we, who know everyone for miles around! So she came in a vehicle. But where is it? I believe she may have jumped from, or perhaps been thrown, from a moving car — hence the state of her. If this is true there may be someone who wishes her harm. And then there is the child. See.' She lifted the limp right hand, which lay on the spotless bedcover. 'No wedding ring, or even a mark where one may have been removed. Is she then a poor unfortunate turned out by her family in her trouble? Or a mistress discarded when she revealed her pregnancy? Perhaps there was a husband once whom she has left — who knows? She will tell us all in her own way once she is better. In the meantime we can keep our ears open and our mouths shut. That never did any harm!'

One did not question Grandmère's decisions, but as the days passed Jean-Yves became worried. 'Do you know her name, Maman?'

'No. As yet she hasn't spoken or fully regained her senses.'

'But we must find out her name — so that we can trace her people. They'll be worried sick. They must be going frantic by now!'

Mme Dubuis looked at him sceptically. She had lived long enough in this world to know that families didn't automatically love one another. Not everyone had her son's good heart. She had seen brother betray brother, father turn against child and husband against wife. She shut her mind against awful memories of Occupied France when as a young woman she had aided the Resistance and known of horrors no one should experience.

'So where are they, this loving family?' she queried, eyebrows raised. 'I don't hear them knocking on the door searching for their lost daughter. Nor has anyone been enquiring in the village. The radio is silent. There is no appeal in the newspapers. So where are these loving people who can mislay a young woman for whom they care and yet make no commotion about it? No, my son. We will hold our peace until the little one can tell us what has happened. Until then she is our young cousin, come to visit and caught in the storm that night.'

Jean-Yves was silenced. As time passed and still the slight figure lay unresponsive in the big guest bed he questioned his wife. 'Is there nothing, Marie-Thérèse? Has she never spoken? Is she mute?'

'I don't know. I don't think so. She has made sounds of pain and distress. But they meant nothing. There was no sense to them. I believe she can speak and is too deeply unconscious to respond to us.'

'Thérèse you must keep on trying. Ask her. It may bring her to herself.'

'Oh, wise one! You who know everything! Do you think I haven't tried? I am as worried about the poor child as you. It will come in God's good time. Le bon Dieu will arrange everything. We must be patient.' She did, however, continue to question the silent figure on the bed as she kept vigil.

* * *

67

One September afternoon the sun streamed through the open bedroom windows, a heat haze shimmered over the fields and the contented clucking of chickens scratching in the yard below tempted the watching Marie-Thérèse to close her tired eyes. As she dozed, her patient became restless. A jumbled muttering passed the till now silent lips. Marie-Thérèse roused and her heart leapt with hope. How could she reach this poor young woman?

'What is your name, little one? Comment t-appelle tu?'

There was no answer, but the restless tossing of the head from side to side. Marie! All good Catholic girls had Marie somewhere in their names. She, herself was Marie-Thérèse, named for the Blessed Virgin and Saint Thérèse of Lisieux. 'Marie,' she called gently, but firmly, 'Marie, answer me.' She took the twitching hands in hers. 'Marie, speak to me,' she commanded. The head tossed more wildly and then stopped moving. Thérèse leaned towards the still figure. Had she done more harm than good? The parched lips opened again.

'Anne,' came the thread of a voice.

Thérèse felt joy and triumph surge through her. She patted the frail hand in hers. 'Marie-Anne, of course. Now you have a name, my dear, we'll soon have you well again.' She dampened the cloth once more to bathe the hot forehead and moistened the dry lips. The girl that the good God had sent her to replace Angélique would not die. She, Marie-Thérèse, would make a vow to hold on to the life that had so nearly slipped away.

★ ★ ★

Another week passed before Grandmère, sitting reading at the bedside, became aware of grey eyes fixed on her, a hint of fear in their depths. Raising the invalid's head, she held a glass of cool barley water to the dry lips, then smoothed the furrowed brow and gently bade the young woman rest.

'All will be well, my child. Have no fear,' she murmured, and was rewarded by seeing her patient slip into a quiet natural sleep.

From then on Marie-Anne rapidly regained her strength. She tried valiantly to eat the dainty meals concocted to tempt her appetite. Yet still she said no word. In answer to their oft repeated enquiries, a look of strain and panic would come into those large grey eyes. A trembling hand crept towards the rapidly healing scar at the side of her skull and a wince of pain twisted her features. So they desisted, unable to bear the sight of her distress.

'In God's good time,' Grandmère would repeat, 'le bon Dieu will arrange all.'

It took three more weeks for Marie-Anne to find her voice. 'Madame,' she croaked in a husky whisper.

'Ah, child! You are with us at last,' beamed Grandmère in delight.

'Where am I?' whispered Marie-Anne.

'Worry not, my dear. You are safe here with us at La Lavandiere.'

'Who are you please, Madame?'

'I am Mme Dubuis and I live here with my son Jean-Yves and his wife Marie-Thérèse whom you already know.'

'And please, Madame, who am I?'

The simple question, so earnestly put, robbed Grandmère of speech. Here she was prepared to receive all the answers she had waited for so long and this child had demolished her hopes in an instant.

'What do you mean, little one?'

'I mean, please, Madame will you tell me my name? Am I related to you? I can't remember and when I try, my head . . . It hurts me so!'

Painful tears ran down the still-pale cheeks. Grandmère gathered the sobbing girl into her motherly arms, rocking and soothing her like a small child. 'There, there, don't cry, my pet. Shush, shush now. Don't distress yourself. All will be well. It may just take a little time. Don't worry.'

★ ★ ★

'But it wasn't well and it had never come right, has it Marie-Thérèse?' said Marie-Anne sadly. 'I still don't know who I am or where I came from. At first I used to worry about it, but when I tried too hard my head hurt so much, I was pleased to push the thoughts away. Gradually I felt safe and at home here. I didn't want anything else. You've all been so good to me. But why didn't you tell me about the baby?'

'It was hard. At first you were so distraught at your memory loss it was all we could do to calm you. Your headaches were appalling. The old doctor gave us strong painkillers for you. It was his opinion that if you led a quiet life with no upsets your memory would return of its own accord. So you see that was not the time to give you such bad news, especially as we knew nothing about the father. The new Inspector of Police eventually came in answer to Grandmère's summons, but all enquiries failed to produce any knowledge of you. As time passed the thoughts of that poor little mite surfaced less and less and it became harder still to broach the subject. You do see that?' queried Marie-Thérèse urgently, willing the young woman to realise that all had been done with the best of intentions, for her benefit.

'Yes. I suppose so.' Marie-Anne was thoughtful, staring down at the worn flagstones of the kitchen floor. 'But do *you* see,' she said, raising her head, 'this changes everything? I can't marry Maurice now. Not without knowing who I am. It could even be possible that I have a husband somewhere.'

Marie-Thérèse shook her head sadly. 'If that were true, my dear, he certainly didn't want to find you. And there was no trace of a ring. Do you remember the photo that was taken of you? When there was no response, we all agreed that, after so much time had passed with no one trying to find you . . . '

'It might be better for me if I were to remain unfound,' finished Marie-Anne quietly.

'Yes, my dear. That was always Grand-mère's opinion. And there was always the hope that your memory would return. Even now! Who can say? Jean-Yves was told by the Gendarmerie that no one had been reported to the Police as missing for months. Except for three poor souls who were drowned in the

Sarthe. Bodies were found far downstream when the floodwaters receded.'

'And there has never been any clue, any indication?'

'Nothing. Your cotton blouse and torn skirt were simple summer clothes, home-made. Your underwear was from Marks and Spencer. But that doesn't mean to say you came from Paris. Since they opened that store, every woman who visits the Capital buys something there. The label has a certain cachet. Grandmère was disgusted,' she smiled reminiscently. 'In her day a 'label' meant Dior or Chanel, not manufacturers of blue-jeans and training shoes. She couldn't believe what the world was coming to! In fact the only odd thing about you, my dear, is your fear of the Abbey in Solesmes.'

An involuntary shudder ran through Marie-Anne. It was true. Even the thought of that forbidding building rising massively above the Sarthe river made her feel sick and desperately sad. Her head started to throb. 'I can't help it. I don't know why it happens. I only have to think of the place, not even go there!'

Seeing her white face Marie-Thérèse cursed herself for her thoughtlessness. 'Forget about that now, my dear. What did you mean? You can't marry Maurice?'

'Of course not. While I thought myself a virgin who had never known another man it was bad enough that I had no memory, but having been with someone else . . . Oh!'

'What is it? What's the matter?'

'She knew! That's what her ravings were all about. Mme La Salle! She thinks I'm no better than I should be!' Marie-Anne said sadly.

'Take no notice, my love. She is a bitter and vindictive old woman.'

'But how did she know? Was it Grandmère? She would never say anything to harm me.'

'I know. And she bitterly regretted it later, but at the time we all thought you would wake and tell us everything. We didn't realise there would be a mystery lingering on for years. They were quite close then. Grandmère and Mme La Salle were of the same generation. They took a perverse pleasure in each other's company, with their opposite viewpoints. Grandmère used to say Violette La Salle kept her on her toes — stopped her brain stultifying.'

Even in her distress Marie-Anne couldn't help smiling. That was so like Grandmère. She would find a good use for anything, even her neighbour's disagreeable nature.

'I can understand how she feels.'

'Rubbish! She has known you as long as we

have. There can be no doubt of your honesty and good character.'

Marie-Anne smiled at her champion. 'Thank you, ma chère, but now even I find myself questioning my roots. Who am I? How did someone come to hate me so much they could abandon me like that? I could be a gangster's moll,' she continued, only half joking. 'Perhaps I knew too much about a drugs deal or a murder?'

'Stop it this instant,' commanded Marie-Thérèse. 'You'll drive yourself distracted with such thoughts. Now you are asking questions we must seek answers, but carefully, child, carefully.'

'So even you think I may still be in danger?'

'Who can say? It is a fact you arrived here in strange circumstances. It is a fact that no one seems to have tried to trace you. Don't you think we have all gone over and over this ourselves? While you were content here and happy to remain as our 'cousin' we have let it lie.' Worriedly she shook her head. 'Perhaps we were wrong. We never meant any harm, believe me.'

Swiftly Marie-Anne crossed the room and gave the older woman a hug. 'I know you've all done everything for my good. Please don't ever think I'm not grateful, you must see that now I have to take responsibility for myself.'

5

During the next few days her thoughts were a constant jumble of questions without answers, and efforts to find a way to get at the truth. At last, one evening she pulled on a headscarf and walked down to the village. Entering the cool gloom of the church she joined the end of the queue for Confession. While the waiting line got shorter she knelt and prayed for guidance.

Marie-Thérèse had been horrified when she discovered that memory loss could wipe out even the words of prayers learnt at a mother's knee, and the Catechism studied before every Catholic child's First Communion. She had taken it upon herself to instruct Marie-Anne as she was convalescing and, once fit again, the young woman had been able to follow the weekly Mass at the Village church.

When her turn came she slipped into the penitent's side of the divided Confessional Box. 'Bless me, Father, for I have sinned,' she began, crossing herself in the usual ritual, but her mind was not on the confession of her little daily sins and their absolution. As her confession ended she asked, 'Father, might I speak with you? I am the last for this evening.'

'Of course, child,' answered the priest. 'Is this a spiritual matter?'

'No, Father, but I need help and advice.'

'Then may I suggest we adjourn to my study where there are seats more comfortable for my old bones and your poor knees.'

Marie-Anne smiled. It was well known that Father Anselm enjoyed his creature comforts; even so he was a good minister. Three years ago the previous Curé, Father Montcalm, had died. He had perhaps let things slip a little in matters of church discipline, and the villagers of Maréchal les Deux Chapeaux had got used to the old man's gentle ways.

The village had waited in some trepidation for his replacement.

Father Anselm blew into their midst like a March wind, stirring up their lives, overturning their comfortable habits and letting light into matters long hidden. When the dust settled they found themselves breathless and shaken. Some feathers were ruffled and dignities tender; now, three years on, there was no one to be found to have anything but praise for the forthright priest who strictly promoted his tenets of right and wrong without fear or favour; he could never be accused of compromising his beliefs to gain popularity. The village thought him omnipotent.

After Father Anselm's motherly house-keeper had served them with coffee, Marie-Anne smoothed her skirt over her knees and, with difficulty, began her tale. She had rehearsed it many times; even to her own ears it sounded implausible and melodramatic. Eyes firmly lowered to the hands clasped in her lap, she continued her recital, uninterrupted. Finally she peeped up at the priest. He sat, head resting on the high back of his upholstered armchair, fingers linked over his ample paunch, eyes closed. For a moment Marie-Anne thought he had fallen asleep and a surge of indignation warred with a desire to giggle.

As she ceased speaking Father Anselm's eyes opened. They were warm and understanding. 'You poor child,' his voice was so kind that tears rushed into Marie-Anne's eyes.

She felt her lips tremble. At the farm she was surrounded by kindness, even love, expressed in practical ways. She had never been encouraged to indulge in self-pity or vain regrets. It took the compassion of this learned priest to reduce her to weeping. She gulped, 'Can you help me, Father? I know it's been a long time; you do see that now I have to know?'

'Yes, indeed, and not before time. Don't worry,' he continued hand upraised, as she would have burst into speech. 'I'm not laying blame anywhere. What's done, is done. People have reasons for their actions which, in hindsight, are sometimes thought to be mistakes, but this is certainly a strange business.'

Patiently he took her through the story again, making careful notes. 'It has been a long time,' he began. Marie-Anne's shoulders slumped in defeat. 'But nothing is impossible to God, my child. If it is His will that you find the truth, then it will happen. In any event, if you wish to marry, steps must be taken to legalise your position. Without an identity you cannot register a marriage, and you will need some kind of papers in lieu of a Birth Certificate. This is for later and for the lawyers to puzzle out. Meantime, we shall do what we can to assist,' he beamed. 'Remember Mother Church and her servants cover the whole globe. Give me time to contact my brother clerics and we shall see what good detectives the Seminaries can produce.'

He smiled and Marie-Anne felt new hope. Surely someone among the hundreds of priests across France must have heard of her.

'You must be patient, Marie-Anne. My letters will be received by busy priests who already have full lists of parish duties and precious little spare time to devote to odd requests. I shall try and make the wording as intriguing as possible. Perhaps we shall whet the curiosity of my brothers-in-Christ to good effect.' He chuckled and Marie-Anne felt herself smiling in response.

'Thank you, Father,' she said rising to leave. 'I shall try and be patient.'

★ ★ ★

This was easier to promise than to carry out. Each Sunday after Mass when shaking the Curé's hand she would raise interrogatory eyebrows to the jovial priest. Each Sunday she was met with a slight shake of the head and the ghost of a shrug, telling her 'these things take time'.

Maurice, too, was impatient. He could see no reason why they must postpone plans for their marriage. With difficulty Marie-Anne had told him of the lost baby, tears filling her eyes for the small son she had never known. Thinking of his own beloved child, Maurice had enfolded her in comforting arms. 'You can have a child of your own, Marie-Anne, of our own. Claude needs a brother or sister. He'd be delighted, as would I.'

The bewildered suitor couldn't understand

why she gently pushed him away and refused to consider becoming his wife. 'Even if you were married once, your husband has given up all rights to you by his neglect. I'm sure you can get an annulment. Ask Father Anselm. I know all about you that I need to know. You are honest and true and good. That's enough for me. I love you Marie-Anne. Please, please, be my wife!'

'And Mme La Salle?'

'Ah!'

Life at Les Rosiers was more uncomfortable than ever. He had told his belle-mère that Marie-Anne had refused to marry him, believing she would cease her campaign of hate against the young woman. At first Mme La Salle had seemed to be grimly satisfied. Then one day, returning from the village, she had entered the kitchen like a whirlwind, flung down her basket and leaned across the table towards him.

'Liar!' she spat. 'Did you think I wouldn't find out? Do you think I am so stupid?'

Open-mouthed Maurice listened to her tirade of abuse. 'What are you raving about woman?' he demanded as she paused for breath.

'No wedding!' she panted. 'Refused to marry you did she? As if she would be so stupid, having managed to get you to declare

81

yourself, fool that you are! You must think I'm simple to be taken in by such a tale. Then she creeps in to see the Curé after Confession to make all the arrangements. Thought there was no one about did she? Thought no one would know she'd been? Not very clever either of you. Mme Beauchamp, the Curé's housekeeper is a friend of mine. You didn't think of that did you?'

It was in vain that Maurice swore Marie-Anne's visit had nothing to do with forthcoming nuptials. The old woman had made up her mind. Maurice was at the end of his tolerance. The sooner he had someone else to care for Claude the better. He was determined to be rid of the vindictive presence of Claudette's mother — but how?

★ ★ ★

Weeks passed. Christmas came and went. At the Christmas Eve Mass Marie-Anne looked at the empty crib in the Nativity scene. On Christmas morning the Christ Child would lie there, but her arms would still be empty. Her heart ached anew. It was as though her body remembered the weight of a babe, the feel of an urgent mouth suckling at her breast. She shook her head, marvelling at how powerful imagination could be.

Father Anselm continued to write to his brother priests across France. It was a painstaking and protracted job. He had divided a map of the country into sections with Maréchal as the centre of a circle. Ignoring the parishes adjacent to his own whose inhabitants were mostly known to him, he spread his search week by week into a new area. So far no one knew of anyone called Marie-Anne, of the description and general age of his young friend who had gone missing from her accustomed place five years ago.

He had approached the Gendarmerie and, like Jean-Yves, drawn a blank. The local man had suggested he try in Sablé-sur-Sarthe, the nearest town of any size. Here, too, he had no luck. The Inspector in charge five years ago had retired, and his successor searched all the files and reports of missing Frenchwomen dating back to the crucial time. There was no one who fitted the description.

With mixed feelings Marie-Anne awaited the coming of spring. It was a time of year she had always loved. Snowdrops dancing bravely in the harsh winds of January; daffodils mimicking the yellow glow of the summer sun in February and the staggering newborn lambs before Easter were all a source of constant delight and faith in renewal. Yet this year her future looked dark. There would be no spring wedding to Maurice.

Sometimes a nameless fear took hold of her. Trying so hard to remember, her head would start to hurt and a depth of sadness welled up inside her. Would it be safer to remain in ignorance? Did she really want to know if someone had tried to kill her?

6

On a sunny morning in Yorkshire, Shirley Brookes addressed the top of her son-in-law's head. 'You should get married again. Or at least think about it.'

Opposite her at the breakfast table Mark Rawlings's eyebrows rose as his paper lowered. His hazel eyes twinkled as he smiled. 'Trying to get rid of us, old darling?' he asked.

'Of course not. You know I love having you here, but I won't be around forever, Mark.' She smiled at him. 'You're thirty-five, a good-looking, normal, healthy male. Quite apart from your needs, my dear, I do feel that a younger woman would be better able to keep up with Fliss when she hits those turbulent teenage years.'

Mark grinned as he remembered the chaos of his eight year old daughter's bedroom when he'd crept in that morning to kiss her goodbye. Boy-band posters jostled for wall-space with pictures of ponies; piles of CDs, books, stickers, abandoned clothes and half-empty bottles of 'dress-up' nail polish and perfume littered every surface. She shared her bed with at least four soft toys, her eternal favourite being Puddles, the long-tailed monkey with the aimless smile. He'd been a First Birthday gift from the mother she barely remembered and Fliss would not be parted from him. She had lain spread-eagled across the bed, her duvet on the floor. Gently he had covered her, then smoothed back the honey-blonde hair before he kissed her forehead. How like her mother she had seemed as she lay sleeping. With tight lips and jaw clenched against the memories that threatened to invade his mind Mark had tiptoed silently from the room.

He looked at Shirley with narrowed eyes. 'There isn't anything you're not telling me is there? You don't seem to be off colour and I know for a fact you can tramp the legs off me any day,' he added with a grimace, as he felt a twinge from overworked muscles in his calf. 'But does having Fliss cut you off from all the things you'd otherwise do? Do you find it tiresome always to have to put her first? After all, you've been there already, done it all before.'

Although in the last five years more grey showed in the glossy dark brown of her hair, and lines of grief now marred her formerly smooth forehead, Shirley Brookes was still a handsome woman. She had a good figure, if slightly thickened at the waist and her vigorous walk and boundless energy would be the envy of someone half her fifty-eight years.

She shook her head. 'You know I love having her. It was the logical thing for her to stay on with me after the accident. You had enough to cope with.'

'I ran away, Shirley,' Mark confessed. 'I couldn't cope with Fliss or our old London life alone. I made an excuse that the far North was neglected and used it as the reason to develop an office in Leeds. I nursed my grief and guilt, hid in my little bachelor pad there and never gave a thought to anyone else. It was totally selfish. I can never repay you for all you did for me then — for us both.'

Shirley smiled at him with real affection. 'It's a two-way street, my dear. Having Fliss saved my sanity. First I lost my husband, then my child. Fliss needed me. Never underestimate the power of being needed Mark. We all want that. But life goes on. I could quote you all the clichés, but you know them already. Is there anyone special these days? I know I'm prying,' she added with a mischievous smile. 'But only with the best *possible* intentions!'

He smiled back. 'There is someone I like. She's called Patricia. We bump into each other here and there. She's great company; we hit it off the first time we met. She's divorced.'

A brief frown creased Shirley's forehead.

'But it wasn't her fault. She was very young when they got married and, from all I've heard, he was a right bastard. Sorry! But he was. She stuck it out as long as she could before she had to escape. If I let myself go, I think I could quite easily feel more for her than just friendship. Underneath that glossy sophistication I think there may be a warm, vulnerable person. It's just that . . . '

'You'd feel guilty?'

'Yes. It doesn't go away, you know. It's always with me . . . I still dream.'

'Oh, my dear!' In quick sympathy her hand reached out to cover his, clenched on the tablecloth. 'You must let go,' she added. 'It's time.'

★ ★ ★

As the English countryside flashed past the carriage window Mark thought again over what Shirley had said. These journeys, from his mother-in-law's home in Yorkshire to visit the London office, gave him plenty of time to work or think. Although his bulging briefcase silently reproached him, Mark let his thoughts range over the happenings of the last few weeks.

* * *

'Patricia, I want you to meet Mark Rawlings.' Ben's high-pitched voice made itself heard over the racket of his birthday party, now in full swing. 'Mark, dear boy, this is Patricia Bannister. Mark is with Rawlings and Thorpe,' he said to the tall, slim blonde he'd brought across the crowded room. 'In fact, I suppose I should say Mark *is* Rawlings and Thorpe. I'll let him explain. Must circulate, duckies,' and with a waggle of his manicured hand he disappeared into the melée.

'*You* are a company?' Her beautifully shaped eyebrows raised, she tilted her head in enquiry with a small smile of shared amusement at their mutual friend. Mark found himself warming to her gentle fun poked at flamboyant Ben.

He had always hated people to introduce unattached females in such a blatant way. The last thing he needed was a woman in his life. 'I've already got two,' he used to say.

This one seemed different somehow and he let himself relax as he responded, 'Half a one. My grandfather and a friend founded the firm. So I'm a Co-owner and Managing Director.'

'Impressive.' She was coolly amused.

Mark returned her smile. 'Very. Don't let

89

my secretary, Rosemary, hear you say so, because,' he lowered his voice, and Patricia leaned forward to hear what he would whisper, 'actually *she's* the one who runs the company. She terrifies me. I'm really a robot. R2D2 is my cousin.'

Patricia's laughter made heads turn as people wondered what they'd missed. Mark's eyes sparkled in appreciation at her genuine mirth. He couldn't remember how long it had been since he'd talked this kind of nonsense with a kindred spirit. 'What about yourself?'

'Self made woman and an avid reader of the books you publish.'

'Glad to hear you have such good taste. And into what have you made yourself?'

'I'm a 'scout'. Not the dib, dib, dib, variety,' she added, amused by his startled look. 'I've always enjoyed travel, done a fair bit in the past and seem to have a knack for photographic composition. I seek out locations for films and advertisement photography, from the slums of Rome to the Lake District right here in England.'

'Is that a lucrative career? Are you full time, or is it just a hobby?'

'I think it could be full time — if that's what I wanted, or needed. I'm lucky enough to be able to pick and choose when I work. If a commission interests me, I go for it. I've built up quite a nice client list,' she informed him with pride. 'What about you? What else do you do, other than tremble when your Rosemary dragon's around?'

'I think I'll call her that in future. I'd like to see her face! You know what I do for a living. Besides that, there's not much to tell. I'm a widower and I have a small daughter. She lives with her grandmother.'

'And where do you live?'

'My time's split between the Northern office in Leeds and Head Office here. I have a house in London, too big for one person, so I rent it out and use the company flat.'

'What about likes and dislikes?'

'I dislike cigarette smoke; those noisy motorbikes that sound like irate wasps, and Party political broadcasts. I like good wine, good books and — ' he fished around in his mind to find something else to give this beautiful, smiling young woman who looked at him with such interest, 'Laurel and Hardy films.'

She laughed. 'I don't believe it! Me too! I love them.'

'Perhaps we could go to one, next time it's possible. I get advance notice when there's a revival on or a special fans' showing anywhere.'

'I'd love that. Goodness knows when it'll

be. Do you dance?'

'Yes. At least I used to, but not lately.'

'I love dancing, but I like my partners to be taller than I am. You'd do nicely,' she laughed.

'We'll have to try it then.'

They were interrupted by their host and, despite seeing her on two or three more occasions, Mark still hadn't fixed a date for their dance.

He accepted most business invitations he received, especially to corporate entertainments, book launches or Theatre First Nights — all good ways to see and be seen. He liked to keep his finger on the pulse of the literary and artistic world. He found Patricia moved in those circles, and they were invited to many of the same functions.

★ ★ ★

Mark gazed unseeing at the landscape and considered what Shirley had said. He loved his small daughter and wanted to be with her as much as possible. He'd killed her mother. The least he could do was try to fill the void. Was it time to put the past behind him? Would Patricia welcome the opportunity to become the second Mrs Rawlings?

There lay the problem. Mark knew the first Mrs Rawlings was still too much a part of his life. Would the marriage be fair to Patricia? Would he make comparisons? Can you ever recapture perfection? For a moment he let go his usual firm control, to let his mind wander over scenes from the past. They had been two young people, so much in love.

★ ★ ★

Elbow to elbow, they'd waited to be served at the bar of the local pub.

'Mark Rawlings, fledgling publisher.'

'Marion Brookes, talented illustrator . . . newly qualified,' she amended. 'I've got my first commission.' She bubbled with enthusiasm.

'Let's drink to our incredibly successful future?'

It was as simple as that. They'd immediately 'clicked' and, from that moment, had spent little time apart until their marriage soon after. Their first home, that tall, narrow London house with the tiny garden behind, had been a wonderful find. Little matter it had needed so much work. They had been young, strong, and enthusiastic. By the time Felicity arrived to bring added joy, there had been a studio in the North-facing attic and Mark could, when he wished, work from home in the ground-floor study. The room behind their bedroom had been transformed into a nursery. Love and happiness increased with the years. They had led a charmed life.

Perhaps that had been the problem, thought Mark with a wry twist of the lips. Perhaps everything had been going too well!

* * *

Which brought him back to Patricia and the future. Should he sell the house? If they married, Patricia would want a home in London, near her friends and business contacts. Would she prefer a house or a flat? Perhaps a service flat would be the answer? Then there was Fliss . . . What if she didn't like Patricia? The questions went round and round. His eyelids drooped, and he slept.

The darkness is total. The deafening din hurts his head. He grabs for her. His questing hands close on empty air. 'Don't go! Don't go! Where are you? You can't go! Don't leave me! Where are you? Come back! Come back!' She is gone; nowhere to be found. She can't come back. There is only emptiness. He searches frantically; screams her name into the storm. It is whipped away on the wind. Rain mingles with his tears. She has gone and his hands are covered in blood.

* * *

As always, at this point he woke up, his brain on fire. He was drenched in sweat. The nightmare still held him. Had anyone noticed? He'd no idea if he'd called out in his dream or in reality. There had been nights in the past when Shirley had heard him. No one seemed to stare. The few passengers in his carriage were immersed in books and newspapers, or fast asleep, their limp bodies rocked to the movement of the train. Once his pounding heartbeat steadied he made his way to the washroom. His hand shook as he smoothed his hair and sluiced cold water over his face and wrists. Haggard eyes looked back at him from the mirror. Will I ever be free of the past and its guilt? Would Patricia even think of marrying me if she knew? I'll have to tell her. Won't I?

I can't take much more of this. If I plan for the future perhaps the nightmares will go away. Perhaps Shirley's right; I'll live in the present, shut off the past. I will be positive about the future. No more vain regrets. I'll make a new start now!

* * *

So Mark Rawlings and Patricia Bannister became a regular couple on the London social scene. The reactions this produced puzzled and surprised Mark. 'What's got into people, Rosemary?' he asked his motherly London secretary who'd been with him since he started with the firm. 'Everyone I know seems to be going round with grins like the Cheshire Cat! Men slap me on the back and the women kiss my cheek, say they're 'so glad', and hug me.'

Rosemary sighed and shook her head at him. 'There's none so blind,' she quoted. 'Just because you gave up on all your friends when things got bad, don't think they gave up on you. You tried to turn everyone away. No!' She held up her hand to stop his protests. 'Don't argue. You did, and we all know why. Just because one of a popular couple is absent, it doesn't take away from the love friends still have for the other.'

Mark blinked. This was a sentimental speech for sensible Rosemary. In the office it secretly amused him to hear her speak with respect of himself as Mr. Rawlings or Mr. Mark to repress familiarity in junior members of staff. When they were alone, she treated him much the same way Shirley treated Fliss. But this kind of observation was different.

'Am I getting a telling off?'

'If the cap fits,' sniffed Rosemary. 'You're just lucky you've got such patient friends. You've kept them without any good news long enough. Let them enjoy it now.'

'Enjoy what, for Heavens' sake?'

'You marrying Miss Bannister, of course.'

'Me what?'

'You and Patricia Bannister,' she repeated slowly as though he were a half-wit.

'What about me and . . . wait a minute. You said marry.'

'Well, you are going to, aren't you? If you're not, you shouldn't get the poor girl's hopes up by all this carry-on.'

'Rosie, I've taken her out to dinner a few times.'

'Don't you 'Rosie' me. Taken her out to dinner, yes. In the most expensive restaurants; with your most important clients; and to the homes of your dearest friends. What else do you think you need do to make your intentions clear?'

'Oh, Lord!' Mark ran his fingers through his hair in dismay. He hadn't intended things to happen so fast. He was a long way from being ready for remarriage. Once he stopped holding her at arm's length, he and Patricia had rapidly slipped into a happy friendship; one he valued. They had common interests, shared many points of view and found they could discuss anything under the sun. In his company she began to drop her brittle guard, relax more and reveal a warmer, more genuine side to her nature. Mark was delighted and reassured by the revelation of this gentler Patricia. It was true he had thought of a meeting between her and Fliss. As the weeks passed he could imagine, somewhere in the future, a life they could all share; a pleasant vision, as yet in the realms of make-believe; a possibility in the far future. But Shirley hadn't been happy with the fact Patricia was divorced. The acid test would be a visit to Yorkshire.

7

'Soon be there,' Mark negotiated the car round yet another roundabout.

It had been an uneventful journey. Both Patricia and Mark had been able to leave work in time to catch the early evening train. Once in Leeds they collected the car from its lock-up garage near his small flat and set out on the last leg.

'Just about an hour to Giggleswick — traffic permitting,' Mark amended. 'Shame your first trip couldn't be made in daylight. It's an attractive journey, especially along the Ribble Valley, but there'll be plenty of other occasions for you to admire the countryside.'

Patricia's heart swelled with happiness. Mark had begun to make occasional references to the future — a shared future, and now she dared to think of it as real: to make sweet daydreams of how it would be. First there was The Meeting to be got through.

Patricia gripped her hands together. She felt her tummy tighten. You idiot, she thought. You're thirty-two years old, not some little schoolgirl being hauled up before the Headmistress. Get a grip!

It wasn't the thought of the adult she was about to meet, which put her on edge. It was Felicity — Mark's beloved daughter. How do you talk to an eight year old? she wondered. Should it be all-girls-together or adult to child or . . . ?

It's hopeless. I haven't got a clue. I'm not used to children. I'll probably make an absolute hash of it and Fliss will hate me, and Mark will see I'm not suitable for her new mother. Patricia's frantic thoughts raced round as the moment of truth drew nearer. She shrank deeper into the protective cocoon of the warm, powerful car as it sped through the darkness towards the moment she dreaded.

'Don't fret.' Mark reached over to give her hand a friendly squeeze. 'It'll be fine.'

'So you're a mind-reader now, are you?'

'I'd be a bit insensitive if I hadn't realised how you feel. And anyway, you should see the expression on your face. Bring on the tumbrils!'

Patricia laughed with him and sat forward to get an impression of the town they were in; narrow streets, old buildings; a cobbled market place; over a bridge then uphill, swinging right and higher still until the car passed through a wooden gate, open in welcome. Neat flower borders were briefly illumined in the headlights; then they stopped before a lighted doorway.

'Come in, come in out of the cold,' welcomed Shirley Brookes, as she ushered Patricia into a pleasant hall. There was an impression of polished wooden furniture, bowls of flowers: a mingled smell of lavender wax and pot-pourri.

'I'm sorry. You won't get any sense out of that pair for some time,' Shirley continued with a laugh. 'I'll take you up and show you your room.'

As they mounted the shallow treads of the staircase, Patricia glanced back and understood what Shirley meant. After a polite, 'How do you do,' to the guest Fliss had flung herself on her father with shrieks of delight and a babble of news. Now he nibbled her ear in a familiar routine to squeals of delight and wriggles of protest.

Patricia smiled.

'You'd think he'd been away for a month instead of a few days,' continued Shirley. 'Although she's the centre of his universe Fliss knows her father has a life beyond us here at Ravenscourt.

'This is your room. If you want to freshen up I'll wait for you downstairs with a sherry. Now that Fliss has met you and seen her Daddy, he'll put her to bed. We can have a civilised dinner in peace. The bed-time ritual can take some time,' she warned.

Patricia unpacked her weekend case. Her bedroom was warm, she noted with gratitude, and pretty; decorated in a William Morris paper with toning fabrics. Here again pot-pourri lay in shallow bowls. Her bedside table held a selection of books and magazines, a carafe of water and a glass, and a tin of 'nibbling' biscuits. Everything was provided for her comfort and welcome. She took several deep breaths to loosen the knot of tension in her stomach and quickly washed her hands at the dainty basin. She dried them on one of the thick fluffy towels set out for her use, then re-did her sleek chignon; a whisk of powder, touch of lipstick and she was ready.

★   ★   ★

The two women sat with their sherry by an open fire of apple logs.

'Courtesy of the winter's gales,' explained Shirley. 'We had no idea the tree was rotten. Fortunately it was at the end of the garden so no harm done and the smell is lovely, isn't it?'

Polite social chitchat soon deepened into a proper conversation and they both relaxed in the comfort of the chintz-covered armchairs set either side of the fire. Patricia realised Shirley, too, had been apprehensive of this meeting.

'You're the first woman friend Mark has brought home, you know. I can't tell you how relieved that makes me. He's been alone, shut away in his world of misery, ever since my daughter died. It's time to let go of the past. I wouldn't normally talk about him behind his back, but I did want to take this opportunity to say how much happier he has seemed lately. We've been delighted, and put the change down to his new friend. I feel as if I know you already, your name crops up so often. Fliss has been longing to meet you.'

In answer to Patricia's raised eyebrows she continued.

'Yes. It's not easy for her you see. I do my best, but I'm the wrong generation for her friends' parents. She needs someone younger to relate to and Mark has told her all about your travels. There you are darling! You can pour us another sherry while I check on the dinner, then we can eat.'

⋆　⋆　⋆

In bed that night Patricia thought over the evening and could laugh at herself for her earlier fears. Shirley was a lovely person, warm, generous and outgoing. Mark had been so happy to be home. He'd teased Shirley, and caught up on local news, and took care to involve Patricia. Shirley, too, had made sure family jokes and references were explained, so her visitor didn't feel left out. Patricia snuggled down under her duvet, wriggled her toes and looked forward to the next day.

* * *

It started with a tap on her door. When Patricia bade the visitor enter Mark appeared, to present her with a morning tea tray. A bright face, with laughing eyes peeped around from behind him.

'Daddy and I are going down to The Naked Man to get some fresh rolls for breakfast. The bathroom's free, but I'm not to annoy you or make you feel you've got to get up *now*,' announced Fliss.

Patricia laughed. 'And good morning to you, too, Felicity. Naked Man?' with a look of enquiry at Mark.

'Behave yourself, pumpkin, or I shall leave you behind. It's our local bakery,' he explained to Patricia, 'lovely fresh bread. You just take your time and we'll see you when we get back. There's plenty of hot water for a bath, or the shower's electric. It's quite easy to work. You may want to save your bath for this evening,' he added with a meaning grin. 'Come on, brat. Let's see if Nana wants anything else while we're at the shops.'

As she sipped her tea, Patricia thought how beautiful it was to see the warmth of love between Fliss and Mark. All she remembered in her own childhood was the distant figure of her father, on the rare occasions he was home. Her offerings of little girl's kisses had been rejected by her discontented mother. The child might smudge her make-up! With a pang of regret for what might have been Patricia pushed such thoughts away and swung her long legs over the side of the bed.

★ ★ ★

Half an hour later, showered and clad in a primrose flannel shirt, neat chestnut cord trousers and a matching warm jumper, she found the kitchen and deposited her tray on the table. Shirley refused her offer of assistance and poured her guest a cup of coffee. She was very happy to talk about Ravenscourt. 'The house is quite old, though not the oldest hereabouts by a long way. When we go round the garden you'll see we're built into the hill for shelter, and the trees behind keep us pretty snug. In front we look over Giggleswick and from the gable window in your bedroom you can see over Settle along the Ribble Valley. That's the advantage of being so high up. We have the best of both sides of the hill. Over the years the rest of Settle has gradually climbed up to join us, but, thank goodness, because of the gradient, we can never be overlooked or have our view blocked.

'I love it here. Latterly my husband worked in Leeds. In those days the roads were much quieter and journeys less stressful. He wouldn't like it now, poor darling. When he died I stayed on. I have my friends and you'd be amazed at the things there are to do here, even if you don't garden, climb or walk. I used to go to several evening classes. Now my activities are restricted to the daytime — unless there's a concert or something. In that case I can easily get a sitter for Fliss. She's not a difficult child.'

'It must have been an upheaval for you, nonetheless, reorganising your life round a child again?'

'I'd be a liar if I said it wasn't. That whole period was so dreadful anyway we just muddled through and did what seemed best at the time. When the dust settled it was a 'fait accompli'. I don't regret it. I'd do it all again if necessary, God forbid. It will be good for Fliss to talk to you this weekend. I'm totally out of touch with fashion, films and the pop scene.'

'Heavens! I hope she's not expecting too much. I can't say I'm a great pop fan myself. I suppose I have some idea of what's 'in' on the fashion front. I think I'd be safer sticking to my travels. Mark says that's what she wants to pump me about most of all.'

'Yes. It's a shame. Her friends go off skiing in the winter and to foreign climes all over the world in summer. Poor lamb, she stays at home with me. Mark may have to travel occasionally on business, but he hasn't voluntarily gone out of England for years. I don't think he'd trust himself to take Fliss abroad.' The arrival of the shoppers put a stop to further confidences and conversation became general.

★   ★   ★

After a hearty breakfast Mark and Fliss cleared away and loaded the dishwasher, obviously a regular routine. Patricia went up to make her bed and spent a long time looking out of her windows at the spectacular views Shirley had described. The house was so high, the village spread out below her like a toy. Brightly dressed cyclists rested on wooden benches by the War Memorial, their cycles propped against beech hedges. Walkers with plastic map cases banging on their chests investigated the church with its square tower. Farther on, large buildings climbed the slope on the other side of the narrow valley; she was eager to explore.

After a quick glance through the morning paper, it was time for a conducted tour of the garden. Shirley had been right when she spoke of the cosy situation of the old stone house, with its slate roof and deep-set windows. The sun was out and they had elevenses on a rustic bench under the remaining apple tree, while Patricia was regaled with snippets of information about the beautiful area in which they lived.

'What's that incredible building on the opposite skyline? It looks rather Oriental; Turkish or something.'

Fliss giggled. 'That's our school chapel. At least it's the Giggleswick chapel. I go to Catteral Hall, the Prep.,' she explained.

'I suppose it does look a bit foreign,' put in Shirley, head on one side as she considered it. 'We're so used to it, that never crossed my mind before, but the shape outlined against the sky . . . yes, I see what you mean. The interior's marvellous, like a miniature St. Paul's. The gilded mosaics on the inside of the dome are incredible. It's private, but we know quite a few of the staff. I'll get a friend to invite us to morning service one day. It's so beautiful, you shouldn't miss it.'

'The views here are wonderful and the air is so clear and fresh.'

'Is that a polite way of saying you're cold?'

'Not at all. Warm as toast. Don't you like my country wardrobe?' she asked preening comically for their inspection. 'What's the village church like?' she went on, not waiting for a reply.

'St. Alkelda's is a lovely old church,' answered Shirley. 'The present building is the third or even fourth on the site. It's early Elizabethan. You'll see the inside tomorrow morning . . . that is, if you want to come? There's no compulsion.'

'Of course I'll come. Just promise me I won't be choked by incense. I can't stand that.' Patricia smiled at Fliss. 'Who's St. Alkelda? I've never heard of her.'

Fliss chuckled again and took up the tale. 'You're not the only one. Nobody's ever heard of her!' Fliss's eyes — her Daddy's hazel eyes — sparkled as she made her pronouncement. 'There's only one other church named after her. She was strangled for being a Christian,' she finished with a ghoulish leer.

'Fliss! You're a grisly child,' admonished Mark. 'It's true though. She's supposed to have been a Saxon Christian lady, martyred by a group of Danish women. You females are so barbaric! No! Get off me, you horrible brat!'

Patricia and Shirley watched in amusement while Mark and Fliss enjoyed their own private wrestling match, which involved much tickling on both sides.

'Lunch!' declared Shirley. 'Just a snack as breakfast was so late and we'll take some fruit with us.'

'With us?' queried Patricia.

'On our walk,' replied Shirley. 'Didn't Mark tell you? We usually go for a stroll on one of the weekend afternoons, weather permitting. You don't have to come or, if you prefer, we could do something else? Do you have any walking boots?'

'Walking boots, no, but I have brought my wellies.'

'Good! That might be even better after the rain we've had. We thought we'd go over to Stocks Reservoir. There are plenty of pretty paths around to choose from.'

'Can we go by the drownded church?' asked Fliss.

'Don't be daft,' replied her Daddy. 'It isn't drowned. That's why we can see it.'

'But it was going to be. Poor little church. They unbuilt it, Patricia, and put it back together stone by stone above the water.'

'That at least is right. It was at the head of the dale they flooded to make Stocks Reservoir so they had to move it or lose it. Now instead of Daleshead Church it's St. James, Stocks-in-Bowland. We may not walk there, but I'll drive home that way so you can see it. I'll bet you haven't got any thick socks for your wellies. Come on. I'll look you out some of mine or you'll end up with blisters.'

★   ★   ★

That evening, as she soaked in a luxurious deep bath filled with relaxing salts, Patricia pondered on how intimate it is to wear someone else's clothes. The best part of her enjoyable day had been the simple act of pulling on Mark's socks. Critically he had watched to see if they fitted; one hand casually on her shoulder.

'A bit big, but they'll do you,' was the verdict. 'See you downstairs.' And with a light kiss on the top of her head he was gone, leaving Patricia to hug this new closeness to her in glee.

111

The outing had been as attractive as promised. Although now she could feel it, the five miles they'd walked hadn't really taxed her. They'd ambled along and stopped now and then to examine plants, appreciate a view or identify a bird.

'If you're into birds, we must take you to the Falconry one day,' said Shirley. 'It's just down the road from us and you can see them up close. We go quite often. You can watch them being worked with a lure. It's marvellous. They're so majestic. Even the smaller birds of prey have that air, don't you think?'

'I've only ever seen them on T.V. Close up that is,' confessed Patricia.

'This is much better,' said Fliss with her usual enthusiasm. 'We could go next weekend, couldn't we? It's a pity you weren't here in May for the Shambles.'

'The what?'

'The Settle Sheep Shambles,' explained Shirley. 'And try saying that after a few drinks! They're held most years. It's just a bit of fun really. The whole of Settle joins in. There's a theme and the shops put on displays. For instance, when it was the Sheep Olympics we had sheep wearing skis, on bicycles, and sheep in running gear. No! No!' she laughed as she watched Patricia's face.

'Not real sheep — dummies. Most ingeniously made, too, I can tell you. That goes on for ten days or a fortnight before the actual weekend when there's a Rare Breeds show in the market place and often a fair; Morris dancers; and all the usual type of thing, produce stalls etc. I think they usually end up with an open-air disco. People come from miles around.'

'I'm not surprised. It sounds like fun.'

'It is,' piped up Fliss. 'You'll see it next year. Are we going to the Falconry next weekend then?' she continued with the single-minded tenacity of the young. There was a minimal pause. They had come to a standstill while talking, communication being difficult on a narrow path.

Mark draped his arm across Patricia's shoulders. He turned his head to look into her blue eyes. A slow smile crossed his face. 'I think we might, don't you?' he asked her. 'Unless you can't get away . . . '

'I shall manage,' she answered. She would be there if she had to crawl over burning coals to catch the train!

*   *   *

Patricia wallowed in the scented hot water, soothing muscles unaccustomed to such

113

exercise and reviewed the sights she'd seen.

They had come home by a different road, seen Fliss's 'drownded church' as promised and finished off the treat with a cream tea at the Inn at Whitewell. This historic gem, hidden in a fold of the wide countryside, had thick stone steps worn into deep hollows by the feet of countless travellers and a fireplace in which you could roast an ox. At one point she had scrabbled in her handbag for the inevitable notebook and pen, 'Where are we? This is perfect! I can see just how it would be. I'd like to put it in my pocket and be able to trot it out for the period films and dramas for telly. I'm always being asked for this kind of thing.'

She used her own form of shorthand to record the old sandstone houses, which lined narrow streets edged with cobbles instead of pavements, and the War Memorial topped by a puttee-wearing soldier, crossed hands resting on his rifle stock. 'You know,' she continued, 'now I've done the train journey I can honestly say it's not logistically too far away. You've no idea how some people in London react when you suggest using the North of England for shoots. They either think it's so far away they might just as well go abroad, or they'll tell you it always rains. Just look at this sunshine. And the air is so

114

clear; any cameraman would swoon with delight. Where did you say we are?'

'I didn't,' replied Mark. 'I couldn't get a word in edgeways,' he teased. 'It's called Slaidburn and yes, it is beautiful in a very period sense.'

A round-eyed Fliss watched Patricia. 'Are you working now, Patricia? Daddy said you were both going to chill,' she giggled at her father trying to use 'in' words to impress her and show he was 'with it'. 'When we get home will you tell me about all your adventures?'

'Adventures? Well, I'm not sure I've had any real . . . ' she started to laugh. 'Oh, yes! I do remember something funny that happened in Greece, and then there was a shoot in Italy. I'd forgotten all about that. Yes, pet, I'll tell you my adventures when I've had a long hot bath and a large gin and tonic!'

★   ★   ★

Held to her promise that evening, Patricia found dinner dominated by Fliss's eager questions and her own amusing memories of 'far away places with strange sounding names'. The little girl was insatiable until Shirley called a halt. 'That's enough now, darling. I'm sure Patricia's been eating her

115

dinner cold trying to satisfy your curiosity. You've got all day tomorrow to chatter. How about helping me clear? Then you can get the cards out and we can play something until your bed-time?'

The 'something' turned out to be Chase-the-Ace, followed by Dominoes, Stop the Bus and an exceedingly noisy and violent game of Grab, at the end of which the adults declared themselves exhausted and, with great reluctance, Fliss went off to bed.

'Thank you,' smiled Mark as he handed Patricia a glass of Drambuie to have with her postponed after-dinner coffee, 'for being so good with Fliss. She doesn't mean to be a pest.'

'She's not a pest. True, I was nervous of meeting her. I haven't had much experience of children, but she is such fun. And look at how my education had been broadened,' she smiled. She appreciated the earnest patience with which Fliss had explained the intricacies of the various card games. 'I love her questions. I never know what she's going to come out with next. She fairly kept me on my toes. It's fascinating to trace her train of thought, so different from an adult's. If she's typical then children obviously go straight to the heart of the matter, whatever the subject.'

'Yes, but not always in the best of taste, I'm afraid.'

Patricia laughed. 'You have to admit, it's a perfectly natural question to ask — how you go to the loo in the middle of the desert?'

'Maybe. But not at the dinner table!'

The rest of the evening passed quietly. The television News was on when Mark caught Patricia in mid-yawn. 'I do apologise. It's all this fresh air and unaccustomed exercise. If you don't mind I think I'll go to bed. Thank you for a lovely day, both of you. Good night.'

★ ★ ★

'Well?' queried Mark. 'Now you've met her what do you think?'

'I like her,' replied Shirley. 'I like her very much. It's a pity she's divorced, but there we are. I must say I expected someone less likely to fit in with a country weekend, but she's a pleasant surprise. She'll be welcome whenever you want to invite her.'

'Thanks. She did fit in, didn't she? I confess to seeing her in a new light here. When we first met she was so sophisticated — a bit brittle. As time passed she relaxed, became more natural. Here she seems just right. I'm glad you like her. I'm sorry I couldn't consult you about next weekend.

117

Without being rude, what could I say while Fliss held a pistol to our heads.'

Shirley laughed. 'Little monkey. You'd almost think she realised, but I'm sure that's not the case. You know what she is. She wanted an answer and wanted it then — so she asked. Fortunately we're all in agreement and if you feel your relationship could grow into something deeper and more permanent then, my dear, I'm glad. Be sure you have my blessing. *She* wouldn't have wanted you to be alone. You know that. Good night, my dear. Sleep well.' She bent and kissed his cheek as she passed his chair.

Mark gazed into the glow of the dying fire for a while longer. He thought of his young wife. She'd loved her work as an illustrator. He remembered her complete absorption, tongue tip touching the middle of her upper lip. She had an unawakened quality, quite belied by her capacity to survive alone in London. It roused protective feelings in the male of the species. A fact she was not above using to advantage, as she related to him with a mischievous twinkle in her eye. He recalled how she cocked her head on one side like a bright robin as she examined her work to assess its merit, her own most severe critic; or kicked off her shoes to sit with bare feet curled beneath her, engrossed in a book. He smiled at the gentle ghost, then sighed and roused himself to perform the nightly ritual of closing up the house.

That weekend was the first of many spent in the welcoming warmth of Ravenscourt. Shirley and Fliss looked on with approval, as Mark and Patricia grew closer. He learned to relax and enjoy the warmer relationship, but still found it impossible totally to put the past behind him. Too much was unresolved.

8

'Is Patricia coming to us for Christmas?' Shirley looked up from her knitting and put the question to Mark as he watched the television. He frowned. Christmas arrangements had niggled at the back of his mind ever since Fliss had innocently included Patricia in her own plans.

'Mark?' persisted Shirley. 'I do need to know soon. There are about eight weeks to go, but I have to get the catering sorted out. I must go into Leeds for a big shop. If Patricia's with us that makes the amounts different and then there'll be extra presents for under the tree. I suppose we'll make her a stocking?' she mused. 'It would be too mean to leave her out when we all have one.'

'You talk as if she's definitely coming,' said Mark.

'Well, yes, dear. I rather thought she would be. Perhaps she has family who want her, too?'

'No. I don't think so.'

'Well then?'

'Shirley, it's not that simple.' In answer to her unspoken question he blundered on. He tried to put into words the feelings, which bothered him. 'A family Christmas is almost a declaration of intent. It's too soon! I know she's been up several times for weekends and we all get on brilliantly. She's lovely with Fliss and I know you enjoy her company, but I feel as if I'm on a helter-skelter. I've taken my place at the top and now I'm out of control. Everything's happening too fast. First Rosie and my friends in London, now you. Everyone takes for granted what's going to happen. Maybe it will, but I'm not ready yet! Something just won't let me make that final commitment.'

Shirley looked troubled. 'I'm sorry. I didn't realise you still felt like that; were still caught in the past. I've been so glad to see the change in you since Patricia came on the scene. I thought we'd nearly got the old Mark back; I shouldn't have presumed; shouldn't have interfered.'

'For heavens sake, Shirley! It's your house. You can ask whomever you like to visit. I feel like the Spectre at the Feast. I'm putting a damper on what should be a joyful occasion. I'd like to say, don't take any notice of me, just go ahead. To be honest, it would be very awkward with me feeling the way I do.'

'I appreciate that, my dear. I just wish she had a loving family to spend the time with.

Will she be all alone?'

'Yes. I'm afraid she will, and no doubt hurt I haven't invited her.' He gazed into the flames of the fire. All he could see were pictures of Patricia spending a miserable Christmas by herself. Then he smiled. 'I've got it! I've got the answer and it will kill the proverbial two birds.'

'What are you talking about?'

'Patricia can spend Christmas with us, and you, my dear, efficient, hard-working, selfless mother-in-law can have a well-deserved rest.'

Shirley laughed at the string of compliments heaped on her. 'Explain.'

'We'll go to an hotel for Christmas — all four of us.'

'An hotel? I'm not sure.'

'I won't hear any arguments. All you have to do is organise your own presents — and give Fliss a hand, no doubt. Buy yourself a posh party frock and be ready to roll when I get back from work. I'm pretty sure we can get a package, which includes Christmas Eve, Christmas Day and Boxing Day. That would make a nice break, wouldn't it?'

'All right, you've sold me. But where?'

'Give me a chance! I've only just thought of it. Not a word to Fliss. I'll do some digging, ask around and see what I can come up with.'

* * *

'Mark! Wait!' laughed a breathless Patricia as she tried to keep up with the tall figure, which cut a path through the airport crowds, their two cases in his hands. 'I haven't got my Passport. When you said come away for the weekend, I didn't know you meant abroad.' What a shame, she thought as she pushed away dreams of the might-have-been warm sunshine and balmy romantic evenings; perhaps the soft sound of the surf as it broke on a foreign shore. But she couldn't go without her Passport.

'I didn't,' he replied and scanned the names above the row of Booking-In desks. 'Come on. That's ours.'

'Scotland!' Patricia's surprise was obvious. 'But won't it be a bit cold?'

'If you're chilly I'll buy you a thermal vest,' he grinned.

As the plane rose above Heathrow, Patricia smiled at Mark. 'What are you up to? You're like a little boy with a big secret. Stop grinning at me like the cat that's had the cream, and tell me what's going on.'

'No.' He laughed at her. 'You'll just have to be patient and see if I can't organise nice surprises. All I'll say is that we're the advance party.'

She frowned. As he'd intended, this statement intrigued her even more, but he was adamant, he wouldn't give her any more clues.

* * *

At Inverness Airport a hire-car was ready for them. Mark confidently turned right, out of the airport and then left at the junction.

'You've been here before,' accused Patricia.

'No. I just made sure I studied the map thoroughly before we left.'

They touched on the outskirts of Inverness, then crossed the Keswick Bridge. From that high vantage point they could look left, over Inverness town and inland up the Beauly Firth, or right, over the Moray Firth to the North Sea. As the short winter day drew in, pinpoints of light sprang up along both coasts to emphasise the shades of blue and grey, which softened the landscape. They drove on. Patricia relaxed in the warm car content to be with Mark wherever he took her. With total confidence in his route, he chose exits from roundabouts, never at a loss.

By the time the car slowed it was fully dark. Patricia just had time to see big stone pillars and open wrought-iron gates illumined in the headlights as the car swung onto a driveway.

Mark slowed right down to avoid the several potholes shown up ahead. On a rise to their right, warm lamplight shone out from a double row of uncurtained windows. To judge by their size and number it was a very big house, or more probably an hotel?

Patricia sat up. The drive curved around behind the building onto a wide sweep of gravel before an open door. She left Mark to deal with the luggage and hurried inside. The short trip from the car left her shivering. Gratefully she moved forward, hands outstretched to a roaring fire. Big as it was it couldn't fill the enormous stone fireplace in which the fire-basket stood. Above the mantel a huge coat-of-arms was carved from the stone that reached up to the vaulted ceiling.

Once her hands were warm Patricia turned around. Comfortable-looking settees and armchairs with squishy cushions were arranged in groups around the large room. Occasional tables, low bookcases and sideboards held glowing lamps, charming arrangements of flowers and foliage, assorted books and a choice of magazines. Despite its size the overall impression was of cosy comfort.

'Patricia! Come and meet our host, Euan Mackay,' called Mark.

She crossed the room to shake hands with a stocky, sandy-haired man who wore a kilt.

She blinked and wondered if this was just for show or his usual dress. She'd visited Scotland before, but never come so far North.

'Welcome to our home. I hope you'll find Calcutta House to your liking,' said Euan with a friendly smile.

He's not exactly good-looking, thought Patricia, but I'd trust him.

'I'll make the explanations in case you're too polite to ask,' Euan went on. 'My great-great-grandfather made a fortune in the East India Company and re-named the house so we should never forget to be grateful to him. He'll be turning in his grave if he can see what we've done to it now,' he grinned. 'Some fortunes don't last for ever and big houses eat money. In these days when private families don't have hordes of servants, the place was much too big for just us. We like folk, so we've turned it into an hotel, as you see.'

'And from what I've been told,' put in Mark, 'a very successful and pleasant one, too.'

'We aim to please. And we try to incorporate our family tradition of hospitality into our business venture. This is my wife, Fiona,' he continued, as he drew into the group the fair-skinned, dark-haired young woman who had entered the room from a side door. Once more greetings were exchanged. 'Fiona will show you up to your rooms and whenever you're ready I'd like to welcome you with a dram down here before dinner.'

'I could get used to this,' Patricia told Mark as they followed their hostess up the main staircase, past portraits of men in Highland dress and women in ball-gowns with a tartan sash across their shoulders.

★　★　★

Their cases were already in their rooms and by the time Mark knocked on her door to accompany her downstairs, Patricia had unpacked, showered and changed. The softly draped lines of the fine woollen dress flattered her elegant figure. Her golden hair shone and Mark wondered yet again why he couldn't declare himself. She was truly a beautiful and intelligent woman.

'You look lovely,' he said as he kissed her cheek. 'How's your room?'

'Wonderful and so warm. Very efficient radiators. Lovely furniture and a colour scheme I could have chosen myself. I don't feel as if I'm in an hotel. More like a friend's country house.'

That feeling persisted throughout the delightful weekend. Their host was friendly and informative, but not encroaching. The food was superb, cooked with artistry from fresh local ingredients. 'Fish, game and meat are plentiful and no problem,' said Euan. 'Scottish beef and lamb can't be bettered, but only in the last twenty years or so have we been able to offer a really good, wide range of fresh fruit and vegetables all year round. Goodness knows how hotels managed before the advent of refrigerated lorries and planes. The world has certainly shrunk since great-great-grandfather's day,' he laughed.

Replete with good food, a fine wine and several drams of malt whisky Mark and Patricia relaxed by the fireside.

'I'm for my bed,' she said. 'I can't keep my eyes open. I love your surprise, Mark. It was worth waiting for.'

'Ah! But that's not all of it,' he smiled.

'I'm too tired to even try to guess the rest. Walk me home?'

After pleasurably kissing Patricia goodnight at her door, Mark wondered yet again how long it would be before he could shake off the past and make plans for the future. Patricia was lovely and desirable. She got on well with Fliss and Shirley. He was truly very fond of her — and yet! He sighed.

Despite her weariness Patricia lay awake. Was it something she'd done? Something she'd said? It was obvious Mark found her attractive and good company. They'd reached the point in their relationship where the next logical step should, hopefully, be an engagement. But just when she felt Mark might declare himself, he drew away.

Patricia had always been fastidious in her personal relationships. When she was on her own, after the divorce, there had been several men who would have been only too glad to 'comfort' her, but she wasn't interested in such affairs. She was convinced Mark was the man she could be happy to spend the rest of her life with, but he made no solid plans for a shared future. Just as it seemed he might say something, she felt him draw back. The shutters came down and he reverted to her pleasant, almost platonic companion. Tiredly she turned her pillow and tried to sleep. She drifted off to lovely dreams of churches and wedding rings.

* * *

Saturday morning was crisp and bright. Not knowing where they might end up, Patricia had packed the walking boots she'd got for use on her trips to Ravenscourt. Mark kept his promise and bought her a tartan body-warmer and a snug hooded jacket from the small well-stocked boutique in the hotel.

After a morning stroll round the extensive grounds, they had a snack lunch and headed for the nearby forest where, Euan told them, they would find marked walks of varying lengths. By the time the short afternoon was over they were back at Calcutta House with huge appetites.

'Scones and jam in front of the fire,' recommended Euan.

Patricia frowned, puzzled for a moment. She wondered what he meant before she recognised his pronunciation of the word 'scones'.

'It's not so much a different language as a different treatment of the same thing,' she mused to Mark.

'Well, of course, the Gaelic is a different language. I know what you mean. What we hear now seems very English. It may be Euan chooses not to use words he knows we wouldn't understand. I'd like to hear some of the locals talk amongst themselves. When you've finished your tea, you might like to go up for a soak in the bath and change.'

'Heavens! Mark. It's not nearly time for

dinner yet, surely?'

'No, but we're not dining here. I've told Euan we'll be out.'

'Where? No! I'm not going to ask.'

He laughed. 'You're learning. Just sit back and enjoy the ride.'

★ ★ ★

The next part of his surprise was a visit to the Eden Court Theatre in Inverness and dinner in its own excellent restaurant. They saw a play Patricia had just missed in the West End. She was impressed

'Don't be such a snob,' chided Mark. 'They have a cracking programme here, ballet, drama, even events on ice!'

'Are you trying to educate me by any chance?'

'Well, sort of. I want you to get a flavour of what's on offer in this area for a very special reason.'

'And that's all you're going to tell me, I suppose?'

'Yep! That's it.'

'Well, I won't pander to you by trying to guess or worm it out of you, so there!'

'Fair enough. If you're ready, we'll get back. There'll be time for a nightcap in front of the fire. That's the only problem with driving anywhere. I can't join you in a drink.'

'Never mind. It's good for your waistline,' she said, mischief in her eyes.

'I'll treat that remark with disdain and refuse to retaliate,' he retorted.

As the powerful car carried them back to the hotel in warmth and comfort, Patricia despaired. Their time together was such fun. They enjoyed the same things; shared ready laughter. Why couldn't it become more? Patience, she told herself. Enjoy what you've got and have patience. It's not as though there's anyone else — for either of us!'

★ ★ ★

Daylight came late on Sunday morning. Heavy clouds kissed the treetops and wreaths of mist draped themselves along the hedges. Mark and Patricia enjoyed the Sunday papers in front of the fire.

'Bar's open,' said Euan as he passed through the lounge.

'I thought it was always open for residents?' queried Mark.

'In the house, yes. But we have a wee local tacked onto the end of the building — used to be the old dairy. There we have to keep licensing hours, as it's open to the public. If you want to have a look, go down the passage past the cloakroom and through the door at the end.'

'Thank you. We might do that,' said Patricia. 'Now you may get your wish, Mark,' she smiled.

'Wish?'

'You know. Hearing the locals talk together.'

'Let's go.'

★ ★ ★

The old dairy had been converted with taste and a desire to keep as many of the original features as would be appropriate, and with a feel for comfort, too. They settled with their drinks at a small table by another generous fire. They recognised four fellow guests, also seated. The other occupants of the room were grouped at the bar. From their cheerful talk they were obviously well known to each other.

Patricia leaned towards Mark with a nod of her head to where they stood. 'Your locals, I think.'

'Yes. I'm trying to do a spot of eavesdropping, but not very successfully.'

'Mark! Bring Patricia over and be introduced to Willie Ross, our local Factor. He'll be able to tell you all about the woods you

133

walked yesterday,' called Euan from behind the bar. 'He's far more knowledgeable than I am about the area, even if I was born here.'

'You knew enough as a bairn, Euan. But your grandfather sent you off to boarding school and then the University. I'm thinking you learned a lot and forgot a lot also,' said Willie with a smile.

Patricia was fascinated by the soft cadences of the voices around her as the conversation became general. It seemed a popular pastime to take a gentle rise out of the good-natured Euan. She was content to let the men-folk talk while she listened for the differences in pronunciation and emphasis. Some words were totally unknown to her, but she got the general drift. 'Excuse me, but you're not local to this area are you?' she demanded of a black-haired young giant who, she gathered, was the star of the local tug-of-war team.

'Well done, Patricia,' put in Euan as the young man shook his head. 'You've obviously got a good ear. I've been watching you listen and try to sort us all out. Hamish is from the Isle of Skye, he's in Forestry.'

'Will you be coming to visit us again, Mistress Rawlings?' asked Hamish smiling down at her. 'You should come in the Summer for the Games. You'd enjoy that.'

'Better for Hogmanay,' chipped in another,

introduced as Iain Macleod. 'Yon Great Hall's a braw sight for Hogmanay, decked out wi' greenery and wi' all the wee lighties twinklin' on the Christmas Tree.'

'Hogmanay?' queried Patricia.

'You'll be calling it New Year, nae doubt, lassie,' offered Willie Ross. 'We make a greater party for that than for Christmas. Christmas is for the bairns and still a religious festival. But any Scot worth his salt will do his best to be by his ain fireside for Hogmanay. Mothers look to see their sons return. Aye, and daughters, too, these day. The drink-driving has put paid to some of the old first-footing, or visiting, far afield. But there's still some good walking done in the week after Hogmanay.'

'A week!'

'Aye, just about. When folk come hame from afar, they've a lot of catching up to do, lots of folk to visit and each visit an excuse for the craic and a wee ceilidh.'

'A what?'

'Ceilidh. A party; a convivial gathering.'

'Oh, Mark! It sounds wonderful. Can we come again, please?' begged Patricia. As she turned to him her eyes shone with excitement. 'It must be such fun.'

Euan winked at Mark who smiled broadly. 'Well,' he answered slowly, 'I think we may be able to manage that. What do you think, Euan?'

'Does this mean you're confirming your booking for Christmas? Nicely filling the cancellation I had last week?'

'Christmas!' Patricia's eyes grew round as she took in what they said. 'Really? Christmas? How marvellous! Is this your surprise?' In answer to his nod she threw her arms around him in a big hug. 'I think it's fabulous.'

There were smiles from the group at the bar. Patricia's joy at the thought of a return visit pleased them all.

'I'm glad you approve,' said Mark. 'Do you think Fliss will like it here?'

'She'll love it. You'll have to be prepared for her to go home speaking broad Scotch. I've never known a child to pick up accents so quickly.'

'Scots, Patricia. Scotch is a drink. You speak the Gaelic or possibly Doric in some parts. There's an ongoing debate among various points of view as to the true Scots tongue. But Scotch is a dram, so have another.' As he spoke, Euan poured drams all round.

'It'll be a lovely rest for Shirley,' said Patricia. 'She'll really enjoy a dinner like Friday's. More so when she hasn't had to cook.'

'She'll need to bring her appetite,' said Euan. 'We have a seven course Gala Christmas Dinner.'

'Seven!'

'Starter, Soup, Fish, Meat, Dessert, Cheeseboard. Then with your coffee and liqueurs we leave fruit and petits-fours on the table for you to nibble during the entertainment while you chat to your fellow guests.'

'Stop! Stop! I feel too full already,' cried Patricia.

'Don't worry, you'll soon work it off dancing reels and The Dashing White Sergeant,' grinned Euan.

'And we can play golf, too,' added Mark. 'There's a nine-hole course in the garden. What Euan calls a pitch'n'putt. Would you like to have a go after lunch?'

* * *

They parted from their new friends with reluctance and promises to meet again at Christmas. When they sat down to Sunday lunch they were no longer surprised at the quality presented.

'You mean it, don't you?' asked Patricia. 'We're all four coming here for Christmas?'

'Yes. A real family party,' promised Mark. He saw the flush rise to her cheeks and the happiness in her eyes. He mentally kicked himself. Family! It implies so much I'm not ready to say. I might as well have invited her to Ravenscourt and left if at that! However he did nothing to spoil Patricia's contentment and joined in the fun of their golf game that afternoon.

'We'll have to get some practice in for the Boxing Day competition,' he told her. 'Euan and his wife organise various events, which are totally optional. No one has to do anything they don't want. Fliss will be able to join in the games for kids. She'll like that. And there's a Treasure Hunt. I have a feeling she'll rope us in on that one. I'm glad you like my surprise. I think the others will, too. I was lucky to get the cancellation. They're booked up months in advance.'

That night Patricia hugged the thought of being part of Mark's family Christmas. Surely this was progress?

9

Helplessly, Marie-Thérèse watched as Marie-Anne crossed the courtyard. Gone was the buoyant skipping step; the younger woman's shoulders drooped; her whole attitude spoke of depression. Marie-Thérèse's motherly heart was filled with compassion; she felt useless. The Curé was doing all he could — so far in vain. She and Jean-Yves kept up an unfailing support of loving kindness, but this didn't stop the shadows under Marie-Anne's eyes darkening daily. She picked at her food and would go off into daydreams, which gave her no joy. Marie-Thérèse was sure the little one was not sleeping well. Coming up to bed in the early hours after tending a sick beast, Jean-Yves had reported a line of light showing under Marie-Anne's door. What was to be done?

'I've racked my brains, Jean-Yves. This can't go on. She's getting thinner and paler by the day. Where's our golden girl gone? At this rate she will soon look as bad as the night she arrived!'

This comment set them both thinking afresh how they could help.

They were not alone. Maurice haunted La Lavendière every minute he could spend away from his own farm. The only time Marie-Anne showed any sign of her old self was when he brought Claude to visit. Then she would make an effort and forget her problems for a while in entertaining her most fervent admirer. 'I do love you, Marie-Anne,' was the child's oft repeated cry, as he threw his arms around her neck. And she would hug him close, welling tears filling her sad eyes.

★ ★ ★

At night Marie-Anne paced the floor of her bedroom. She was on the point of collapse when Marie-Thérèse decided to take things in hand. Without telling the younger woman, she doctored her bedtime drink with a mild sleeping draught Grandmère used to recommend. So tired was Marie-Anne, she dragged herself upstairs and fell heavily asleep.

Some hours later Marie-Thérèse and Jean-Yves were jerked awake by terrified screams from the young woman's room. Grabbing dressing gowns on the run, they hurried to her door. A light burned on the bedside table. The screams were now a mutter. Marie-Anne clawed at the air, her seeking hands encountering only empty space. Sweat ran from her agitated body.

'Go and make a hot drink, Father,' commanded Thérèse and hitched her ample form onto the bed to take the thrashing figure in her arms. 'Wake up, Marie-Anne, wake up!' She shook the young woman and again called her, 'Marie-Anne, wake up!' At this last command, Marie-Anne's eyes flew open, wide yet unseeing. 'It's all right, little one, you're safe, quite safe.'

At the reassurance in the kind voice, Marie-Anne burst into wild sobs. As she rocked her in motherly arms, Thérèse uttered soothing little murmurs of childish nonsense. At last the paroxysm ended and the slight body rested slumped against Marie-Thérèse's shoulder, only an occasional shuddering gasp for breath showed Marie-Anne's efforts at control.

There was a tap at the door and Jean-Yves appeared with a cup of tisane.

'Put it down on the table, Father, and then you might as well go back to bed. There's nothing more you can do here.'

Once he had departed, Thérèse helped the exhausted Marie-Anne to take off her soaked cotton nightdress. Firmly and capably she dried the shivering body and helped the girl into a clean, dry gown. She insisted Marie-Anne drink the tisane before beginning her questions.

'It was the dream, Thérèse. It's always the same one. It's pitch black and the needles of rain are stinging my skin. I'm crawling, trying to get upwards. I've broken my fingernails and the heather and rocks are grazing my knees and my bare feet. My hands are cut and my knuckles are bleeding.' Marie-Anne looked down at the hands clenching the bed sheet and seemed almost surprised to see the smooth lightly tanned skin, covering her fingers, with no sign of blemish.

'It's so real,' she whispered. 'After a while I feel no pain, because I am so cold, so deathly cold.' She shivered, remembering. 'I'm frightened and lost, and so sad. I've never been so sad in all my life. I'm trying to . . . trying to find . . . '

'What?'

'I don't know,' the young woman wailed in distress. 'I don't know what I'm looking for. I just know if I don't find it I want to die.'

Once again tears got the better of her and she sobbed against the comforting shoulder. At length she quietened again.

'Do you think I'm searching for my baby? Is that why I'm so sad? The dream has only started since I knew about him.'

142

Thérèse pondered a moment. 'No. I don't think that's it,' she answered slowly. 'Since you found out about the child you've never been cold and wet, and I don't see why you should appear that way in a dream-search for the little one. What you have described — your injuries — are exactly the same as the night you arrived here.' She paused. 'I think you're starting to remember.'

A whimper of fear escaped from Marie-Anne's throat. 'I'm not sure I want to, if this is how it's going to be!'

'Don't be afraid. We are here with you. You're quite safe. If you wish I will sleep here in your room. There is still the little bed we used when you were so ill. One of us watched over you each night.'

Marie-Anne's heart filled with gratitude at the love and care these good friends had shown for her. 'I can't let you do that. I'm not ill now, and Jean-Yves wouldn't sleep well without you beside him,' she smiled. 'You know he wouldn't.'

Thérèse puffed out her lips and arched her neck like a young coquette.

'No doubt it would do him good to be reminded how much he would miss me if I weren't there,' she said complacently, 'but at least we can leave both doors open. I will hear you immediately then. My 'mother's ear' hasn't lost its edge. And I believe you shouldn't fight this dream, just let it take you and teach you more.'

Marie-Anne was doubtful. 'You don't know what it's like. I am in such — anguish! And so afraid.'

Thérèse covered the slim fingers with her own work-roughened hand. 'I know, ma chère. It must be terrible. Now you have talked about it I have a feeling it won't be quite so bad again. We shall see. Trust in le bon Dieu, little one. He is watching over us all.'

She tucked Marie-Anne up in bed like a child, left the lamp alight and returned to her feather bed, to snuggle up to the welcoming warmth of Jean-Yves's back.

'He may be watching over us,' she murmured, 'but that doesn't mean we can't give Him a hand.'

'Now, Mother, what are you plotting this time,' he asked warningly. 'Look how upset she was tonight. That was the sleeping draught.'

'Nonsense. She would have had the dream anyway as soon as she fell asleep from sheer exhaustion, but now here memory has started to return I think we should help it along.'

'I think you should leave well enough alone and not meddle in things you don't understand. Perhaps we should call the doctor?'

'That one? No! What can he know of life at his age? He doesn't even look old enough to shave!' Thus she dismissed young Doctor Rougemont who had passed out from his training the top of his class. 'If the good Doctor le Brun were still with us I may consider consulting him, but that young lad? Never!'

By the morning Jean-Yves's words had borne fruit and, after making sure that all was well with a pale-faced Marie-Anne, Thérèse pulled her shawl over her head and set off for the village. Not finding the Curè at the church she pulled the bell at his front door — out of respect for his calling.

Father Anselm listened intently to her recital of the previous night's happenings. Unlike Jean-Yves, he agreed that things could not be left in their present state. With just a few words of caution, and promising to be at hand if needed, he approved of the plan she had hatched.

★   ★   ★

'Hmm!' grunted Jean-Yves, seated at the kitchen table. 'You've got *that* look.'

'What look?'

'It's either 'the cat's got the cream' or 'I know something you don't know',' he replied warily. Marie-Anne smiled at the familiar exchange between these two people she loved best in the world. Rounded and comfortable, with her soft bun on top of her head, Marie-Thérèse was the image of Mrs. Bun the Baker's wife in the set of cards Marie-Anne played with little Claude. Jean-Yves, leaner, lined and nut-brown from his days working the farm, was more like one of the friendlier trolls in Claude's fairy-story books. Now she laughed aloud as Marie-Thérèse put a finger to the side of her nose and nodded her head at her husband. The sound of her amusement lifted everyone's spirits. It seemed so long since there had been anything to laugh about.

'Tomorrow we are going into Sablé,' announced Thérèse, 'so you two had better get your shopping lists ready. If you see Maurice, Marie-Anne, you could tell him. There may be something he needs.'

She knew it was no use asking the girl to pop over to Les Rosiers as she had done in the old days. Mme La Salle's attitude was getting worse as time passed. Maurice was at his wits' end. As often as possible he brought Claude to La Lavendiére to get him away from the hostile atmosphere, which poisoned his own home.

He had always believed the old woman would never hurt the child, but now he was worried that, rather than let anyone else come near him, she may do something desperate. Mme La Salle couldn't prevent Claude leaving the house with his father, but there was no way she would let Marie-Anne approach Les Rosiers.

★ ★ ★

The following day the three set off for the town of Sablé-sur-Sarthe. Maurice had visited the previous afternoon and Claude's favourite pair of wooden sabots were in the bottom of Marie-Thérèse's large basket. New rubber soles and heels were needed, and a short list of personal items for Maurice was tucked inside one of the clogs. He wouldn't need to ask Mme La Salle to do him any favours, which she might spitefully forget if the mood took her.

As the big old Citroen swung to the right out of the farm gate Marie-Anne raised enquiring brows at Thérèse. She had always appreciated Jean-Yves's habit of taking the longer road to Sablé, down the hill and through the local village of Maréchal les

Deux Chapeaux, in order to avoid passing within sight of the Abbey at Solesmes. This route was shorter by at least four kilometres, but it crossed the crest of the hill behind the farmhouse and dropped down into the valley of the Sarthe, hugging the river and passing Solesmes on the opposite bank before arriving in Sablé. Thérèse affected not to see the question in Marie-Anne's eyes and Jean-Yves kept his attention fixed on the road ahead. Marie-Anne shrugged; since talking with Thérèse and speaking of her nightmares she had felt so much better. Last night she had had her first good sleep for weeks and wakened strengthened and refreshed.

But as they neared Le Port de Juigné opposite the Abbey, her nerves tightened. Thérèse turned and smiled at her. 'See, ma chère, how the sun shines on the Abbey. The stones look warm today. What a marvellous edifice it is, built with skill and worship. I think it's amazing what they could achieve in the old days without all our modern technology.'

Marie-Anne gave her a tight smile and did as she was bidden. She took a good look at the impressive building. It was true. The massive Abbey soared heavenwards from its foundations rooted in the solid rock that formed the high bank of the river. It was a monument to craft and devotion, bathed in the spring sunlight. She let out the breath she had been holding and felt herself relax. Warmly she smiled at Marie-Thérèse, who had been observing her, and felt as pleased as if she had passed some difficult test.

Just before they turned the corner, Marie-Anne looked back to confirm her new-found courage, but the sun had hidden behind a cloud and the Abbey rose once more black and forbidding. She shivered.

Sablé-sur-Sarthe was filled with holiday-makers. Some had come for Easter Mass at the world-famous Abbey at Solesmes. Seats needed to be booked more than a year in advance, so great was the demand from Catholics worldwide who wished to share in one of the most important occasions in the Church calendar. The monks sang their worship in the unaccompanied Gregorian plain chant. It raised the level of praise to heights those attending never forgot. They bought copies of the service and the other great rituals on cassette and CD to take home and relive the experience, enriching their spiritual lives long after their visits were over. Other visitors to the little market town were on their way from Angers or Le Mans, turning aside for a while from the main Autoroute, which sliced the country from Paris to Nantes.

With her habitual efficiency, Thérèse fulfilled her commissions, dispatching her companions on errands she was content to leave to them. The more important matters she kept in her own control, bargaining for the best prices with various stallholders in a mutually respectful routine as old as commerce itself. Finally they gathered, as arranged, outside the cordonnier. Claude's little sabots had been left for repair with the kindly owner, and the lists of commissions were complete.

It remained only to go back to the car and load their purchases when there was a tentative tap on Marie-Anne's shoulder. 'Excuse me, Miss, can you 'elp me?' enquired a stranger's voice. 'I've got a plan 'ere, but I'm 'avin' a spot of bovver wiv it. Can you tell us 'ow to get to the Bus Station?'

Marie-Anne smiled. 'Of course. You are here,' she indicated on the map the man held out to her. 'If you follow this road to the junction and turn left, then first right, you will see the Bus Station in front of you.'

'Sorry, ducks. I fort you was a Frenchie. Well, fanks. We'll be awright nah. Come on, Muvver.'

They moved away and Marie-Anne turned back to her friends. 'What's the matter? Why are you looking at me like that?'

'What were you doing?'

'You know what I was doing. They asked me the way. You must have heard them. They wanted the Bus Station.'

'But they were speaking in English! I could hardly understand a word they said. But you . . . '

Marie-Anne went cold. She thought back. Yes. The strangers certainly weren't speaking in French, but how did she understand them? Few foreigners penetrated the countryside to Maréchal. There was nothing there to attract them. She rarely came to Sablé, and then only to shop. So far as she was aware she had never heard anyone speak English, or maybe just a snatch of conversation, a few words from passers-by. Yet she had completely understood what the man was saying. Her head throbbed. 'Please. Let's go home. I don't want to think about it now.'

★   ★   ★

They sat in conference round the kitchen table. 'And he, the man, he thought I was English,' said Marie-Anne.

'But that is ridiculous!' exclaimed Thérèse.

'I know. But he distinctly said, 'Sorry I

thought you were a Frenchie',' repeated Marie-Anne.

'But what of that? It is no more than the truth?'

'Mother, you're missing the point,' put in Jean-Yves quietly. 'He was surprised. At first he thought she was French. After he heard her speak he believed her to be English — like him. So she must speak it very well.'

'Say something,' demanded Thérèse. 'Say the sky is blue.'

Marie-Anne tried to think of an alternative to 'le ciel est bleu', but the more she tried the more confused she felt, and the throb in her head was now developing into a full blown migraine. 'I can't,' she cried. 'My head hurts.'

'There. You see,' proclaimed Thérèse in satisfaction. Although what she was seeing she couldn't have said. Like a cat with its fur ruffled the wrong way, she felt thoroughly disturbed. Something alien had crept into her ordered world — something she couldn't explain, and she didn't like it. No, she didn't like it at all.

She packed Marie-Anne off to bed in a darkened room, placing a hot water bottle in her bed for comfort despite the warmth of the day. Leaving Jean-Yves to see to the chores, Thérèse pulled her shawl over her head and left the farm.

'Is there any significance, Father Anselm? What does it mean?'

The Curé shook his head. 'It could mean simply that she went to a good school; that she was an apt pupil with a flair for languages,' he said keeping his face impassive. Inwardly his heart sank. He had begun to get a little dispirited himself when his search through France for Marie-Anne's identity stubbornly failed to unearth any clues. If now he had to extend that search to England! 'And the dreams? Is there anything new there?'

'Not so far. I got her to look at the Abbey today and for a while it seemed to be all right. Then the sun went in and she was afraid again.'

Bright eyes fixed on his face; she sat with her head cocked on one side awaiting his words of wisdom. Father Anselm sighed. There were times when the unwavering confidence of his flock placed upon him burdens he felt unqualified to carry. This good woman was relying on him to give her the answers she craved. He knew himself to have nothing to offer by way of comfort — except . . . 'We must be thankful for what little progress we have made so far. I believe the rest will come, don't press her any more. Faith, Marie-Thérèse, faith and prayer. Le bon Dieu hears us all. We must trust in Him.'

He gave her his blessing and she hurried home, a little comforted. That night she spent much longer than usual over her evening prayers. Of course le bon Dieu saw all things, but it wouldn't hurt to explain to Him how important it was for Marie-Anne to know the truth so that she could marry Maurice.

10

'Mark, darling, have you made any plans for Easter?'

'I usually spend the holidays with Fliss. You know that, Patricia.'

'Yes, of course. It's just that I have to do a 'scout' in France and I thought it might be fun if you came along?'

'Not during the holidays when there are tourists everywhere!'

'No. You're right! Why didn't I think of that? It would be far better if we could actually see the places without hordes of bodies. Who's a clever boy, then?' she teased. After the success of Christmas in Scotland she had hoped he would ask her to join him for Easter at Ravenscourt, but no such invitation was forthcoming. 'Well, can I go ahead and book us rooms for a week after the holidays?'

'Yes, I think that'll be all right. I'll have the Leeds office all tied up during the Easter break, and when we get back I've got a couple of projects to keep me in Town, so that would fit in nicely.'

'Good. I'll make the arrangements. You

don't have any particular place you want to visit?'

'No. I don't mind. Where were you thinking of going?'

'We'll start in Paris and then probably down the Loire. Everyone has done the chateaux to death, but I might find something in the wine caves of the region. The scenery is spectacular all around there.'

Mark exhaled the breath he had unconsciously held in. The Loire Valley was fine with him, just as long as they kept away from the Sarthe.

★ ★ ★

Patricia's ex-husband, Robert, had been spoiled, weak, and wealthy. Her mouth twisted at the labels. These days, with those traits in mind, she could think of him without pain as 'Wobert the Womaniser'! At nineteen she'd fallen for his easy charm. Stars in her eyes, she had been eager to marry him. Only afterwards, did she realise he believed her total adoration would prevent any awkward scenes if she ever found out he cheated on her. Confident of his ability to sweet-talk her out of any recriminations, he had bowed to family pressure to get married. His Trustees were fed up with bailing him out of scrapes.

He let them believe he would mend his ways and settle down with his young and pretty bride at his side. So she was enthusiastically welcomed into their world and Robert carried on his usual path regardless.

The ten years of her marriage left Patricia with an encyclopaedic knowledge of the best hotels in all the resorts of the world where the Jet Set played. Her husband had the attention span of a demented gnat and would rush from one country to another looking for 'fun'. He cared nothing for her wishes and, it was due to the whim of yet another last minute journey, she lost the child she carried. At that time she still loved her dashing, mercurial husband. She tried hard to believe him when he insisted the miscarriage might have been providential. Certainly it would have been difficult to fit a baby into their lifestyle. True, she was still young and healthy, so there was plenty of time, as he said, for 'all that kind of thing'. But she mourned her lost child and cracks appeared in her rose-tinted glasses.

Patricia had a good brain. By the time she finally divorced Robert she was reasonably fluent in six languages, with a useful smattering of another three or four. She could unravel the mysteries of foreign timetables and plan her own journeys with meticulous attention to detail. She had been accustomed to travelling with a maid and trunks of clothes; now she fended for herself and could appear cool and soignée from the contents of a weekend case for days on end.

Her pleasant two-bedroom flat near Sloane Square, and an adequate income from her divorce settlement, meant she didn't have to work to support herself. But she had already experienced the emptiness of a life spent flitting from one hectic party or race meeting to another. It was time for change. She enjoyed the career she had invented for herself. It was flexible enough to allow her to pick and choose her working hours. She still had plenty of leisure and could make herself available to accompany Mark whenever he invited her.

Christmas had been wonderful; now another happy memory they shared. They saw each other at least three times a week. His weekends, of course, were still spent in Yorkshire. Sometimes Patricia went with him; sometimes not. If an engagement kept Mark in London on a Friday, he caught the last train from Kings Cross to Leeds, picked up his car and was at the breakfast table to greet Fliss on Saturday morning.

Patricia repressed an unworthy twinge of jealousy at the thought of the unconditional love Mark lavished on his small daughter.

Despite her outward appearance of self-contained sophistication, she craved a settled home with a loving husband and family. Her biological clock ticked on. Sometimes she panicked at the thought her chance of ever having a child of her own had been lost for ever. These days that seemed less and less likely. Mark was a good father. Everyone knew it was best for a child to have siblings. Surely he would like to have a brother or sister for Fliss?

★   ★   ★

'Here we are then, Madam. Sorry to have kept you.' Patricia accepted the wallet offered to her. 'Your tickets and itinerary are all in there, together with the hotel reservations for your first night. You can pick up your Travellers Cheques at the desk over there, and if Mr. Rawlings comes in tomorrow he can sign his.' Patricia placed the wallet in the depths of her handbag and collected the Travellers Cheques. She tucked her Credit Card away as she stepped out of the Agency onto the Knightsbridge pavement.

'Woops! Sorry!' called a familiar voice as the sharp edge of a hatbox dug viciously into Patricia's shin. 'Oh, Patricia, it's you,' continued the woman, laden down with bags and parcels. 'So sorry, darling. Do come and let me buy you a coffee to make up. I haven't seen you for ages.'

Patricia's smile was cool. 'It's OK, Mandy. You don't have to do penance. I can see you've been busy.'

'Yes, and I'm absolutely shattered, darling. Do come and tell me all the 'goss'. We can go and get a cup of tea in 'Horrids' and listen to that divine young man who plays the piano. Have you seen him? He is absolutely gorgeous. Swedish, I think.'

Mandy Hamilton-ffrench was not Patricia's favourite acquaintance, but she was related to half Debrett, and therefore not a person to upset. If Patricia wanted to use a country house for a photo shoot, or a Scottish Castle for a film set she could be sure the owner was in some way connected to Mandy Hamilton-ffrench.

With an inward sigh, Patricia accepted the invitation and the two women crossed the busy street to enter the world-famous store. Patricia was not required, at this stage, to say anything. Mandy could, and did, talk for both of them. Her conversation was sprinkled with semi-slanderous comments and her own deliberate mis-pronunciations.

Once they were settled with tea Patricia became the target of a barrage of personal questions. Secretly Mandy was delighted to have met her by accident. Had this not happened today, she intended to create an opportunity to bump into Patricia Bannister in the near future.

Some years previously Mandy had propositioned Mark Rawlings, confident no man would ever decline her overtures. What and who she wanted, she got. At that time, he had been alone for barely six months, but Mandy had no conception of any man preferring to lick his wounds in private when she was offering to 'kiss it better'. His rejection of her had never been forgotten, or forgiven! She could still see the distaste in his eyes as he made it clear he had no interest in her. Mandy certainly agreed with the adage, 'revenge is a dish best eaten cold!' She had waited so long for an opportunity to hurt Mark Rawlings and now, if her acquaintances were to be believed, she had found his Achilles heel. Her chance had come. 'And are you still seeing as much as ever of the dashing Mark? Rumour has it you two are quite an item,' she asked archly.

'I'd hardly call him dashing,' replied Patricia, quite determined not to discuss her personal life with the most prodigious gossip in London.

'Well, darling, all I can say is do be careful.

If you are thinking of cosying up to that one you'd better watch your back.'

'What on earth are you talking about?' asked Patricia, with what she hoped sounded like an unconcerned laugh.

'You know about his wife, of course?'

'Yes. I know he was widowered about six years ago.'

'Ah! But how?'

'How what?'

'How did it happen? Do you know that?'

Patricia had to confess she didn't. Mark was a very private person. He didn't discuss his family and had never mentioned his wife.

'Well, just tell me this, my dear,' asked Mandy with deliberate emphasis. 'Where's the body? They both went off to France, but only one came back.'

'Well, if she died in France, I suppose she must be buried there.'

'I have no doubt of it. But not in any proper graveyard. If there was a decent burial in France her mother would have gone, wouldn't she?'

'Well, yes. I suppose so.'

'She didn't. She didn't stir from home the whole of that summer. My great-aunt lives in Giggleswick. The mother has a house there. They meet in church every Sunday, so you see she would know. And the body wasn't brought back here for burial either. She would have mentioned visiting the grave to Great-Aunt Lucy. So what happened to it? Tell me that!'

'I'm sure there must be a logical explanation.'

'Logical? Or criminal?'

'Mandy! For heaven's sake!'

'Think about it. He's a loner. He dropped all their mutual friends. He never grieved for her or talked about her. I remember her, actually. Rather an insipid type, I thought, but they couldn't get enough of each other. At first that is. But then that's how it happens isn't it? Remember Othello.'

'Othello?'

'Yes. You know — Shakespeare.'

'I know who Othello was,' retorted Patricia, irritated. 'I just don't see what he has to do with anything.'

'He caught her out, didn't he? Great passion turned to hate and Bingo! He bumped her off.'

'But you're not suggesting surely that . . . '

'It happens every day,' Mandy interrupted. 'Look at that chap in the papers this morning. No one suspected a thing until his second wife disappeared. And tell me this, darling, if they were so potty about the child as everyone says, why, just on that occasion, did he insist they leave her behind?'

Patricia had no answer. 'I have no idea why they didn't take her and I'm sure it's nothing to do with us. This whole conversation is ludicrous and besides, Desdemona was innocent,' she averred. Perhaps she could steer Mandy onto a new tack.

'Des . . . ? Othello's wife! Yes, well that's irrelevant. All I say is, 'Watch yourself.' What do you know about him after all? Have you even met his family?'

Patricia didn't resist the temptation to emphasize how close she was to Mark, 'Yes, I've often visited them in Yorkshire. They are perfectly charming and thoroughly normal.'

Mandy couldn't suppress the rage that swept through her. 'Well, of course, darling, they would seem to be all cosy to an outsider, like you.' Adding spitefully, 'Perhaps the mother doesn't know the truth. I still say the conspicuous lack of a body is fishy.'

'Good heavens is that the time,' exclaimed Patricia with a glance at her watch. 'I must fly. Thank you for the tea Mandy and the whodunit.' She laughed, determined Mandy should not see how these malicious digs at Mark had upset her guest.

'We must do this again sometime . . . such fun.' Patricia kissed the air at the side of Mandy's cheeks, bade the other woman goodbye and hurried out of the store.

With narrowed eyes and the hint of a satisfied smile on her lips Mandy Hamilton-ffrench watched her go. At last she had found a way to pay Mark Rawlings back. Rumour had it he was very keen on the Bannister woman. If Mandy could queer his pitch and ruin his relationship she would be well pleased. Behind her off-hand air she had watched Patricia closely. She hadn't missed the look of consternation cross her face at the mention of the child left behind. No! It didn't fit, and Mandy was determined to make the most of every opportunity to remind Patricia of this fact. She was a firm believer in the power of suggestion.

To congratulate herself on this first success she helped herself to a cream cake and indulged in a pleasant reverie. Mark Rawlings, a broken man, would somehow have to beg her to save him and grant him her favours. With great delight, she would refuse him — at first! She smiled.

★   ★   ★

Patricia's shaking hands finally managed to unlock her own front door. She had hurried all the way home, desperate to be away from prying eyes. Her thoughts were chaotic. There just couldn't be anything in the nonsense Mandy spouted over tea. And yet there were loose ends, unanswered questions. She was determined to push the whole subject from her mind, and was glad she had a free evening. Before she saw Mark again she needed to think through what Mandy had implied. Of course it was nonsense! But there were one or two rather odd things. If she could just get them straight in her head!

* * *

'How did Fliss cope with the loss of her mother?' she asked Mark at their next meeting. 'It must have been very hard for her.'

'She was so young when it happened. She is very happy with Shirley. I believe her to be a well-adjusted child.' His answers were stilted. He forced himself to talk about Fliss's life without a mother. After all, he reasoned, Patricia had a right to some kind of explanation.

'How did she die?' she asked, her heart in her throat as she waited for his reply. For a moment there was silence.

'I'll tell you anything you want about Fliss and Shirley. You know pretty much everything about my business and social life, but please understand I will never discuss my wife with you, or anyone else.'

If he had struck her, Patricia couldn't have been more shocked. Mouth open, eyes huge, she stared at him.

As Mark saw her stricken expression, he groaned. 'Oh no! Patricia, I'm so sorry.' He took her cold hands in his. 'Please forgive me. I should never have spoken to you like that. I know you don't mean to pry.'

Patricia flushed. She felt that was exactly what she had been doing.

'You see, the fact is, even now the circumstances of my wife's death are so painful I can't bear to even think about it, let alone discuss it. I killed her.'

Patricia started.

'It was my fault she died and I can never forgive myself.' His hoarse voice filled with tragic emotion matched the haunted look in his eyes.

Surely, she thought, he couldn't pretend such grief? 'Othello was sorry, too — afterwards,' said Mandy's voice in her head.

'You are the first person I have spoken to about this. I've tried so hard to put it all behind me. Now you've given me hope for a happy future. I want you to be a permanent part of my life.'

A week ago that invitation would have

made Patricia the happiest woman in London. Now she simply felt numb. She forced a smile to her stiff lips. Mark said he had killed his wife! But surely he didn't mean it, not literally. There had obviously been some kind of accident. He'd felt responsible. If only he would talk about it — lay the ghosts. She longed to comfort him; to wipe away that haunted look. Perhaps their trip to France would turn out to be a catalyst?

11

'Just there. That's fine,' Patricia called to Mark standing in front of Angers's massive, fortified walls. He looked happy and relaxed as he struck an exaggerated pose, his open-necked shirt, casual slacks and bomber jacket so different from his usual business suit.

'You're not really going to show any of these to your clients are you?' he protested.

'Not this one at any rate,' thought Patricia seeing his smiling face in the viewfinder. 'This one is strictly for private consumption!'

'I just need a body to give the sense of height and the vastness of the stones,' she explained as she clicked away. 'Your dark jacket makes a perfect contrast to the white masonry.'

This was the third day of their working holiday and so far it had been an unqualified success. Mark was determined to drop his guard and let her into his life at last. Arriving by the Wednesday teatime shuttle to Paris they had found a gleaming Peuguot 406 ready for them at Charles de Gaulle Airport. Once out of the capital they bowled along and reached their hotel in Chartres in time for an excellent dinner. Careful not to do anything to spoil their new closeness, Patricia had booked two rooms on separate floors. She would give Mark all the space and time he wanted to realise he needed her permanently in his life. It would be up to him to make the next move.

★ ★ ★

After they'd wandered around Chartres on Thursday morning they followed the Autoroute 11 direct to Le Mans. Patricia took a few shots of the track, the pit lane and the empty seating of the famous 24 Hour Race. There might be a possibility of doing something with a racing theme. But it didn't really satisfy her. Beautiful girls draped over sports cars were 'old hat'. She was searching for something new, something fresh.

So on Friday they'd travelled on to Angers in Maine et Loire. Patricia's professional antennae began to twitch as she took in the immense walls and the vast central Place. Here was a distinct possibility. She worked industriously for two hours then, having got all the records she needed, she was ready to indulge Mark in his role as tourist.

When they entered the reception area of

the local distillery, they were invited to join a small party for the conducted tour. Not Patricia's idea of fun, but Mark had been so patient while she was working, it was his turn to be humoured. A lovely smell of oranges filled the air. She sniffed appreciatively. Such a romantic aroma, but it was very strong. What would it be like to have to work in it, and be surrounded by it all day? Trailing the little group she glanced idly about her, lagging behind the others.

Being the last to enter the great hall there was a considerable distance between them — space enough to bring her up with a gasp of excitement at the sight that met her eyes. 'Yes!' This was it. She had found her location.

Enormous, rounded, shining, copper pot-stills ranged both sides of the huge room. Sitting with their bulbous bases on low supports, their tapering bodies reached gracefully high above her head like strange birds nesting in two rows. Drunk with satisfaction she darted this way and that, camera flashing. Totally focused on her own work, she urged people to move in or out of frame and only came back to earth when Mark took her arm.

'We're leaving now, Patricia.' He looked amused. 'Are you sure you've got enough pictures?'

She looked at him, dazed. 'Oh, Mark! My goodness! I'm so sorry,' she laughed with a rueful grin. 'I'm afraid when I hit a really spot-on location nothing else matters. Did I offend anyone? You do see I had to get the shots, don't you?' she queried anxiously.

'Not to worry,' he reassured her. 'They just think you're a batty tourist. Of course, I disowned you,' he finished, his deadpan expression only spoilt by the quirk of his lips.

'Wretch! I suppose I couldn't have blamed you if you had. I'm so grateful you wanted to come and see this. It's wonderful; the colours in the copper; the size of the stills; the lights reflected off them, even the distortions, and that gallery overhead, it's perfect.' Her enthusiasm carried them out of the building, accepting on the way courtesy miniatures of the potent liqueur from a smiling attendant. Patricia examined the small square brown bottle in her hand. 'Cointreau, Angers. I always thought it was made in Algiers? I suppose it's because of the orange flavour. I like to pour mine into a cup of black coffee. Yummy! Let's go and find one.'

Replete after a delicious lunch they spent the rest of the day wandering around Angers, fascinated by some of the older narrow streets. They strolled by the river and searched the shops for presents to take home.

Mark chose a wonderful warm-orange casserole dish for Shirley and then grimaced at the weight of it.

'I'll probably be charged excess baggage,' he moaned.

'Is Shirley really fond of cooking?'

'Oh yes! We all enjoy our food, and Fliss has been brought up to try dishes from different cultures.'

'Does she like dolls?'

'She doesn't have many. I don't know why. I think she's more into soft toys and pop music.'

'Do you think she'd like this?' Patricia held up a doll, beautifully dressed in the national costume of the region. On the hair perched a lace headdress of intricate design. 'I know it's not exactly a plaything, perhaps she might like to start a collection? You know, dolls from different countries? I'm off to Spain in the autumn, perhaps I could bring her back a Senorita to keep her Mademoiselle company?'

The question was casually put, but she hoped he wouldn't think she was trying to force the pace of their relationship, by worming her way into his daughter's affections. Fortunately he took the gesture at its true value.

'How kind. That is a good idea. It might

encourage her to pay more attention to her Geography lessons, and that wouldn't be a bad thing.'

They dined in their hotel and once again their food was delicious.

'Maybe it's as well our visit is so short. My waistbands are getting noticeably snug!' Patricia said in mock despair.

Mark studied her elegant appearance, in a soft gold silk trouser suit with a burnt orange top, which just showed the valley between her breasts. He thought she had never looked better. Gone was the brittle gloss of sophistication so evident in London. The woman he sat opposite was warm and relaxed.

'You look lovely,' he said sincerely. 'If that's what an extra inch does, don't lose it again.'

Ridiculously Patricia found herself blushing and was aware of her quickened heartbeat. How could this man get her in such a state with a few words?

★ ★ ★

The following morning they dawdled over coffee and croissants. Once more they were lucky with the weather.

'I'll drive,' Patricia announced gaily. 'You deserve a rest from chauffeuring. Now that

I've got my location I don't need to be constantly scanning the countryside, making notes.'

'Have you got everything you need?'

'For this commission, yes. The distillery is ideal for a fashion shoot. So much contrast — the rough texture of the concrete and bricks, the matt black metal rails and the smooth glow of the copper will be superb. But I'm always on the lookout for places to add to my files for future reference. We don't need to hurry back to Paris. If I see anything as we go we can detour.'

As they rolled along, Mark was happy to let Patricia chat away. He sat comfortably, contributing the odd comment to the conversation. This had been a good idea. He needed the break. Apart from the visits to Fliss and Shirley he hadn't let up for years. Even his social life was work oriented — until Patricia came along. He smiled across at her and, feeling his gaze, she grinned back at him. They fell into a companionable silence.

With the passing miles something about the countryside impinged on Mark's con-sciousness. A prickle of awareness lifted his scalp. He looked around in dismay. 'Where are we?'

'We're just a few kilometres from Sablé-sur-Sarthe. It's a typical market town, and a few K's farther on, the guide book said there's a fantastic Abbey, at a village called Solesmes. We could go and have a look.'

'NO!'

Patricia jumped. The big car swerved. She struggled to get the powerful machine under control. Then she showed, pulled into the verge and stopped. She turned to Mark, shock in every line of her body. 'What on earth . . . ?'

His head hung forward. He slumped in his seat. What bitter fate had caused Patricia to choose this of all places? Could he bear it? Was this the opportunity to tell her the truth? Or was it meant to be a time of farewell? Should he say a final goodbye to the past and build a new life with the woman beside him? He took a shuddering breath. 'I'm sorry. I'm so sorry. I don't know what came over me and I'm thoroughly ashamed. I should never have shouted at you; it was unforgivable. We could have had an accident and it would have been all my fault. Call it a mental aberration. Perhaps I'm not very fond of churches.' He knew he was babbling, trying to pass off the incident.

'If you'd rather not go to . . . ?'

'No. Of course we'll go. I think I must have been half-asleep. Perhaps I was having a daydream. Please, carry on.' He continued talking as she started up the car and drove the short distance to Sablé. He tried to blot out his exclamation, restore a feeling of normality to the day. Patricia had obviously been shaken by the whole episode, but she followed his lead and they tried to put it behind them.

★   ★   ★

The Easter visitors were gone and the small town was simply busy with the normal weekend crowds. They parked the car near the Tourist Office in the Place Raphael Elize just before noon. The helpful elderly man in charge recommended an hotel. With Easter past there would be no problem at this time of year. He provided them with brochures of the area and promised to alert the Hôtel Bretagne to their arrival for dinner. Ignoring the lure of the pavement tables they penetrated the gloom of a restaurant and spread out the map.

'Bonjour m'sieur, madame,' a pleasant young woman greeted them.

Patricia ordered coffee with the little cakes or 'sablés', typical of the region, and made no comment on Mark's request for a double cognac to go with it. She didn't understand what the scene on the road had meant, but had sense enough to realise she couldn't push him. He would tell her in his own good time — she hoped. 'Is there a market in the town?' she asked when the smiling waitress brought their order.

'But yes, Madame. The market is held twice a week, on Mondays and Fridays. You are on holiday?'

'Yes. We're just passing through. I'm sorry we missed the market. We thought we might go and see the Abbey in Solesmes. I'm told it's a great spectacle at Easter, though of course we've missed that, too.'

The young girl giggled. 'You have also missed the weekly spectacle at Solesmes, Madame.'

'Another one?'

'But yes. You know the monks are very devout. All the time they are not sleeping or praying, they work very hard. On Saturday they are allowed out for a promenade — not alone, you understand.' She rolled her eyes suggestively with a saucy smile. 'They would be afraid of meeting a woman! But they are allowed out in groups and they look so funny in their sandals with their black robes flapping — a flock of crows! They have no watches so, when it is time for them to return, the great bell tolls, calling them home for lunch. One hundred times and on the hundredth, the Abbot enters the Refectory and they eat. It happens every Saturday!'

'Celeste!'

'J'arrive!' She hurried off in answer to the summons.

'I should like to have seen the monks,' said Mark, trying hard to appear interested. The cognac had helped, but he still felt ill at ease.

'Yes. No doubt that little monkey would have got a rocket if Madame, la Patronne, had heard her mocking the Brothers. Look, Mark, there's a village not far from here called Maréchal les Deux Chapeaux. What an extraordinary name! I wonder how that came about?'

'Perhaps one of Bonaparte's Marshals changed sides, thereby wearing two hats, and came from there, or died there?' he offered. 'There's a village where de Gaulle lived with a similar name, but I think it's 'something les Deux Eglises' or 'Chappelles'. I suppose, because there are, or were, two churches there.' They both tried hard to recapture the happy exchanges of snippets of knowledge and experience, which had made their former conversations so enjoyable.

★　★　★

After consultation over the brochures so kindly provided, they glanced at the recommended 15th century glass in the church

179

windows, agreed not to visit the Museum or Library, or hire the offered bicycles to explore the countryside. They wandered contentedly around the town, taking streets as the fancy took them, until the smell of freshly baked bread wafting out through the open door of the boulangerie left them drooling. They sniffed in appreciation and greedily studied the array of pastries so temptingly displayed. Bread of every shape and size was piled on shelves inside the shop; long thin twists; shorter, fatter loaves; rolls topped with seeds and breads with shiny crusts. The smell and the sight of typical French 'sandwiches', comprising a half baguette sliced lengthways and stuffed with delicious ham and salad, made them realise it was a long time since breakfast.

They turned into the nearest bistro and, by the time they had finished a lunch of plain omelettes and fresh green salad, some semblance of their former companionship had been achieved.

'Why does something so simple taste so much better here?' Patricia commented.

'Perhaps because we're on holiday?'

She wasn't convinced. 'Maybe. But I think they have a secret ingredient they don't tell anyone about. Perhaps you have to be born here to learn it.' She leaned forward lowering her voice dramatically.

Mark took his cue from her.

'Perhaps there's an omelette secret society. You know, like the Masons,' he whispered, joining in the fun.

Patricia's peal of laughter brought an answering smile to his face and from then on they were both relaxed.

They continued their unhurried inspection of the town, passed a pleasant hour writing postcards in the Park, and watched the patient fishermen tend their rods on the banks of the lazily flowing river. Mark was very quiet.

'Not a pastime for me,' commented Patricia. 'I prefer something with a bit more action.'

They wandered on.

'Look Mark! There's a shoe shop. I wonder if they have sandals in my size? Do you mind? I promise not to try on every pair they've got.'

The mingled smells of new leather and fish-glue filled the low ceilinged 'magasin a chaussures'. They sniffed appreciatively. As Patricia tried on her various finds, Mark wandered around looking at the assortment of footwear for sale — everything from baby's first little shoe to elegant ladies' high heels, and sturdy working boots for the farming population. At a wide wooden bench under the rear window lay piles of boots and shoes obviously awaiting repair. So, the proprietor was a cordonnier as well as a salesman. Mark was happy to see a sight from his childhood. To find a good old-fashioned cobbler in England was more difficult these days than finding the gold at the end of the rainbow.

At last Patricia had finished her shopping. She was delighted with her purchase of two pairs of attractive sandals.

As they walked on following their Town Plan and gradually making their way to the hotel, she threw a couple of amused glances at Mark. Finally he caught her looking at him.

'What?'

'What's that tune you're humming?'

'Tune?'

'Yes. Ever since we left the shoe shop you've been humming the same tune over and over. What is it?'

Mark frowned. He'd been totally unaware of any tune. He tried to recapture it.

'Yes,' cried Patricia. 'That's it.'

Again Mark hummed the short refrain, wondering where it came from and trying to fish words from his memory. 'A little mouse with clogs on, going clip-clippety-clop.' He stopped short, heart pounding.

'Patricia. Are there windmills in the Sarthe?'

'No. I don't think so. I can't remember seeing any. Why?'

Mark had left her side, retracing their steps to the shoe-shop.

'Ah, m'sieur,' beamed the welcoming proprietor. 'You wish something more for Madame? Or perhaps for yourself, this time?'

Mark ignored him and strode over to the table beneath the window. He pushed aside the piles of shoes requiring attention until he found what he sought — a pair of child's clogs. He stared down at them. On the background of plain, golden, varnished wood danced merry mice in trousers and jackets, dresses and bonnets. Each wore an outsize pair of clogs. The whole effect was guaranteed to delight the child who owned them. 'Where do these come from?' Mark asked hoarsely.

'Ah, the sabots of the little Claude need to be re-soled. The young Dubuis painted them for him herself. She has a talent that one, n'est-çe pas? And it is hard to say who loves her more, Claude or his Papa.' He smiled and nodded knowingly.

'And how old is he, this little Claude?'

'He must be five or nearly six by now. Soon these will be too small for him.'

Mark stared dully at the little sabots in his

hands. For one crazy moment he had seen her slim artist's hands painting Fliss's cot as she sang about a little mouse that wore clogs and lived in a windmill. What a damnable coincidence!

How he envied the little family of young Claude and his mother and father. Had things been different he, Mark, might have had a son now. With a word of thanks and farewell he left the shop.

'Mark?' Patricia was looking at him in concern. 'What was all that about?'

'While you were shopping I saw them on the bench. It didn't register until we were walking along. I thought they might fit Fliss,' he lied. 'But they were too small.' How could he tell Patricia he had been consumed with such a longing for his dead wife?

★ ★ ★

Sleep was a long time coming to Patricia that night. 'People are like icebergs,' she thought. 'What you see is only a fraction of the whole. So much is hidden. What was it that haunted Mark? Here in France, were they near the place his wife died? Why wouldn't he let her comfort him as she longed to do?'

In spite of herself, she heard Mandy Hamilton-ffrench's words: 'They both went off to France, but only one came back!' She sat up and punched her pillow into submission, turning it to find a cool place to lay her aching head. 'What happened to the body?'

It was no good. She couldn't sleep. Getting out of bed she rifled through her big briefcase and spread out the quick notes she had made of the various possible sites they had visited. She opened up her laptop and settled down to translate the cryptic remarks into a comprehensive presentation for her client. When in doubt — work. With luck it would make her sleepy. At worst it would be a good job done.

★   ★   ★

On Sunday morning the sun had disappeared. Grey skies reflected Mark's mood, but he made an effort to at least appear cheerful, and listened politely to their smiling host who told them the clouds would pass. It would be bright again before lunchtime. Having been assured that many non-Catholics attended such services, they loaded the car and set off in good time for Mass at the Abbey. As they had come so far it would be foolish to miss the chance to hear the world-famous Gregorian chant in its original setting.

They left Sablé on the Port de Juigné road, which took them past the cinema and the swimming pool. The last of the houses dropped behind. Countryside surrounded them. Their view of the river was obstructed by trees. Mark sat with fists so tightly clenched his knuckle bones shone white through the tanned skin. His tension was beginning to affect Patricia when they rounded a bend and she involuntarily stopped the car. They gasped, awe-struck: through a rent in the clouds a bright beam of sunlight illumined the Abbey. Behind it the sky was still dark with threatening rain, but this one spot was detailed in shining brilliance.

Speechless they took in the sheer size and impression of ageless power represented there as the Abbey dominated the whole landscape in front of them. Solid and impassive it watched over man's puny endeavours. The passing ages had only added to its magnificence and strength. This permanent memorial to Man's relationship with his Maker stood inviolate, its pinnacles soaring to the sky. Together they sighed on the breath they had been unconsciously holding.

Subdued, they carried on through the small village ahead, turned right onto the bridge crossing the Sarthe and entered Solesmes. Once they had parked near the Square, the trance was broken. Patricia quickly went to work with her camera. Then it was time to take their seats.

Unaccompanied Plainsong rose and fell. Voices climbed in patterns, now one, then another, to achieve the summit, reaching up higher and higher to God in a glory of pure praise, which held their attention throughout the service. Patricia stood and sat when everyone else did. Mark, she noticed, was engrossed. She was frankly bored by the time the Mass ended. The hard wooden seats had soon made her regret her lack of padding and she found the smell of incense distinctly unpleasant.

Mark wanted to linger and examine the intricate carvings and inspect the amazing vaulted ceiling of the church so, promising to wait for him, Patricia hurried out into the fresh air.

The rainsquall had passed while they had been indoors. She looked around the Square with interest as the church emptied. Her professional eye categorised each member of the crowd. Some were tourists, each national-ity with its own idiosyncrasy; Japanese strung with cameras; well-fed Americans and studi-ous Germans. The French worshippers wore everything from haute couture to the 'good Sunday best' with that dash of chic, which only a Frenchwoman can produce.

Best of all, Patricia liked the old men. They replaced their black berets as they emerged into the sunlight, and fished in the pockets of their blouson jackets to find blue packets of Gauloise cigarettes, or produced oily pouches from trouser pockets. Appreciatively she inhaled the aroma of black tobacco as they lit up. Gauloise, garlic and soapy drains! For her that was the smell of France.

Her professional attention noted the bright eyes, in the weather-beaten faces covered with networks of wrinkles. She watched in fascination as big, horny hands with earth-blackened nails completed the delicate manoeuvre of rolling cigarettes from flimsy papers without spilling one shred of tobacco.

As she stood near the church entrance, someone tapped her shoulder and courteously asked her to make way for a middle-aged couple supporting a third person. As she moved aside Patricia noted the younger woman appeared unwell. Correctly pigeonholing them as country folk by their dress she looked at their faces and caught the strained expression in the young woman's eyes before the lids fluttered down. Idly she watched as the small party made its way across the road and down a side street, out of sight.

★   ★   ★

Another pair of eyes also followed the trio's progress. Emil Fourgeon was waiting for his wife to come out of the patisserie opposite the church. He held his small son safely by the hand and watched the milling crowd. The couple supporting a young woman passed close by. Not until they drew level with him did he realise who it was — the woman he had left at the farm the night of the storm! His first instinct was to turn away, but he saw her eyes were closed. There was no danger of recognition. How strange life was. Had he not gone against all his usual instincts and taken her to safety, who could say where he would be today?'

'Maman, maman!' called the child at his side jerking him out of his reverie. They smiled and waved to the approaching woman. Emil rescued the bag of pastries from his wife who had to cope with the small body, which hurled itself into her arms. The little family regained their car and drove away.

★ ★ ★

Patricia was happily snapping 'characters' when Mark joined her. They intended to stay off the main Autoroutes if possible, so drove through the Forêt de Charnie, and grabbed a late lunch in Sillé le Guillaume. From there the D310 took them through the countryside towards Paris. An early flight would get them into London in time for work on Monday.

Patricia had expected to feel flat and sad at the end of their holiday. Instead she felt a tingle of excitement. How? When? Where it had happened she didn't know or care, but Mark was a changed being. The man who came out of the Abbey was relaxed, smiling and attentive. Also there was a new sense of purpose in his attitude.

This break had accomplished everything she had hoped for. 'Oh! please,' she prayed, 'please let it last!'

*　★　★*

Mark hadn't felt so at peace with himself for years. He had some religious faith, he supposed. He enjoyed accompanying Shirley and Fliss to church on Sundays, but hadn't the habit of personal daily pray.

When the church in Solesmes had emptied, he'd walked forward and sunk to his knees in a pew near the front. Not even sure if he was praying to God or his dead wife, he sent up all his accumulated grief and guilt, begging to be forgiven.

In the quiet moment after this offering he felt such a sense of relief and freedom come over him it seemed a mantle of regret slithered down his body to leave him for ever. His eyes stung as he whispered a silent, 'Thank you' and left the church. His mind was made up. He would go forward into the future with certainty. No looking back! Fliss should have a new mother and, in time perhaps, a brother or sister. They would be happy together, Fliss, Shirley, Patricia and himself.

12

Three weeks later Mark and Patricia were once again at Ravenscourt. The mini-drought, which had prompted talk of a scorching summer to come, had broken on their arrival.

'This is what I want,' thought Patricia as she looked out of the kitchen window at the pouring rain. The house was snug and cosy inside. She and Shirley had been baking and a wonderful smell emanated from the big Aga. Hoots of laughter came from the sitting room where Mark and Fliss played some game that obviously involved much cheating on both sides. She smiled; for this I would gladly give up London, Paris and Rome. To have my own home and child, with the man I love. What could be better? If only Mark feels the same.

The following morning she was wakened by a squeal, abruptly cut off. The walls of the old house were thick. The doors fitted snugly so she could only suppose Fliss was on the landing directly outside her room. She slipped on a dressing gown, and opened the door to find Mark, his hand held securely across Fliss's mouth, in the act of hoisting her over his shoulder to carry her away.

'What's going on?' she queried.

'I'm sorry she woke you. Go back to sleep . . . if you can. Have a lie in. Fliss normally creeps into my bed, but this morning apparently you were to be the favoured one. I hoped I'd caught her in time, but obviously not.'

'It's all right. She can come and snuggle in with me. I've had a lovely sleep and feel fine - honestly!'

Fliss hardly waited for the end of the invitation before she wriggled out of Mark's grasp and bolted into Patricia's room.

'Does that invitation include me?' asked Mark with a distinct twinkle in his eye. He stood there in bare feet, hair on end, his pyjamas rumpled from his tussle with Fliss.

Patricia's heart said, 'Yes,' but her lips said, 'Sorry. This is a girlie thing. It's present time. Bye, bye,' and she shut the door.

★　★　★

At breakfast Felicity was enthusing about her beautiful doll and her new hobby. 'Patricia's going to bring me a Senorita - that's what you call a Spanish lady, Nana,' she informed Shirley. 'And she's promised to send me postcards wherever she goes so I shall have to ask for an album for my birthday, and put them all in. I was going to stick them on my bedroom wall, but Patricia says they might fade and it would be nicer to be able to carry my album to school and show my class.'

Patricia winked at Shirley out of Fliss's sight. Shirley silently blessed her for preserving the wallpaper in Fliss's room, and wondered how often she would have to hear, 'Patricia says' in the next few days. Fliss was quite obviously a total fan of her Daddy's new friend, which, under the circumstances, is no bad thing, thought Shirley.

★ ★ ★

Although they usually walked down to church, Patricia had been so busy weaving pleasant daydreams she'd forgotten the state of the path. Fliss's surprise on seeing the car drawn up before the front door, reminded her. She frowned.

'Not to worry,' said Mark. 'Being a sharp-thinking kind of guy I noticed Madame's elegant high heels - with appreciation,' he added with a smile.

'Nana! The bread!' called Fliss.

'It's all right. I've got it,' assured Shirley.

Patricia wondered if there would be

Communion at church until Mark smiled at her.

'Not for our consumption. You'll see.'

They descended The Mains, crossed the main road and drove down Belle Hill to St Alkelda's. Patricia was glad they were in the car. There was no pavement and the road was so steep she could easily have sprained her ankle. They managed to park by the pub, and walked through the lych gate and along the path to the church door. As soon as they got out of the car Mark, Shirley and Fliss exchanged greetings with everyone they met. This is what it's like to live in a small community, thought Patricia, used to the anonymity of London. She was happy to be able to exchange nods of recognition with two or three people she'd seen previously

As they waited for the service to begin her eyes wandered over the lovely old church. She smiled at the amateurish painting of a huge Royal Coat of Arms on wood attached to the church wall. Which local worthy had executed it, she wondered? Perhaps in the days when loyalty to the Crown was in doubt.

For a moment, her contented mood was shaken as she looked round the congregation and wondered if Mandy Hamilton-ffrench's great aunt was among them. Then she deliberately pushed such distasteful thoughts away and concentrated instead on the brass chandelier with its real candles suspended above the main aisle.

When the service started she found she knew some of the hymn tunes. Surprised, she realised she was enjoying herself. She gave hearty thanks for her blessings and prayed they might continue.

★ ★ ★

When they emerged from the church porch Shirley was accosted by friends; Mark turned aside to answer some question of Fliss's, and Patricia was left to wander at will. She looked at the huge slabs, which made up the path. As she looked more closely she saw they were old memorial stones and wondered if the bodies were buried underneath or elsewhere. It seemed irreverent to walk on them. There were whole families listed, many children had died in infancy or barely into their teens. She strolled in the sunshine admiring the comfortable, solid shape of the stone-built church with its square tower.

'Come on, Patricia,' Fliss urged and grabbed her by the arm. She led the way out of the West Gate, past golden stone houses with mullioned windows. Patricia just had time to read dates of 1677 and even 1663 carved above the doors as Fliss rushed her along.

Their goal was soon reached when Fliss stopped on a broad pavement above a shallow stream.

'It's called a beck in this part of the world,' offered Shirley. 'It's only inches deep even after all the rain yesterday, but come back in an hour or two and it'll be a different story. Because this is a limestone area full of caves, sinkholes and springs, rivers rise and fall rapidly. It can deepen to feet in a matter of hours, then these houses behind get out the sandbags.'

Loud quacks heralded their arrival as ducks appeared from every direction, and converged just below the humans' feet. The bullies forced the more timid out of the way as Fliss broadcast pieces of bread over the water. Patricia entered into the spirit of the fun. She seized some bread and tried, by accurate throwing, to get her pieces to land beside the smaller or less aggressive ducks, thereby, she reasoned laughing she had saved their lives. She felt Mark's eyes on her and turned her head. His expression made her knees go weak, she blushed, smiled at him, and as she returned to her life-saving mission she wondered if everyone could hear the thumping of her heart?

'Now it's our turn to eat.' Shirley had obviously been up long before anyone else. A full Sunday roast dinner with all the trimmings, and a very fattening Pavlova with lashings of cream for afters, left them all incapable of movement. For a good hour the silence was broken only by the rustle of the Sunday papers. Even Fliss was quietly occupied in finishing off her homework.

An after-the-party feeling threatened their contented mood until Mark had the happy notion of making plans for the next weekend. Fliss cheered up. Shirley made notes in her diary, and Patricia went up to pack with a lighter heart. This wasn't the end. In fact it was just a lovely beginning. Since France, she felt so close to Mark. All barriers were gone.

She left her case in the hall, and joined Shirley in the sitting room. 'Where is everybody?'

'They've gone to fill the car up. Fliss likes to have a private minute with her Daddy before he goes. You don't mind?'

'Of course not. Shirley, thank you so much for this weekend. In spite of the rain it has been lovely.'

'Good. I thought you wouldn't mind spending just a lazy weekend at home, without any special arrangements. If the weather's better next week we could walk, or

198

go to the Falconry - we still haven't done that.'

As they talked, Patricia wandered round the pleasant sitting room examining the pictures, admiring ornaments. On the baby grand piano there was a group of silver-framed photos of Mark and Shirley, with Fliss at various ages. She reached over and lifted a small heart-shaped frame, and peered at it closely. 'Who's this,' she asked Shirley.

'That's my daughter.'

'Oh! I didn't know you had two?'

'Two what?'

'Daughters. I didn't know there were two of them.'

'There aren't. That's Fliss's mother. Mark's wife.'

Patricia gaped, then frowned. For a moment the room swung round. 'But . . . I don't understand,' she whispered.

'What?'

'I saw her. When we were in France. I saw her in Solesmes.'

Shirley's face whitened. With a hand that shook she took the frame from Patricia and tenderly touched the glass over the face of the young woman below. 'No. She's gone. My dear girl is gone.' She swallowed. 'We lost her in France, when she and Mark were on holiday. A dreadful accident. But she left us darling Fliss, so I suppose we have to be grateful for that at least. This isn't even a particularly good photo of her, but I have so few. She was the one who always took the family snaps. I can't remember why she was looking so strained, but there we are.' She replaced the frame on the piano.

'Shirley, I don't know what to think. The woman I saw was the girl in that photograph. I'd swear to it.'

'Please, Patricia. Don't say any more. It's just not possible. We're all supposed to have a double somewhere in the world, you know,' said Shirley, trying to lighten the moment. 'And please don't mention this to Mark. It would be too cruel. He would be so distressed, and we've had such a lovely time. That'll be them now. You'll have to get a wiggle on, just in case the traffic's bad. You won't want to miss your train.' She moved out into the hall followed by Patricia, who lifted her weekend case.

'Here. Let me take that,' said Mark. 'I'll pop it in the boot. Fliss, you can unlock it for me. Here are the keys.'

Shirley supervised the opening of the boot. Mark waited beside Fliss who, with fierce concentration, was trying to put the wrong key in the lock.

Patricia put her hands in her pockets. 'Drat

it, I've left my gloves in the sitting room. No, don't worry, Shirley. I know just where they are.'

She hurried back into the house and crossed the sitting room to the piano. With a quick glance over her shoulder, she scooped up the heart-shaped frame and thrust it into the depths of her handbag. Hurriedly, she rearranged the photograph frames on the piano to hide the gap, and pulled her gloves out of the pocket in which she'd hidden them. She was putting them on as she went back to join the others.

★   ★   ★

'You're very quiet,' said Mark as they drove towards Leeds. 'Tired?'

'A little. And a bit sad the weekend's over.'

'Not to worry.' He gave her hand a squeeze. 'Plenty more where that came from.'

'Oh, God! I hope so,' prayed Patricia, but she could feel the outline of the purloined photograph frame through the suede of her handbag. A heavy knot of foreboding gathered in her chest.

13

'So, little one, did you sleep well?' queried Marie-Thérèse.

'Yes, I dreamed; but it was the happy one. I just know that's my mother I see, Thérèse. I'm sure it's my mother, because I'm there, too, playing in a garden. There are big rocks beyond and I sit under a tree and watch. Thérèse, we were so happy. There was a swing on the apple tree and Maman pushed me higher and higher. I was flying and I laughed and kicked my legs. She warned me I'd fall, but I knew I wouldn't. I was so safe, because she loved me. She wouldn't ever let anything hurt me. I watched it all. What do you call that? Do you think it was my childhood, Thérèse? I was such a sweet little girl in my cute jeans.'

'It could have been. Why not?'

'So! I know I was loved as a child. What went wrong?'

'Who knows? And the other? Nothing more there?'

'No. After we came back from the Abbey — that night I saw it in my dream, a huge flash of light, I cried out and then the falling.

After that nothing, but this sense of loss and always the searching for I don't know what.'

'Well, write it all down. You know Father Anselm wants everything, no matter how bizarre. When do you see him again?'

'This evening, do you think there's any point in it, Thérèse?'

'He's a very learned priest, little one. Trust him. He's doing his best.'

'I know and I'm not ungrateful. It's just that sometimes I give up hope and I get so frightened, I don't want to know the truth! What if there's some ghastly secret?'

'Rubbish. Don't talk nonsense. Whatever it is we'll face it together. We all love you and we'll always be here for you. You don't need to be afraid.' She gave the younger woman a swift hug. 'Now then, it's time you fed the hens.'

★   ★   ★

'Well, Father?' said Marie-Anne expectantly.

He finished examining the lined notebook she had given him and looked at her over his spectacles. 'Well, Marie-Anne?'

'What do you think? Is it useful?'

'When I asked you to keep this notebook, or diary, after your visit to the Abbey, did you wonder why?'

'You told me it would be useful to record any memories or dreams I may have, so I did. It's been over a month now, so, what's the result?'

'Let's do a little experiment. Here are paper and pen. From memory write down all you have learned about yourself and I shall use the notebook and do the same. Then we'll compare.' For a few moments nothing could be heard in the priest's study, but an occasional sigh and the scratch of pen on paper. 'What have we?' said Father Anselm. 'A name, not Dubuis obviously. You have put Marie-Anne. Why?'

'Apparently, even though I was semi-conscious, I told Marie-Thérèse my name.'

'Good. That's something solid. Your age we think is about twenty-eight or twenty-nine — close enough, and not vitally important. You ladies always seem to look younger than your years. You believe you have seen yourself as a child, with your mother in a dream? In a garden with apple trees and rocks. Apple trees could mean Normandie perhaps or even here in Anjou there are many orchards.'

'No. It's not an orchard, Father. Just a garden.'

'Ah! In the other dreams. You are climbing on hands and knees in the rain. You see the Abbey and then you fall. Is that right?'

'Yes, Father. And then I am searching, too — before — in the first dream.'

'When you see the Abbey, Marie-Anne. Where are you? Are you in the square in Solesmes looking up at the Abbey behind the church?'

She paused — recreated her dream in her mind's eye. 'No. I'm on the other side. When you come along the road to Juigné from Sablé you go round the bend and see the Abbey ahead on the right. That's how it is.'

'Good. Now, what if we turn the dreams around. A bright light — could be lightning. It was the night of the great storm after all. You see the Abbey, then you fall, then you try to crawl upwards in the rain. Why?' He shot the question at her in a sharp tone unlike the musing voice he had used to this point.

'To get away from the water,' she replied immediately. 'Oh!'

'What water is that, Marie-Anne?'

'The river, I think. Yes, the river is behind and below me,' she shut her eyes tight and frowned in the effort to put herself back into that scene of fear. 'It's no good. I can't see any more.'

'Don't worry. You've done well. Whatever happened to frighten you so much you lost your memory, occurred on the Sablé to Juigné road on the night of the storm. Don't try to force it. Let it come to you. I truly believe the mental block you have created is like a brick wall and now, one by one, the bricks are falling out. Give it time. The mind is so complex even great specialists don't fully understand how it works. I've been doing some study on your behalf.'

'Oh, Father! I'm sorry to be such a nuisance.'

'Don't apologise. I've enjoyed it. It's good for me to stretch my own brain beyond the doings of my little flock here. There was a time when I believed I wished to become an academic, but my destiny was obviously set on another path. I've left that life behind, but gain great enjoyment in paying legitimate visits to Academia.'

He smiled and explained. 'Emotion has a greater effect on the way our brain and body functions than one would believe possible. In the case of amnesia, unless it is caused by damage to the brain, it can be termed as voluntary amnesia. In this case the brain shuts away memories that are too painful to face. However, it does monitor the situation and memory can be restored. Sometimes it needs a trigger.'

'What's a trigger?'

'Apparently the senses are very important here. Smells and sounds, music, or perhaps a particular type of engine or running water start a train of thought or memory, which leads to a revelation. I don't suppose you've experienced anything like that?'

'Actually, Father, I wasn't going to mention it. It all seemed too silly.'

'What's that?'

'The other day, little Claude, showed me a new book his Papa had bought him. I picked it up and opened it, and brought it to my face to smell it. I closed my eyes and breathed in that smell of fresh paper and new print. It's like no other and I knew, Father. I knew I'd done that often before. It was like a reflex action, no thought involved. I love books, but though I make up stories for Claude, I'm sure I'm no author!'

'Interesting. And you also paint, I believe?'

'Yes. I seem to have a little talent in that direction.'

'I wonder if you could have trained to be a teacher? You're very fond of children, and good with them, too. You have patience, talent and love books. There is also the question of your apparent fluency in English. Yes. I think that's a distinct possibility.'

'Does that help in finding the truth?' Marie-Anne put the eager question with hope in her eyes.

'Not immediately. But if we get an answer

to my letters describing someone who is missing it could all help to decide if it is you.'

Marie-Anne's shoulders slumped. For a moment there she had got quite excited at the idea of a breakthrough. But they were back to 'if' again. 'Do I really want to know, Father? I used to think it was vital, but now as time has passed perhaps it would be better to let it go. Something bad happened by the river there. I know it. If someone tried to kill me, there must be a reason. Do you think I could be a bad person, Father? I mean really bad, so that I shouldn't marry or have children of my own?'

The good priest hid a smile. 'No, Marie-Anne. I believe you to be a very good, kind, honest and God-fearing young woman. Remember I have heard your confession for years now and I would detect any wickedness in you. God has forgiven your little sins and if, in your heart, you truly repent of any sin, even those you cannot recall, you know He will forgive. Whatever you cannot remember, I don't believe it to be a wickedness you have committed. Were you to marry I should need to seek guidance from Mother Church. There are formalities to be completed, legal affidavits to be sworn, no doubt, and, where there is no background, certain assumptions would have to be made.'

'Then if it is, as Marie-Thérèse fears, a sin committed against me, should I be afraid of the truth?'

This thought had also occupied the priest's mind on numerous occasions. 'I believe not,' he began judiciously. 'Consider! Nearly six years have passed. If, as Marie-Thérèse thought, you had had dangerous knowledge affecting criminals or the like, then that knowledge is surely so old it is no longer a threat. In all this time you haven't appeared to confront anyone or denounce him or her to the Police. If the threat to you was more personal then it couldn't have been meant to kill you, as you were delivered to the farm for help. Abandonment, yes! Attempted murder, no!'

Marie-Anne gave a huge sigh of relief. 'Thank you, Father. You've put it so clearly. You don't know what a weight you've taken off my mind. Even though Grandmère 'adopted' me to give me the protection of the family, I've been on my guard. In the background there was always the fear of someone unknown, yet who knows me, being able to harm me. No way could I protect myself against that. It was always there, a shadow to cloud every pleasure. Now I can relax.'

'My poor child! I had no idea you felt so

vulnerable; that you have carried this burden for so long. Why did you never mention it?'

'What could you have done, Father? What could anyone do? I did mention it once to Maurice, but made light of it. I didn't want to put more cares on those who love me.'

'You see,' said Father Anselm. 'You are a good, thoughtful person — not wicked at all. Beyond the usual daily sins, you know,' he added hurriedly in case she was in danger of believing herself to be perfect. But in truth it was a caveat he knew to be unnecessary with Marie-Anne.

'Father, I believe I'm going to ask you to stop writing your letters. I know you've been so good, but it's yet one more burden in your busy day. I'll think about it and let you know. At the moment I feel content. I want to just enjoy my life here with my new family.'

'And pray, Marie-Anne. Never underestimate the power of prayer.'

'No, Father. In fact I shall do what Grandmère always advised. I shall leave it to le bon Dieu to decide what happens to me.'

'An excellent idea.'

He shook her hand, gave her his blessing and bade her goodbye, happy to see a new glow in her eyes. He watched her go down the path and saw that she walked with purpose. Marie-Anne was at peace with her world.

*   *   *

The new lightness in Marie-Anne's step was not lost on Marie-Thérèse. 'Well, child? What has happened? You left the house dragging your feet and now you practically dance across the yard.' Marie-Anne clasped Thérèse by the waist and attempted to waltz her ample form around the big kitchen. 'Put me down, Marie-Anne. Have you gone mad?'

'Yes! Mad, mad, mad with relief and thankfulness and happiness! Thérèse, I can't tell you how I feel,' cried Marie-Anne. She threw herself into the old rocking chair with such force the heavy piece of furniture skidded across the flagstones. 'I'm going to dig out the notes Maurice did for Grand-mère. I'll start a co-operative for the aromatherapy and I'll make it work. Grand-mère would have wanted that, wouldn't she?' She sprang up again and danced around the kitchen. Merlin barked in alarm.

'Calm down. Stop it, now this minute, before you break something.' Marie-Thérèse tried hard to sound severe, but tears swam in her eyes as she saw the change in the younger woman. This was what she had prayed for so hard. She crossed herself and raised silent thanks to the Almighty for His answer. 'Does this mean you've found the truth? And it has made you happy, God be thanked?'

'No. At least . . . Father Anselm showed me a sort of truth. I don't have to worry any more about who I am. It doesn't matter. I'm Marie-Anne Dubuis of La Lavendière. That's all that's important now. The rest — what happened before — is immaterial. I don't care if I never know the truth. I'm satisfied with what I have here, you and Jean-Yves, that's the new me. The me I'm meant to be.'

'And Claude and Maurice?' added Marie-Thérèse slyly. 'You know he's never given up hope.'

'Ah! That's something else. But don't forget, there's still Madame La Salle to consider. I've tried to see her point of view, Thérèse, but it is as Maurice says: she has had five years to come to terms with the fact he would surely remarry at some time. Perhaps if it were anyone but me? She hates me! When I think of that look in her eyes, I shudder. She looked like one possessed.'

14

That night the raucous clamour of the bell roused the sleeping household. Jean-Yves grumbled as he pushed bare feet into his slippers and dragged a dressing gown around his shoulders. Marie-Thérèse strained her ears and had a feeling of 'déjà-vu'. This was how it had happened the night Marie-Anne arrived. Dear God, not again, she prayed. She heaved herself from the depths of the bed and moved to the door. Marie-Anne was out on the landing before her and together the two women descended the stairs fearful of what they might find.

In the hall below Maurice, white-faced, his hair on end, spoke, quietly, urgently to Jean-Yves. As they approached he swung round and they saw the bundle he carried was Claude swathed in a blanket, half tucked into his Daddy's large jacket.

'Le pauvre petit!' exclaimed Marie-Anne as she ran forward, arms outstretched. 'Give him to me, Maurice. He's not ill?' She took the small boy from his father, waiting only for reassurance it was not illness that brought him to their door at this hour. Claude's huge eyes regarded Marie-Anne from a small pale face where the trembling lower lip presaged a bout of tears. 'Shush, mon petit gars,' she crooned as she led the way into the comfortable kitchen. 'Hot chocolate I think, Thérèse?' she suggested as Marie-Thérèse threw open the big range to release its welcome heat. The early June night was not cold, but Thérèse knew warmth was good for shock. She sensed there were shocks in store for all of them!

Marie-Anne settled herself into the old rocking chair and cuddled the little boy to her. She could feel the tension in him and, at this stage, didn't care what had caused it. All she knew was Claude needed her to comfort and reassure him. Gradually as she rocked and talked baby nonsense to him she felt him relax against her in trust and surrender. How he had prevented himself from weeping she didn't know. He no longer needed to be a 'brave soldier' and his eyelids drooped over less strained eyes. Soon he was asleep on her breast; the hot chocolate rapidly formed a skin in the mug Marie-Anne held for him.

With the child asleep Marie-Anne looked up to take in what was going on around her. Maurice gulped great mouthfuls of hot coffee, with a stiffener of brandy in it, if the bottle in Jean-Yves's hand was any indication!

He spoke quietly, but Marie-Anne could hear every word. 'Will you keep him until I can return?'

'What a question? Of course we will care for him,' replied Marie-Thérèse indignantly. 'He must stay just as long as you think necessary.'

'But what has happened?' asked Marie-Anne softly. 'Why did you have to bring him here at dead of night?'

'I had no choice. I had to get him away.'

'From Les Rosiers?'

'From his grandmother.'

'Tiens! Whatever do you mean?' queried Marie-Thérèse.

'Claude has always been a happy child, but lately he's been nervy, not sleeping well. He has nightmares he can't remember, but enough to wake him. So, I've been sleeping more lightly myself. Tonight I woke suddenly; there was no sound from Claude's room, but I rose to check on him. His room was empty. I tried the bathroom. Empty also. At that point I heard him. He was downstairs — whimpering in fear. I raced down and couldn't believe my eyes. In the kitchen Mémère La Salle was trying to stuff his arm into the sleeve of his outdoor coat! She pulled and pushed at him, muttering all the while. Her hair hung in wisps around her face where it had escaped from her bun. The child was clearly terrified. He saw me and called out. I shouted her name. She took no notice so I grasped her arm. She whirled and attacked me, her fingers hooked into claws.'

Beads of blood oozed from two deep scratches on his face. He put a hand up to his cheek, conscious of the pain for the first time. 'I consider myself to be strong, but I had to use all my strength against her. She was possessed. And all the time the child watched in fear. I managed to manhandle her out of the kitchen and into the hall and there, God forgive me, I hit her. It was the only thing I could think of. I punched her as I would a man and she dropped at my feet. I must get back. I've left her tied up on the bed in her room, but I don't know if it'll hold her. May I use your telephone? She may have gone mad, but she was artful enough to pull out the telephone wire. Yes, and smash the handset, too. I must call the doctor. He'll know what to do — I hope!'

Young Doctor Rougemont wasted no time asking for long explanations. He quickly grasped the problem and agreed to come at once. Maurice stooped to kiss his son's head where he slept in Marie-Anne's arms, and left the kitchen to return to the horrors that awaited him at Les Rosiers.

It was a long night. Jean-Yves returned to his bed. It wouldn't help anyone for him to be too tired to care for the beasts in the morning. Marie-Anne managed to lower Claude into her own bed and cover him, but when she would have tiptoed away, he roused and called her, begged her to stay. She slipped beneath the covers and cradled him in her arms. He slept, but she lay awake and wondered how all these extraordinary events had come about. In the kitchen Marie-Thérèse dozed in the rocker before the glowing range.

★   ★   ★

With the dawn a haggard Maurice returned to La Lavendière. His red-rimmed eyes were sunk into sockets darkened with the shadows of fatigue. 'I've left Jean-Luc Sabbatier to tend the beasts. How's Claude?'

'Sleeping like the baby he is. Marie-Anne has only just managed to wriggle out of the bed without disturbing him. He's quite calm now and resting peacefully. She'll be down in a minute, so why don't you eat and wait for her before you tell us what's happened.'

Thankfully Maurice lifted the large bowl of coffee she put in front of him and demolished a pile of thick tartines spread liberally with butter and topped with home-cured ham. He was lost in his own thoughts, none of which seemed to give him much pleasure, when Marie-Anne entered the kitchen and greeted him. She took her coffee and seated herself beside him at the table. The three friends waited in companionable silence until Maurice should feel ready to speak.

'She's quite mad. When I got back she was conscious and raving; she struggled and shrieked. She cut her arms on the ropes I had tied her up with, but seemed to feel no pain. When she saw me the hate in her eyes was palpable.' He shuddered. 'It was like looking into the pit of Hell. Please God I never have to see the like again. She knew me though, and if she had her way I should be cursed from now through all eternity.'

'But why?' exclaimed Marie-Thérèse, shocked at the pain in Maurice's eyes.

'You've been so good to her. You took her in; let her stay on when Claudette died. She's been allowed to get away with so much; ordering all to her own satisfaction,' she added indignantly.

'Be honest,' reminded Maurice wearily. 'It suited me to have her stay for Claude's sake — at first. Then cowardice held me back from sending her away. When I had finally steeled myself to it, the need no longer seemed

218

urgent,' he concluded, with a glance at Marie-Anne.

'What happened then?' Marie-Thérèse prompted.

'When Doctor Rougemont arrived he gave her an injection, to sedate her. He made the arrangements, and I had to wait with her until an ambulance came to take her to the hospital. She will have to be assessed, then — who knows?'

He gave a fatalistic shrug. 'I've told the Doctor I will be responsible for all expenses, but I cannot and will not have her back at Les Rosiers. She's not actually criminally insane. Perhaps they'll find her a place with the Sisters of Mercy or some such Order. I never want to see her again,' he concluded bitterly.

'But what will you do? How will you manage?' queried Marie-Thérèse.

Maurice shook his head hopelessly. 'I have no idea at the moment, none whatsoever. I can't even think straight. Good friends, can I ask you to keep Claude until I have made arrangements?'

'But of course,' averred Marie-Thérèse. 'How can you ask?' she demanded. 'The little one will be safe and happy with us until it is time for him to go back to Les Rosiers. He's never any trouble, and Marie-Anne can take him to school in the mornings. The Lepâtre children pass by the farm on their way home; they can bring him along with them.'

Maurice smiled, shaking his head fondly. 'Marie-Thérèse what would we do without you? Half a minute and you have sorted out half my problems. Would that you could do the same with the rest,' he added almost to himself.

'Come, Maurice,' invited Marie-Anne. She rose from the table and held out her hand. 'You need some fresh air to blow the cobwebs away. Thérèse will listen for Claude to stir. She doesn't need us to sit around with gloomy faces, getting under her feet.'

She led him out, across the yard, through the fragrant old milking parlour and into the herb garden. There she sat him down on the wooden bench in the sunshine. 'Rest and relax, Maurice. You're wound up tighter than a spring. None of this is your fault. She's always been a hard, bitter woman. You can't take the blame for whatever it is that has pushed her into this state.'

'Hush, Marie-Anne. You don't know the worst of it. Before the doctor came she calmed down a bit. But only enough to speak sensibly, which made what she said so much worse!' He turned tormented eyes towards her. 'Oh God! Marie-Anne. Claude is not my son!'

'What?'

'She told me. At least she said he was hers that she had more right to him than I. That's what she was doing. Taking him away with her; away from me!'

'But that's crazy! Of course he's yours. She's his grandmother, but only a madwoman would say that gives her more right to him than his father. You mustn't take any notice. She's obviously very disturbed. She must have been grieving for Claudette all this time and it's warped her understanding.'

'Claudette! I knew I should never have married her. I couldn't really understand how anyone so wonderful and glamorous could fall for a country boy like me. Well, it appears my instinct was right. She didn't want me. She just wanted to get her own way. Apparently there was a lover, a married man in Paris who wouldn't leave his wife when Claudette gave him an ultimatum. Her revenge was to marry me. But he came back to get her — and she welcomed him with open arms!' he concluded bitterly. 'What a fool I was. I know just when it happened. I was so pleased at last she seemed happy. The trips to Angers and Le Mans. My God, I made it easy for them.'

'Stop it, Maurice! Stop torturing yourself. This is what Mme La Salle was shouting about that day at Les Rosiers. But Claudette must have changed her mind about the fellow, surely. After all she stayed with you.'

'Not voluntarily,' he replied dully. 'He wanted them to leave together the day of the storm. He came to the farm. They had a blazing row. He left in a rage. Then she took the truck and went after him. He never knew. The truck ran out of fuel a few miles outside the village. She tried to walk back, the storm hit and the rest you know.' He hung his weary head, too defeated to continue.

'Why do you say Claude's not your son? Look at him!'

'Yes. Look at him with his mother's yellow hair!'

'His mother's yellow hair and his father's straight hair. You told me once she had curls. And he has your eyes Maurice. Have you no photographs of yourself as a child? I bet he looks just as you did then.'

Hope flared briefly, then faded. 'The old woman was taking him away, because he's not mine to keep. She said so.'

'Then she's a liar! She would do anything to hurt you. She believes, if Claudette hadn't married you, she would still be alive today. Claude is your son. She told me.'

He raised his head to look at her, not daring to believe. 'When?'

'While she ranted at me. She spoke of Claudette and the lover from Paris. She said the child was yours. Claudette didn't want it and obviously neither did her lover, but Madame La Salle did. I believe the original plan was for Claudette to stay at the farm until after the birth. Then, when her strength had returned, she would go away with him and leave Madame La Salle to care for the child. Obviously something happened to change all that and they had the argument. I don't suppose we'll ever know the truth of it. But Claude is your son, Maurice. You have to believe that!'

For a moment he stared into her eyes trying to read if she spoke the truth or merely tried to comfort him. Then his head dropped; painful tears squeezed between his closed lids. His big frame shook with tearing sobs.

'Oh! Maurice,' cried Marie-Anne and gathered him into her arms like a hurt child.

His head fell to her shoulder as he battled for control. All the while her hand traced a comforting rhythm across his back. Finally he heaved a sigh and his breath came more calmly. Gently he extricated himself from her embrace and sat up. 'Thank you, Marie-Anne. I do believe you. What a fiend that woman is. Thank God I woke when I did. If she had . . . '

He was stopped by Marie-Anne's finger on his lips. 'Don't go down that road, Maurice. I've just learned not to say 'if only' and I assure you, it's the best way. What do you intend to do now?'

'I can't leave Claude here for ever, nor would I want to. I shall have to hire a housekeeper I suppose.'

'May I apply for the job?' Marie-Anne looked up at him, with the hint of a smile in her eyes.

'You? You're not serious?'

'Yes and no. I don't fancy being your housekeeper, but keeping house for you and Claude sounds like heaven to me. Once Maurice you asked me to marry you when we sat on this bench. Now I'm asking you. Will you marry me, Maurice? Do you still want me?'

For a moment he sat and stared at her, trying to take it in, then joy blazed in his face as he realised she was serious. His fatigue disappeared. With a muffled exclamation he leapt to his feet and gathered her into his arms. Clasped to him from head to toe, Marie-Anne returned his kisses. So passionate was his embrace she could barely breathe. In the depths of her mind a memory stirred; of being held like this against another man's aroused body; of feeling such intimacy make them one. Ruthlessly she thrust it aside and concentrated fiercely on Maurice. Softly the ethereal memory floated away.

Marie-Anne pummelled Maurice's back with her clenched fists. As he let her go she staggered and would have fallen.

'What's wrong, my heart?' he panted.

'If you don't let me breath occasionally I won't last until the wedding,' she laughed, rosy-cheeked and gasping. 'And I think we should get back to the kitchen before we both get carried away,' she added shyly. Lovemaking was so new to her, she wasn't sure she could handle this side of Maurice. Although she had found it enjoyable, some spark of reason warned it was up to her to keep control of things before the wedding day.

We've been here before, she thought as they made their way arm in arm to the kitchen to break the good news, but this time nothing can go wrong. Unknown strangers no longer bother me. My life is here and nothing can hurt me now.

★ ★ ★

'Impossible,' declared Marie-Thérèse.

'But Thérèse, it's the most logical thing. Neither Maurice nor I want a great fuss. If we get married quietly as soon as possible then

Claude can stay here until the wedding and we'll all go back to Les Rosiers together.'

'And what will the world say?'

'What do you mean?'

'I excuse you only because you are in love,' said Marie-Thérèse shaking her head. 'Think child. You, too, Maurice. Mme La Salle may not have been universally popular, but she still had her cronies among the older women. What a juicy source of gossip! Maurice has his mother-in-law locked up so he can wed Marie-Anne. The whole valley knows she would never have got a foot over the threshold if the old woman were still at Les Rosiers!'

Marie-Anne and Maurice exchanged glances of consternation. Marie-Thérèse was right. They could just hear the tittle-tattle that would follow the announcement of their imminent marriage, then the counting of the months to see if the haste had been forced upon them in order to have a legitimate child! The very thought put a blight on the enjoyment of their happiness.

'Damn and blast Madame La Salle, she is still ruining everything! What can we do, Thérèse?' Marie-Anne asked angrily. 'There's Claude to be considered and Maurice can't manage the house alone.'

'Peace, child. You're not the only ones to have been making plans this morning. Leave the announcement of your engagement for a couple of weeks. Then we'll have a proper party and do the thing in style. By that time Violette La Salle's breakdown will have ceased to be of interest — a nine days wonder, no more. In the meantime, we must consult with a lawyer, Father Anselm will know someone. The question of establishing a legal identity for you, my child, can be left no longer. All arrangements will be made in due form, and you shall be married while the whole world looks on in approval.'

'But Claude . . . '

'Let me finish, Marie-Anne! I shall ask Madame Lepâtre if her eldest daughter, Françoise, would be so obliging as to come and keep house for Maurice and take care of little Claude. You remember her, Maurice. She was in the school a few years below you.'

He nodded.

'They're a clever family. She's the second of twelve children. Her older brother has no interest in the farm. He went to University in Angers and became a lawyer. The next sister down is a teacher, then there's a nurse. The second boy is the farmer with his father.'

'Yes. They belong to the Cooperative. I see them at meetings, but I don't think I've seen Françoise for years,' said Maurice.

'The reason Françoise didn't leave home

and study like the rest is because of her infirmity. She was born with a twisted hip and walks with a pronounced limp. The poor girl is so conscious of it she hates to leave the farm. It's a shame; she's a pretty little thing. She's used to children; she helped to raise her younger brothers and sisters. She would be an ideal housekeeper. Her disability doesn't stop her being an excellent housewife. Her mother was only bewailing the fact to me after Mass on Sunday that the girl is wasted staying at home, but has no vocation to become a nun. Of course they won't push her out, this might be a Godsend for everyone concerned.' She nodded her head, certain her plans would suit everyone.

'Naturally, if Maurice was a bachelor it would never do. But a widower and an engaged man besides . . . I'm sure Monsieur and Madame Lepâtre would be agreeable, especially to oblige in time of trouble. They're a good Christian family. Françoise would live in, but return home after lunch each Saturday and spend Sunday with her family. Her duties would recommence at breakfast on Monday mornings. What are you laughing at?' she finished indignantly.

'Thérèse, you are wonderful,' said Marie-Anne. She put her arms around the older woman. 'Here we swing between high joy and despair and you calmly take charge and organise everything. Isn't she wonderful, Maurice?'

'Indeed she is,' agreed Maurice. He took Marie-Thérèse's work-worn hands in his and kissed her cheek. 'I am indebted, Thérèse, more than I can say. If ever a time comes when I can repay you for your kindness — but I'm sure that can never be. I owe you too much. But I hope we can have the wedding reasonably soon?'

'I've always loved a harvest wedding,' replied Marie-Thérèse. 'So suitable I always feel. There's a little break then when you could get away for a short honeymoon. Let us make our plans and trust the lawyers can sort out the legalities by then.'

She fished in the table drawer for writing materials and, licked the lead of her pencil, making notes as she spoke. 'We'll have to start thinking of booking dates. You'll go to the Mairie first for the civil ceremony, then on to the church to take your vows before God. After that a short stop for champagne at the hotel so the village can drink your health, then back here for the wedding feast. We can put trestles up in the courtyard and string fairy lights around the walls for the dancing in the evening. I'll lay the food out under covers in the old milking parlour. It's cooler there.' She wrote rapidly, compiling her lists and thoroughly enjoying herself.

'The only thing left for us to do will be to turn up on time,' laughed Marie-Anne to Maurice.

'I shall be early,' he declared with a glowing look, which made her blush.

'And I shan't keep you waiting,' she said softly. 'Not any more. Right Thérèse, it shall be as you say. We shall be wed with the blessings of the whole parish — thanks to you. With Madame La Salle no longer a bar to our marriage, at last things seem to be going our way. Merci, ma chère.'

15

'Will you marry me, Patricia?'

She looked down at Settle and Giggleswick spread out below. 'The world at her feet', and, as all the best fairy stories go, she was being offered a 'happy ever after'. Mark's arm was round her shoulders. The sun shone warmly on them as they sat on the short turf of Attermire Hill, high above the valley. It was a beautiful day and she should have been the happiest woman on earth — and yet . . . The photo-frame she had filched from Shirley's sitting room had been returned the following weekend, surreptitiously wedged lightly between the baby grand and the wall. No one had mentioned its absence and Patricia didn't have long to wait for its discovery. During a particularly boisterous mime in 'Give us a Clue', Fliss cannoned into the piano and the frame dropped to the ground.

'Good heavens!' cried Shirley. 'That's where it was. It must have slipped down the back. I thought Mrs Jennings had moved it to the study. Fliss, child, do try to be more careful. You're like a wild pony let loose in here!'

The copy of the photograph Patricia had commissioned was tucked into the back of her Filofax. Many times over the past month she had determined to destroy it, but what would be the use? The original would still look at her each weekend when she arrived at Ravenscourt. Anxiety made her fanciful. She imagined the young woman watched her reproachfully out of the picture, prodding at her conscience.

Surely, she thought impatiently, they can't be wrong. A mother and a husband can't both be mistaken. She must be dead. How on earth could it be anything else? Shirley's right. It's her double.

'Patricia?' Mark turned her head to face him. 'I haven't got it wrong have I? I'm sorry I'm no good at fancy speeches. A terrible confession for a publisher I suppose, but every time I tried to rehearse what I'd say to you is sounded so false. I do love you, you know. We all do. You realise I come as a package. 'Love me, love my dog',' he laughed self-consciously, 'or in this case, my daughter. I want you for my wife — not just to be Fliss's mother. I thought that's what you wanted, too, but perhaps I've got it all wrong?' Mark frowned.

'No, Mark. I mean, yes, Mark. You haven't got it wrong and yes, I will be your wife and,

I hope, not a wicked stepmother for Fliss.'

'Mother,' he corrected. 'We're going to be a proper family, mother, father and daughter. Do you want a child, Patricia? If so, I'm quite willing. My own little brat has given me quite a taste for parenthood.'

'I think so, but perhaps not right away,' she suggested shyly. 'I'd like to get used to being a parent to Fliss a bit first. In the early months of my marriage I did think of cuddly babies, but the mad lifestyle we had wouldn't have suited a child, so perhaps it was as well we didn't have a family. Later, when I got to know my husband better, there was no way I would inflict him as a father on any child. I got used to not having children and haven't really thought that much about it since.' The thought of bearing Mark's child was such a joy her eyes shone as she looked up to him.

'Well, there's no hurry. You've got a good few childbearing years yet!' he joked giving her a hug. 'Hey! Less chatter, wench. We haven't sealed the bargain yet.' He took her in his arms and proceeded to show her, with no possibility of misunderstanding, that a mother for Fliss was the last thing on his mind!

'Mark, behave,' she cried, breaking free. 'Remember where we are. If we can see them, they can see us,' she laughed, indicating the houses and streets laid out so clearly below them.

'True,' he conceded reluctantly. 'Come on, let's go and tell the troops.'

'Will they be very surprised?' asked Patricia as hand in hand they helped each other down the steep hill.

'I doubt it, considering Fliss was asking me only yesterday when I was going to make an honest woman of you. Tell me. Where does she get hold of these expressions? Precocious little brat!'

'Paperbacks probably, or old films on the telly. Then, too, she spends a lot of her time with people of an older generation here.'

'Yes, that's true. That reminds me. Where would you like to live? I'm assuming you don't want to give up work, though you can if you wish. I can certainly afford to keep you in the manner to which you're accustomed, my lady,' he teased. 'But I know how much you enjoy your job, so where is it to be?'

'I hadn't thought that far . . . ' she blushed as she realised she had given away her private daydreams of being Mark's wife, but he didn't appear to have made the connection. 'I can live anywhere. All I have to do is let all my clients have my new address. They can get hold of me on my mobile or e-mail anyway, so that's really no problem. But you'll need to be in striking distance of London, or rather Leeds, which is your particular baby, isn't it?'

'Leeds is well off the ground now. I could easily put a manager in there and concentrate on London, but the real question is Fliss. Thankfully she's at an age when changing schools shouldn't be too much of a problem, but there would still be the question of who takes care of her if we're both away on business.'

'Yes. I would try and arrange my trips not to coincide with yours, but the fact is I'm sometimes called away at really short notice once a job is underway. If, or when we have a child of our own we'll have to think again and perhaps get a Nanny, but I think Fliss would be a bit peeved at having a Nanny imported — it would ruin her street-cred,' she laughed.

'It seems we have two options. She can stay where she is, live with Shirley — I'm sure she won't mind having her during the term — and come to us for holidays. Or she can move in with us, go to a new school and we'll hire a housekeeper — we'll probably need one anyway, to cover the phone when we're away and the house will always be ready for us to come back to.'

'That's introducing another stranger to look after Fliss. Surely she's had enough upsets already?'

'True it's not ideal, but what else is there?'

'How would it be if we bought a house between Settle and Leeds? Fliss could stay with Shirley during the week and continue at the school she loves. We'd be close enough for her to come home for weekends and the holidays. That way, she'd have the best of both worlds. Shirley wouldn't be so tied, and still wouldn't lose touch with Fliss. I think the housekeeper is a good idea, though. I'm not over-fond of housework and it would be lovely to come home to roaring fires and the smell of furniture polish after a cold journey in a crowded train!'

Mark looked at her in surprise. 'Are you sure? I didn't like to ask you to transplant to the frozen North. It can be a bit bleak in winter.'

'I expect it can, but so can London; bleak and grey and wet and overcrowded and miserable; battling to get onto the Tube; being suffocated by the smell of wet steaming wool; having your tights splashed by passing cars just when you're going into an important meeting. Over the last few weeks I've really come to appreciate Yorkshire. I love the roundy hills and the stone walls; the rocky outcrops and the beautiful golden cottages. I've seen lots of super barn conversions. Perhaps we could find something like that, with a garden for Fliss and a lovely view.'

'Winds tend to come with good views,' he warned.

'OK. So we'll have triple-glazing,' she retorted. 'Don't be such a killjoy. Are you trying to put me off?'

'Never. I just want you to be sure. I ask nothing better than to have our home here. If I sell the London house, we should be able to afford something really nice and not have a huge mortgage round our necks.'

Full of plans they strolled back to Ravenscourt where Fliss was on watch for them. She wasn't used to being left behind on walks and had a pretty good idea of the reason behind her banishment.

'Open the champagne, Nana,' she shouted in excitement. 'They're coming and they're holding hands!'

★   ★   ★

In the following weeks Patricia was busy with details of the wedding. There seemed no reason to have a long engagement so they decided on a date towards the end of September. A quiet family service in the old church, followed by a reception in the largest of the local hotels. All were agreed a London wedding was out of the question. The thought of possibly seeing Mandy Hamilton-ffrench's face in the crowds, which inevitably gather on such occasions made Patricia shiver. On their return to London they would have a celebration party for the friends who hadn't made the trip to Settle.

Mark promised to take care of all the legal document side of the arrangements and Patricia threw herself into her work and all the wedding preparations. She was an efficient person who worked well under pressure so, despite her attempts to occupy herself fully, her thoughts would occasionally stray to the picture of Mark's dead wife. She slept badly and became impatient with silly little things.

★ ★ ★

One hot July night she tossed in her stuffy bedroom. The wide-open windows didn't help. There was no air in London. The dusty city was enfolded in the torpor of a heat wave. Tar bubbled on pavements ruining the shoes of the unwary. The parks were filled with office workers stripped off to sunbathe in their lunch hours. Heat haze shimmered everywhere, distorting images of buildings and people. The wailing sirens of fire engines were a constant background to the usual bustle of the city where apathy seemed even to mute the habitual roar of traffic and commerce.

Whoever would have thought I should be glad Mark's gone away, Patricia mused. The relief she had felt at his announcement of a business trip had surprised her. It wasn't his absence she welcomed, but the thinking space this afforded. When they were together she was so content. They made plans, went house hunting on weekends with Fliss in tow, and accepted the congratulations of their friends. Admiringly she twisted the solitaire emerald flanked by two square-cut diamonds, which she had chosen so happily with Mark. She loved her ring. She loved Fliss. She loved Mark. She wanted to be his wife — but! When she was alone she couldn't rid herself of the thought of the girl in Solesmes. As the days passed and her wedding date drew nearer her unease had grown.

At last she accepted the fact she could never be happy until this particular ghost was laid to rest. Tomorrow, she would take action!

★   ★   ★

SAINT PETER AND SAINT PAUL the Noticeboard read.

'How does one go about contacting a

priest?' wondered Patricia, hovering on the pavement. What do priests do at ten o'clock on a Tuesday morning? She wondered idly what they did on any day other than Sunday.

As she turned away from the church entrance a black-robed figure came round the side of the building. 'Can I help you?'

'I don't know. I hope so. I'm not a Catholic. I don't belong to your church, but I do need some advice — and help — I suppose.'

'Come inside and tell me all about it. The church will be empty just now. Mass is over for this morning, so I'm all yours for a while.' The smiling priest led the way into the cool dimness of his church.

She had expected someone older, more mature, and her heart sank. Could she tell her ridiculous tale to this young man?

'Take a seat. They're more comfortable than they look. The ladies of the parish have embroidered these beautiful cushions, to the glory of God and the relief of the senior members of our congregation. I'm Father Benedict. How can I help?'

With much backtracking to clarify points, Patricia told her implausible story. 'I'm probably being stupid, but you do see, don't you? What if that girl is Mark's wife? I don't know how she could be, but I just have this dreadful feeling. I know Mark thinks I'm being cold. You see we've never slept together. We'd both rather wait, but now, even when he kisses me, I think of her and it spoils everything.' She felt awkward speaking of sex to a priest, but he didn't seem to mind. 'She's coming between us.'

'So how do you think I can help you?'

'When we were in Solesmes they said a bit in English for the sake of the visiting tourists, I suppose. I just remember something about the catholic church being universal, one body. If that's right then I thought, perhaps you could write to Solesmes, to the Abbey, to see if anyone knows who she is. Look, I've got the photo here. You could send it with the letter. She may live in the village. They certainly didn't look like tourists. I'd say they were country folk by their clothes. I notice that kind of thing in my line of work,' she explained.

Father Benedict looked at the picture. 'And who is this?' he asked.

'That's Mark, her husband, my fiancé.'

'And you want to send the complete photograph? You could cut him off if you wished.'

'No. If there's any doubt in anyone's mind, when she sees the picture of her husband that'll make it certain, won't it?' she said painfully.

'You really believe this young woman is alive, don't you?' the priest asked with sympathy.

The tears she had valiantly held back overflowed. 'Yes, Father,' she sobbed into her handkerchief. 'I really do and I wish I didn't. I want to ignore it. I tried, but I can't.'

'If it turns out you're right, what do you think will happen?'

She looked puzzled. 'They'll get back together again I suppose.'

'I don't know. We have no idea why she's kept quiet all these years.'

Visions of Mandy Hamilton-ffrench's spiteful face rose before Patricia's eyes. Reluctantly she told Father Benedict what the other woman had suggested.

To her relief he smiled. 'A bit melodramatic don't you think? Was it a case of a woman scorned? It sounds like sour grapes to me. Just because she doesn't know what happened in France doesn't mean to say the facts are not known — to those whose business it is.'

'Oh, Father! Why didn't I think of that? Of course he wouldn't tell Mandy, or any of the casual London crowd such details. He's a very private man. What an idiot I am!'

'I think you're being a little hard on yourself, but yes, a bit silly, a bit of a doubting Thomas. You love him and so I think you should trust him.'

'What if I haven't the right to love him?' Patricia bit her lip.

'Nothing is going to change that fact, whether you acknowledge it or not,' said the priest uncompromisingly. 'You know that don't you? I think you've been very brave in what you're doing to reach the truth. I also believe you to be a very honest person. You could never be happy to live a lie. If you wish, I shall send the photograph with a letter to the Curé in Solesmes who looks after the villagers. If she's there, he will know.'

16

Père Dominic, Monsieur le Curé de Solesmes, tapped his thick-lensed glasses against
his nose and studied the letter from England.
A strange business! The Curé's mild blue eyes
and vague manner hid a brain that could have
gained him academic honours or great
business wealth in the secular world. His
parishioners would have been astonished to
be told this; but it was true. Over the years he
had learned many people fear to speak
frankly with those they believe to be brainier
than themselves.

That would be a disaster for a parish priest,
so Father Dominic practised his little
deception, and daily asked God's forgiveness.
His conscience was in a constant state of
warfare. He knew he learned more from
people, and could better help those who
confided in him, if they believed him to be a
simple unworldly soul with his weak eyes and
snow-white hair. Yet, on the other hand, his
natural humility rejected the thought he
should consider himself in any way superior
to his flock. When he allowed himself to
contemplate his dilemma he always came to

the conclusion that God gave him his brain to use for the good of his fellow men, and his conscience to keep him from becoming puffed up in his own pride.

The problem before him was a case for brain power. How to find one young woman out of the thousands who came each year to the Abbey? When in doubt — ask. Unconsciously he copied Father Anselm's method, but started closer to home. 'Marthe!' he called, on his way to the kitchen of his modest house. It stood at the Sablé end of the village, close to the garden wall of the Sisters' convent. 'Do you recognise this young woman?' he held out the picture to his housekeeper, whose rounded arms were plunged into a large pile of dough.

She peered forward and scrutinised the face carefully before shaking her head. 'No, Father. Should I? Who is she?'

'If I knew that, dear Marthe, I shouldn't have to ask you. You're quite sure you've never seen her? At Mass perhaps?'

'No, Father, never. I should have remembered. She's a taking little thing — not beautiful precisely, but sweet-faced.'

'Yes, she is, isn't she?' the old priest muttered, his spare frame hunched over the picture as he went back to his study. 'And where might you be, my little sweet-faced stranger?'

Over the course of the next few days he showed the photograph to everyone he met in the village, until it became quite a joke. Those who hadn't seen it came up to him in the street and asked for a sight of the Father's mystery lady. Since his object was to canvass as many people as possible he minded not at all, but no one seemed to recognise the unknown girl.

On Mondays, Father Dominic enjoyed an evening off. It was his habit to ride into Sablé on the Velosolex he used to visit his parishioners. This useful cross between a bicycle and a motor cycle seemed to him the ideal steed for a man of the cloth, neither too ostentatious for one committed to poverty and service, nor too slow to render speedy aid in time of need. He could putt-putt along at twenty kilometres an hour so he soon covered the three, which separated his home from the house of his good friend, Bertrand March-and, the retired Chef des Pompiers. Here the chessboard lay ready for their weekly battle of wits. Almost the entire evening passed in silence as each gave the other's skill the respect it deserved in intense concentration.

★ ★ ★

Each Monday evening, before her departure to pass the time with her married daughter, Madame Marchand prepared a cold supper for the combatants. Its consumption was the only break in hostilities. That completed, battle was on again. Only the chime of the handsome mantel clock, presented to Bertrand on his retirement from the Fire Brigade, brought the two antagonists back to the mundane needs of everyday life. Midnight! If Father Dominic were to say Matins at the appointed hour, he needed sleep. Reluctantly he prepared to depart. He wrapped his wide scarf firmly across his thin chest and shrugged himself into his overcoat to keep off the night's chill on his lonely ride. As he tucked his spectacles case into his pocket, his hand encountered the envelope from England. 'Ha! My old friend. Here is a mystery for you. Have you seen this young woman? She was in Solesmes at Easter. Now a friend is trying to contact her.'

Betrand Marchand examined the photo with careful attention. 'No. I'm sure I've never seen her before.' He shook his head and held out his hand to return the picture. 'But wait a minute! Who's the fellow?'

'Her husband.'

Once more Bertrand bent over, frowning. Then, once again he handed the picture back.

'For a moment there, I thought there was something. Not the girl, but her husband. It just seemed to ring a bell, but I can't remember why. If it comes to me, I'll let you know. Ride carefully now, mon père. Until next week.'

'Goodnight my friend. Le bon Dieu be with you.'

★ ★ ★

Days passed and Father Dominic was all but convinced the unknown had been a visitor from outside the region. No one he approached knew her face and, in a small close-knit community, such as those existing in rural France, everyone knew everyone else. A stranger was always remarked on — except in Solesmes where so many foreigners came to visit the Abbey! How could he progress the investigation? He was just a parish priest who had no access to the media, nothing to advertise his quest, beyond his own persistence and a certain faith that all would happen for the greatest good. He was nearly prepared to admit defeat, yet still he carried the photograph in his wallet.

★ ★ ★

One day he was in Sablé. Faithfully he worked down the list of errands the efficient Marthe had given him. The last stop would be the cobbler's low-ceilinged shop. Father Dominic loved the smell of new leather and enjoyed a lingering gossip with his old acquaintance Monsieur Blanche. On this occasion it was Marthe's best shoes to be left for re-heeling.

'Take great care of the ticket, Father,' laughed the cobbler. 'Marthe will ask you for it when you get home.'

'Indeed,' replied Father Dominic. 'I shall tuck it safely in my pocketbook. There we are,' he continued as he restored the wallet to its place.

'Well, well, Father.' The cobbler shook his head. 'You have the ticket safe, but what have you dropped here?' He bent down to retrieve the card, which had fluttered to the floor.

'The photograph! Oh, my son! I would not have lost that for a fortune,' exclaimed Father Dominic. 'Thank you.'

'But why do you carry a picture of the little Dubuis with you, Father?'

'Who?'

'Marie-Anne Dubuis, the young woman in the photograph. I don't recognise the fellow, but that is certainly Marie-Anne.'

'Are you sure?'

'Of course. I have mended her shoes and sabots for more than four years now — ever since she came to stay with her cousins at La Lavendière. A delightful young woman.'

'And where is this place of which you speak?'

'La Lavendière is the farm of the Dubuis family. Over the other side of the hill from Le Port de Juigné, just above Maréchal.'

'Maréchal! No wonder she wasn't recognised in Solesmes. She would normally go to Mass in Maréchal les Deux Chapeaux!'

'Certainly, Father. You can ask Father Anselm about the family. I'm sure he'll know them well. They are all devout.'

★ ★ ★

To follow this good advice, the next day, Father Dominic made a telephone appointment with Father Anselm. The proposed journey to Maréchal les Deux Chapeaux gave him some pause for thought. Although he possessed a keener than average brain, he had a total antipathy for anything mechanical. The only reason he could cope with the Velosolex was the simplicity of its workings. You pedal hard enough and the motor starts, then you can take your feet off the pedals, rest them on the frame and whizz along. You brake, slow down and it stops — simple!

Altogether he was contemplating a round trip of over twenty-eight kilometres — somewhat far for his motorised bicycle. He frowned in deliberation. He could, as so often in the past, beg a lift from one of his parishioners who would be only too willing to oblige, no matter how far off their own way it may take them — anything to keep Father Dominic from driving himself. It was true he had a driving licence, though le bon Dieu only knew how that had happened! It was also true he had an ancient and battered 'deux chevaux' at his disposal. But such was the fear he instilled in other road users every means possible was taken to keep him away from its steering wheel.

Christian Lemaître, the garage proprietor, serviced the baby Citroen and over the years had repaired and resprayed every part of it. He gave his expertise free of charge on condition he might use whatever colour spray he happened to have available. So, with the passage of time, the deux chevaux had two blue wings, one red one, and one yellow one; one door was black, another green and the back was a deep, very papal, purple. Only the canvas roof of the little car retained its original muddy brown colour. Strangers might stare and mock, but the population of

Solesmes and its environs were only too thankful. The recognition of Father's 'car of many colours' in the distance, gave them ample time to get out of the way before he reached them.

This morning, as his errand seemed to be of a delicate nature, Father Dominic decided to drive himself. He reversed out of the garage, adding only a small scrape to the interesting shape of his rear wing. Finally he managed to engage a forward gear and set off for Maréchal. In his efforts to be discreet, the good Father was unaware that the sight of him driving his car in its normal erratic way along the road set every mind and tongue to consider where he was going and why? The grapevine would soon provide the answers to the former, but the why of it provided pleasurable speculation for many days to come.

★ ★ ★

In the privacy of Father Anselm's study, Father Dominic lost no time in laying the complete story before the younger priest. His face impassive, to hide the rising tide of excitement and amazement, Father Anselm listened courteously, without interruption, to the flow of knowledge for which he had waited so long — sought so diligently. God moves in a mysterious way, he thought. He remembered the hundreds of letters he had written on Marie-Anne's behalf, and all, it seemed, to the wrong country!

'So is it true you know this little one, Father Anselm?'

'Indeed. She is a regular worshipper and belongs to a well-known and respected family.'

'But how can this be? It says in the letter she is English!'

'I know. And that's what bothers me. It's true she came here in strange circumstances, with no memory and therefore no history, but if these people are her real family, do we believe they, too, have all lost their memories? Why has no effort been made before to find the child?'

'No memory? No history?' Father Dominic was puzzled. Father Anselm apologised. Briefly and concisely he told Marie-Anne's story. 'So, in fact, you are already searching for her past, her identity? How overjoyed she will be at your success,' said the old priest, generously laying aside his own part in the triumph.

'Will she, Father? I believe we mustn't tell her what we've learned — not just yet.'

'But why? How can you keep this from her?

There's not only the girl to be considered. Apparently this young man in the picture with her is her husband. Imagine what he must feel!'

'That is precisely what I cannot do, Father. It seems his wife has been missing for six years and yet even now it is not he who seeks her, but the woman he intends to marry! I don't like it, Father. I don't like it at all and, until we know more, I believe we should say nothing to her. I will, however, tell the gist of it to her cousin, Marie-Thérèse, a sensible woman, who shares my concerns for the little one. Then I think we should ask this English Father for more information.'

'Yes. We could certainly do that. Now you tell me the strange history, I tend to agree with your reasoning. And there's no hurry. After all, the parties involved have waited this long. A few more weeks or so won't make any difference.'

'I'm afraid that's where you're wrong, Father. Time is passing. Caution is necessary, but speed is essential. Two weddings are being arranged!'

★ ★ ★

On a sunny Wednesday morning, Antoine Grosmenil, the retired Inspector of Police, was thoughtful as he made his way towards Les Deux Magots, his usual weekday morning haunt. His memories carried him far from the bustle that surrounded him. He had a duty to perform, which stirred up old matters long forgotten, re-opened old wounds. Just before he reached the doorway, he smiled as an old friend approached from the opposite direction. 'Salut, Bertrand! Comment ça va?' Antoine greeted the newcomer.

'Bonjour, Antoine, ça va,' The two shook hands and clapped each other on the shoulder. One could be forgiven for thinking they hadn't laid eyes on each other for months. Yet this was their usual method of salutation!

'Come and take a glass with me,' invited Antoine. 'You're just the chap I wanted to meet. I need to pick your brains.'

The two friends entered the bistro and, once settled with glasses of chilled Stella beer, Bertrand Marchand quizzed the ex-Inspector of Police. 'So, mon vieux, what great mystery have you for me to solve today?'

'You can mock, but it was a bit of a mystery, a tragedy rather, in its day. Do you remember the great storm of six years ago?'

'I wish I could forget it. A dreadful time. My men and I worked with yours round the clock for three days. There was loss and a great deal of hardship as a result of all the flooding and the damage it wrought.'

'Do you remember an accident involving an Englishman? Sadly he lost his young wife. Poor soul. He was as one demented trying to find her.'

'Yes. I remember the one! We had to restrain him from injuring himself. Then they took him away and I never saw him again. Why?'

'He's written to me. It seems at long last he's been able to bury the past and now intends to marry again. There's a child you know. He wants me to send an account of the tragedy to simplify the issue of a Presumption of Death, or Dissolution of Marriage certificate in England. Of course I shall do so at once. I'm just glad he's found happiness again. It's taken him long enough. Anything I can do to assist the marriage will be my pleasure. I thought it might be useful to compare my notes with yours.'

'Of course — anything I can do to help. No! Wait a minute!'

He frowned in thought; tried to recall the features briefly seen in a small photograph and match them with a memory from the past. 'He can't get married! At least I don't think so. It's him! I'm sure it is! We'll need to speak to Father Dominic. I have to have another look at that photograph. You, too!'

'What are you raving about?'

'He's the man in the photograph! I knew he rang a bell somewhere! I never saw the wife so she meant nothing, but I'm sure he's the man in the photograph.'

'Explain!'

'Father Dominic is searching for a young woman seen just after Easter in Solesmes. He has a photograph of her with her husband. I don't know the girl, but the husband is definitely our Englishman!'

'And she's alive you say? But that's impossible. We searched everywhere. The river was dragged. She can't be alive. Perhaps this is another wife or a second husband?'

'Who knows? But if it is she, and she was seen at Easter, and he turns out to be her husband, he's not free to be marrying anyone else! Come on. We must see Father Dominic.'

* * *

'We must go to Maréchal, to speak with Father Anselm,' exclaimed Father Dominic when the two friends had told their tale.

He folded his tall frame into the back seat of Antoine's Dauphine and they set off. All three were keyed up with anticipation. Since their retirement the two friends had led quiet lives, in sharp contrast to their drama-filled careers, and Father Dominic's major excitements were the rituals of Confirmation and Marriage. This quest was something quite out of the ordinary. They would all enjoy it to the full.

★ ★ ★

'I don't understand,' said Father Anselm. 'How can you lose a body?'

'It was the great storm,' explained Antoine.

'Before your time here,' put in Father Dominic.

'Everything was disrupted. No communications, no power, roads blocked, people and animals swept away,' contributed Bertrand.

'Wait. Let's start at the beginning. You, Antoine, were Inspector of Police at the time. You tell me your story.'

'A farm labourer going to his work at dawn after the Great Storm spotted a body on the riverbank. We investigated and found the Englishman just coming to his senses. Betrand was called as we could see the roof of a car in the floodwater below. The vehicle was pulled out. We found a woman's sandal inside. Later its twin and various articles from the handbag were recovered from the river, but no body. When he thought his wife was in the water it was all we could do to stop him diving in to find her. At last the doctor gave him a sedative and he was taken to hospital where he developed pneumonia.

'When he was finally discharged he had to return to England — there is a child. I assured him it was hopeless; everything had been done. We even dragged the river. I promised he should be informed if there was ever any news, but as it has happened before, once swept past the town, bodies are seldom recovered.

'When the waters receded, we did find a piece of cloth he identified as being from her skirt, about two kilometres downstream, caught on a weir, but no trace of the body. There were two false alarms, but the corpses were identified as two other unfortunate women who had been swept away and drowned that night. I tell you, Father, you cannot have any idea of the ferocity of the storm, or how swiftly the floodwater rose. Anyone going into the river stood no chance. The body must have been swept kilometres away, perhaps wedged underwater, never to be recovered. But we did search. Again and again.'

'Where?'

'In the water, of course. We had divers down for days. And all along the banks of the river we had notices posted asking for any information.'

'Along both banks?'

'But of course!'

'Up and down stream?'

The Inspector of Police and the Chief of the Fire Brigade looked at each other in puzzlement. It had never been considered necessary to seek the lost woman upstream from the car's point of entry. What was the priest trying to imply?

'It appears the young woman arrived on the doorstep of a farmhouse just up the hill from here that very night.' Despite himself, Father Anselm could not help but revel in the drama of the situation. He watched the faces in front of him.

'Impossible!'

'Never. It can't be the same woman. She could never have got out of the river and if she were thrown clear she couldn't have walked any distance in that storm,' exclaimed Antoine.

'And in bare feet,' added Bertrand. 'I found her sandals, myself.'

'True,' agreed Father Anselm. 'Apparently she was driven there in a vehicle of some kind and dumped, battered and bruised. The vehicle then drove away unseen. Did it, only later, appear in the river by Solesmes?'

'Mon père! What do you suggest here? The Englishman tried to kill his wife, dumped her body to be found and then drove his car into the river?'

'It is a possibility you must confess.'

'You didn't see him. No one could act such grief. And he begged me not to give up the search. No! I don't believe it.'

'It would certainly be of an unsurpassed wickedness,' came the gentle voice of Father Dominic. 'And yet if he wished to kill her, why deliver her to a place of safety?'

'There is that to be considered, of course. I should like to know who exactly brought her to the farm,' said Father Anselm judiciously.

'Farm!' exclaimed Antoine. 'You say she arrived at a farm? And upstream?'

Father Anselm gave them a brief resume of Marie-Anne's history.

'But then Henri Mercier has seen her! I remember him telling me of a poor young woman who had lost her memory. There was an appeal in the paper. But I never dreamed . . . I made no connection . . . I had never seen Madame Rawlings, not even a picture. Her Passport was never found. And the little one at La Lavendière was French, he swore she was. She spoke with the accent of the region. That was one reason he was so convinced she was playing games or would speedily be reclaimed. When no one recognised her, the Dubuis gave her a home. Other things took precedence in my life. Truth to tell I forgot all about her.'

'So, it would appear did her husband. But until we know more we cannot accuse him of any wrongdoing. Now he wishes to re-marry and must provide some proof of her death to the Court in England. He must show all has been done to trace her. This is where our friend, Antoine, comes in,' recapped Father Dominic.

'Meantime, his fiancée, makes enquiries through Father Benedict in London to verify the wife is alive,' added Bertrand. 'What complications! Whatever the truth, someone is going to be left unhappy.'

'More than one, my son,' put in Father Anselm. 'There are hopes for two weddings. The little one is to marry Maurice Boucher at harvest-time. She has searched for the truth of her past, for her very identity. For many months the need has haunted her. At last, when she has come to terms with her lack of knowledge; has turned her back on a fruitless quest and made happy plans for the future, everything is thrown once more into confusion.

'The 'cousin', Marie-Thérèse, knows all I knew until today. She agrees with me that

Marie-Anne should be kept in the dark at the moment. When we have a clearer picture it will be time enough to tell her of our finds. I charge you all to speak of this affair to no one; not even your wives,' he said to the two laymen.

'Least of all our wives!' agreed Bertrand fervently.

'Meantime I have asked Father Benedict to send us more proof that these people are kin to Marie-Anne. I want to know more about them before I reveal the whereabouts of the little one. She has suffered enough. I am not ready to expose her to more now if it can be avoided. Although, if the husband is innocent as you seem to think, I look more favourably on him. I am still concerned that anyone can be missing in this day and age and yet turn up under the very noses of the authorities, as you might say,' he said ironically with a questioning look at the two erstwhile officials.

'Father,' protested Antoine. 'We're not psychic. If you had seen how the river raged, you, too, would be certain no one could survive the torrent. There was no sign she had ever been on the bank and Madame Rawlings knew no one who could have given her a lift. Even if she had hitched . . . why there, so far from the main road? I still cannot believe it is the same woman. It doesn't make sense.

There's no connection.'

'I agree it is strange. It appears Marie-Anne did not regain consciousness for many days and afterwards for some weeks could not, or would not, speak. At first, they expected her to tell them who she was. Marie-Thérèse tells me they scoured the newspapers and listened avidly to the radio for appeals to trace a lost woman. There was nothing. You thought you knew where your woman was, or at least her dead body. Add that to the method of her arrival at the farm, the fact she had, it seemed, been badly beaten up. Madame Dubuis Senior, the grandmother had lived through the Occupation of the Second World War. As a young woman, before she came to the Sarthe, she had aided the Maquis, the Underground movement who fought the Germans all through that time. She had seen many dreadful things and heard of more. The grandmother trusted in her own judgement and le bon Dieu. She decided to give the child sanctuary, instead of immediately handing her over to the authorities. Perhaps, in this case, that was a mistake?'

'Perhaps not,' offered Father Dominic. 'The little one has been well cared for. She has had the peace necessary for her mind to begin to restore itself. Can we say she would have been discovered before this had she been in an institution? Who can say if memory would have returned, or if she would for ever have been condemned to live with strangers, yearning for familiarity?'

Silently, the other three exchanged looks of accord: the old priest was being romantically fanciful, but no one voiced dissent to his mild hypothesis. They all agreed nothing more should be done until Father Benedict provided further information. Antoine, with Bertrand's collaboration, would put together a detailed account of the events of six years ago. Whatever happened, such a report would be useful. But he would not send it to England until the four conspirators had met again.

17

'Shirley?' queried Patricia. She held the telephone with an ice-cold hand. She just couldn't get warm these days. 'I must see you. Can I come up to Ravenscourt tomorrow?'

'Of course, my dear. You know you're welcome anytime. Is Mark coming, too?'

'No. He's busy and I have some free time. In fact, I'd rather you didn't say anything about my visit if you're talking to him.'

'Ah! Wedding secrets, is it?'

'Something like that, yes. Will it be all right if I catch the night train? I'll get the connection to Settle and take a taxi up.'

'Nonsense, dear. I'll meet your train with the car. I'll pack Fliss off to her friend Jane for the day. Now school's broken up it's a constant round of visiting. I'll see you tomorrow then. Such fun! I love surprises.'

★   ★   ★

'Good journey, dear?' asked Shirley, as she hugged a pale-faced Patricia. 'You do look tired — no sleep?' As she spoke, she ushered the younger woman out to the car and stowed her, complete with overnight bag, into the passenger seat.

'Shirley. Can we stop by the hotel for a minute, please? I just need to pop in. I promise not to keep you waiting.'

'I'm all yours today, until Fliss gets back. Jane's mother will bring her home for supper — unless they decide to have a sleepover, which is the latest craze. We can have a cosy day and go through all the plans. Have you got your dress yet?' Chatting happily she drove up to the front of the hotel and stopped the car. 'Take your time. I know how difficult it can be to get all the arrangements just right,' she commented with a laugh. 'I shall be quite happy waiting here. I'll listen to the radio.' But it was barely five minutes before Patricia rejoined her.

'All done? You really are an efficient girl. I'm sure these things would take me ages.' She pulled out into the early morning traffic and headed for home.

*   *   *

'Here we are. Let's put the kettle on. Would you like some breakfast? I've got beautiful fresh mushrooms.'

'No! That is, no thank you. Just coffee will

267

be fine.' *If she doesn't stop prattling I shall scream.* Patricia massaged her temples to try and relieve her throbbing head.

'Right you are then. Now let me in on the secret. What's so special you've got to arrange it without Mark knowing? You can count on my help — and discretion — I promise,' said Shirley leaning forward eagerly.

'Shirley,' Patricia stopped, not knowing how to go on. During the long journey north, she had tried to work out what she would say, each version sounded worse than the last.

'Yes, dear?'

'Shirley. I've misled you — a bit. It's not really about the wedding I've come, at least it is, but only indirectly.' She stumbled on, and watched the changing expressions on Shirley's face, surprise, puzzlement, confusion. 'I'll go back to the beginning. Please try and hear me out before you comment, otherwise I don't think I'll be able to keep going.'

Strain was evident in her face and a hint of suppressed tears in her voice. She swallowed convulsively. Shirley reached over and gave Patricia's hand a sympathetic squeeze. It was jerked away as though it had been stung.

'No. Please don't. It makes it worse.' Patricia took a deep breath and tried again. 'You remember the day a photo frame dropped down from the back of the piano?

You'd missed it. You thought your cleaning lady had put it in another room. Well, she didn't. I'd . . . borrowed it. I took it to Town and had a copy of the picture made. Then I replaced the frame behind the piano and hoped you'd think exactly as you did. I never knew I could be so devious,' she remarked with a shaky laugh.

Shirley's face showed simple puzzlement. She waited, as requested, for the story to continue.

'I kept the copy in my Filofax and tried to forget it. When Mark asked me to marry him I was so happy, but there was this niggling doubt. Not that I loved him, but that I had the right to. I couldn't forget the girl I saw in Solesmes.'

She saw Shirley's body stiffen at the name.

'But I argued myself out of it. If someone's husband, and own mother believed them to be dead, who was I to question? So I said yes to Mark and we made plans. I was so happy. I do love him, Shirley, and Fliss, and you, too. I knew I could be a good mother to her and make our marriage work. And I wanted it so much. Please forgive me.'

For a moment she sat and looked down at her hands, where the restless fingers had shredded a paper tissue. Then she raised sad eyes to Shirley. 'It couldn't go on. I was living

269

in a Fool's Paradise. As the wedding date drew nearer I couldn't stand it any more. I found a Catholic priest who said he would help. I gave him the photo and he sent it to France. He's had an answer. I don't know how to say this gently, Shirley, but I believe, and so does he, that your daughter is still alive.'

'No!' After that first exclamation of disbelief, Shirley sat, the back of her fist pressed against her mouth, her eyes huge, as she tried to come to terms with the words she heard.

Patricia waited in silence.

At last Shirley expelled a long sighing breath. 'I don't believe you, or anyone, could be so cruel as to think this could be a joke, however sick. I give you that much credit. But I mourned the death of my daughter six years ago. I mourn her still. Every day I think of her. I keep her fresh in Fliss's memory and in mine. Perhaps you mean well, Patricia, but I told you before, whoever you saw in Solesmes must have been a double or had a strong likeness to Marion. That's all. To try and pass some French girl off as my Marion — well! I don't understand what you hope to gain by this.'

'Gain!' The word was torn from Patricia. 'Gain! You think I wanted to do this? You think I didn't try to keep my head in the sand? You think this is for my benefit? Well, just stop for a minute and think what I've lost! I've proved the man I love belongs to someone else. I've given up my chance of happiness. I'm letting him go!

'Do you know why I went to the hotel? Not for any arrangements. I cancelled the reception. The wedding's off! I can't marry Mark. He's already married! Your daughter's alive, Shirley. Here read this.' She threw Father Dominic's letter across the table and burst into a storm of weeping.

Shirley sat frozen. Patricia's passionate outburst of words had barely penetrated her mind, but, as she heard the bitter sobs of loss, the faintest thread of hope stirred in her heart. She felt as if she were made of fragile glass: one false move and she would shatter into a thousand pieces. She took small shallow breaths, tried to remain quite still, tried to take in what she had heard. If she stretched out her hand to that paper, whatever it said, nothing would ever be the same again.

With a muffled apology, Patricia left the room.

Shirley looked down at the letter, and tried to summon the courage to read it. She wouldn't hope for anything. She dare not let herself hope. And yet, despite her good intentions, a bubble of optimism grew. It expanded in her chest. She took a deep breath, reached out and unfolded the single sheet covered in closely written script that had a foreign look.

★ ★ ★

Solesmes, 14 ième août

Dear Father Benedict,

You will see I enclose a letter from our brother, Father Anselm, through whom, I believe, we have traced the young woman you seek.

He is reluctant to disclose the actual whereabouts of her present home in order to shield her from further pain. Having appointed himself her protector he must be reassured the people who now seek her have her welfare at heart. He intends to vet them very carefully before allowing them to communicate with her.

One natural question he raises is simply, why has it taken so long for them to search for her? She has been in his parish for six years, with no one making any enquiries. To him, this seems strange, to say the least. 'Unnatural' was the word he used. If they care for the little one, they will have to prove it conclusively to our brother, who, I may add, is not an easy man to dupe.

I have every belief she is the one you seek, but to claim her may be less straightforward than your contacts believe. There are those here who love her and would not wish to part with her. I put my trust in le bon Dieu and await the outcome with interest. Go with God.

Yours in the Faith,
Dominic
Curé de Solesmes

★ ★ ★

Shirley read and reread the letter, smoothing the words with her fingertips as though it would bring the writer and his subject closer. When the door opened she raised her head and looked at Patricia who had bravely tried to repair the ravages of her grief.

'I'm sorry, my dear. I am so, so sorry to have misjudged you. What must I do now?' She felt numb. Mentally she accepted the fact her daughter was almost certainly alive. Emotionally she couldn't yet handle it. Like a child she turned to the young woman whose efficiency she admired.

Patricia realised Shirley's state of helplessness and steeled herself to take charge, and face even more heartache. She had set the enquiry in motion, now she must follow it through to a conclusion. Then, she promised herself, she would go far away to lick her wounds in private. For now, Shirley needed her. 'Here's the letter from the other priest, Father Anselm. He's playing it very close to his chest. He doesn't even mention where he is, let alone her address. See, he's asking for all sorts of proof of identity. Have you got all this?'

'Well, I think I can lay hands on her Birth Certificate. She needed it for her Passport and then gave it to me for safe-keeping. She was hopeless with paperwork — I mean, she is hopeless. It's all so difficult! Yes, and I have her Confirmation Certificate. Her Marriage Lines were at the London house. I suppose Mark has them, but I can't ask him, can I?'

'He'll have to know!'

'But not until we're one hundred per cent sure. I couldn't bear it for him if we're wrong.'

'No. And he'd never trust me again, would he?'

'So, we're agreed. Now then what else? I can find old photos of Marion with her Daddy and I, and I have a few of her with Fliss in an album I made up of memories of her Mummy. I didn't want her to forget,' she continued. Her lips quivered. 'But, of course, she did. She was only three. What she thinks she remembers, she's taken from the pictures. But I don't understand! Why didn't she come home? It's not like her to put us through all this! Do you think she may have been badly disfigured in the accident? But surely she would realise it wouldn't make any difference to us. We loved her!'

'I don't know. There couldn't have been — some-one else?' Patricia tried to put the question as delicately as possible.

'Another man, you mean? No! Impossible! She and Mark were besotted with each other. And she would never have left Fliss.'

'It's a mystery. But one I hope we're about to solve. If you gather together all the photos, certificates, letters she wrote to you and anything else that might prove your relation-ship, I'll try to contact the priest by telephone. At least we have the address in Solesmes. I'll start there.'

While Shirley turned out cupboards and drawers, looked in old handbags and retrieved the treasured album from Fliss's room, Patricia set to work to track down Father Anselm. She made contact with Father Dominic, without too much difficulty, who agreed to give her his friend's telephone number. But then came the hitch: Father

Anselm was away from home and the housekeeper couldn't say when he would return. Exhausted by her efforts to converse in French via an international line with a person speaking in broad patois Patricia made yet another cup of coffee and slumped in her chair. 'I'll keep on trying,' she told Shirley. 'I think you should dig out your Passport and go to the bank for some Euros and Travellers Cheques. I'll stay by the phone.'

Shirley's eyes became huge as she took in the implications of Patricia's words. 'You mean — me? Go to France?'

'You want to, don't you? You mustn't worry. I'll arrange it all for you. I have friends in Paris and once I've contacted the priest we can organise the other end.'

'I'd give anything, but I can't. There's Fliss!'

'I'll stay here and look after Fliss. I can't go back to London or do anything until this is sorted out. What are we going to tell her?'

'Not the truth, at this stage, that's for sure. We'll say I've been called away to help a friend, and she'll be so excited you're here I don't think she'll question it.'

'It's as close to the truth as we can get. Who said you had to have a good memory to be a successful liar? I'll tell Mark the same tale when he rings to say goodnight to Fliss; that is if we can get you off today.'

She was making a huge effort to lighten the strange mood that had gripped them both. Nothing seemed real. They were actors in a play. Would they wake and find it was all a dream?

'I've left our number with the housekeeper, but I'm not sure she understood my French, and I'm also not sure the priest would ring back at once. He seems to have taken an awful lot of judgement on himself. He might want to keep us waiting, as a kind of punishment. He obviously believes us to be at fault in some way.'

★   ★   ★

It wasn't until the early evening that, at last, Patricia made contact with Father Anselm. Having read his demands and the words of Father Dominic, Patricia was pleasantly surprised at the warmth of his tone. She was not to know that, since writing to Father Benedict in great indignation, Father Anselm had heard the story of Mark's demented and unsuccessful search for his lost wife. This had disposed the good Father more favourably towards Marie-Anne's kin. Nevertheless, he was still not prepared to release more

277

information, except to say she was safe and well. He pondered a minute when confronted with the idea of the mother's arrival, but was then pleased to give it his blessing. 'If Madame will telephone me from Paris the time of arrival of her train in Sablé, I shall, myself, come to collect her and bring her to the hotel here. When we have met and spoken I will then make arrangements for the two women to meet — probably,' he added. He still reserved the option of refusing to reveal Marie-Anne's whereabouts.

'But he can't do that!' stormed Shirley when told of the arrangements. 'He has no right, either legal or moral, to keep me from my daughter.'

'Hey! I'm on your side,' said Patricia, half-amused in the face of Shirley's wrath. 'You're quite right, and I'm sure he knows that. I think he's still trying, as he sees it, to protect Marion. Just in case you're unsuitable or want to do her harm.'

'The man must be mad,' snorted Shirley. 'As if I'd harm my own child.'

'You wouldn't,' agreed Patricia. 'But such things have been known and he doesn't know you like we do. It's too late for you to travel today so I'll get you there as early as possible tomorrow. Jeanne will meet you at Charles de Gaulle, and put you on the train for Sablé.

She'll also phone Father Anselm for you so you don't have to worry about French telephones. Now I think you should pack for a stay of at least two or three days. You'll phone me when you arrive and let me know what's happening? I think that's all we can do for now.'

★   ★   ★

When Fliss arrived home, she was joyously surprised to find Patricia already installed for a few days holiday while Nana went away. Immediately she drew up an exhaustive programme of events to fill their days and was only persuaded to go to sleep when reminded it would make the morning come quicker.

★   ★   ★

That night, as she lay in her usual bed at Ravenscourt, Patricia replayed in her head the events of the day. Everything was now out of her hands. Whatever happened next she would never be Mark's wife or a mother to Fliss. She'd heard of Mark's devotion to Marion. She couldn't believe he would want a divorce. She supposed she might be expected to feel virtuous. She'd done the right thing. All she felt was stupid. She'd thrown away her happiness. She was so lonely. She tried hard to be glad for Shirley; hoped all would go well with the reunion, but her own heart was heavy.

What if she doesn't want Mark after all this time? The questions ran round in her brain. What if they don't want to be married any more? What if she's married to someone else? After all Mark nearly was! And where has she been all this time? Why didn't she come home? Perhaps there is someone else for her, but where would that leave Mark's love for me? I think I've always been second best for him. While Marion was dead I could accept that, but now . . .

It was at times like this Patricia wished she were a smoker. Then she could pace the floor puffing on a cigarette as she had seen countless heroines do in films. It seemed to help them. Instead, after she'd tossed and turned for what seemed like hours, she crept downstairs. She felt her way in darkness until she reached the kitchen.

Someone was there before her. A strip of light shone under the door. Patricia pushed it open, and surprised Shirley at the cooker. 'Hush! Come in and shut the door. Cocoa?'

Patricia nodded.

'I couldn't sleep either.' smiled Shirley wanly. 'There's so much to think about. I'm not used to travelling alone, at least not abroad. It was very kind of you, and your friend, to make everything easy for me. I can't help thinking of our meeting. Will we throw our arms around each other? There are so many questions. Why hasn't she come home? The priest seems to think we should have searched for her earlier. But we did! At least, Mark and the local police did. Was she hiding? If so why? Perhaps someone kept her against her will? The priest wrote of people who loved her and wouldn't want to let her go. Do you think they'll stop her coming home?'

Patricia could only shake her head. She had no answers. The same questions had bothered her. She had turned them over for hours, but was no nearer to an answer. She accepted the mug of cocoa Shirley proffered and sat at the table opposite Marion's mother.

Strange, she thought. I feel so close to Shirley. I suppose I could claim to have found and restored her daughter to her yet, apart from the photograph, I know nothing about her. 'What's she like,' she asked.

Shirley looked into her mug, thought a moment, and smiled up at Patricia. 'Clever — in her own way. She was a very talented and successful book illustrator. Full of fun — she loved to laugh. There was always something to be happy or amused about. I missed that so much, first when she left home to marry Mark, and then after she died. Their house was always filled with laughter and bits of songs they would sing or hum, she in her attic studio and he in his office on the first floor. They had a two-way communication system. It was such a tall house they didn't like to be so far apart. So Mark had a pal rig up this sort of microphone thing. They could talk to each other from their work places, just as though they were in the same room. And when Fliss came they extended it to her nursery. It kept them close together.'

'Why didn't they take Fliss with them on holiday?' The question had bothered Patricia ever since Mandy Hamilton-ffrench's vicious remarks.

Tears filled Shirley's eyes. 'That was another heartbreak for us, especially Mark. You see they left Fliss with me, because it was a sort of second honeymoon. It would have been the last chance of a holiday alone for a while. Marion was pregnant again and they were so happy.'

She stopped and looked at Patricia in consternation. 'The baby! What happened to the baby? We thought we'd lost them both. When you told me this morning about Marion, I just didn't taken in everything. No one's mentioned the baby. Oh, Dear Lord! I don't think I can take any more.'

'Here.' Patricia took a little bottle of pills from her dressing gown pocket. 'They're not strong, honestly. My London doctor prescribed them for me, to get some rest. You can take a half if you like, just to relax you.

'I found I couldn't cope with any more either, so I came down for a hot drink and to take one of these. We're going to be no use if we're out on our feet tomorrow. You've got a journey and I've got Fliss!' she smiled. 'Of the two I think the journey may well be less tiring. She seems to have made all sorts of plans.'

Shirley hesitated only a moment before she swallowed a little pill. The more she puzzled over her daughter the worse the unanswered questions grew. She felt overwhelmed by her brain's constant demands for facts she didn't have. God willing, by this time tomorrow she would have solved the mystery. She pulled herself up the stairs to bed like an old woman. Patricia watched and pitied her, but could offer no help or comfort. She had done all she could. Now she was helpless. From tomorrow she would hold the fort here, with Fliss, and have to wait impatiently for news from France.

18

Father Anselm had no difficulty in picking out Shirley Brookes from the bustling crowd at the Sablé-sur-Sarthe station. She looked so very English, and a little flustered. He produced his most soothing and delightful manner, introduced himself, loaded her into his car and set off for Maréchal les Deux Chapeaux. On the way he chatted lightly about her journey, her family, her home circumstances and deftly possessed himself of various items of information, which added pieces to the jigsaw of Marie-Anne's former life. He booked Shirley into the Hôtel de Ville, recommended the Plat du Jour for her dinner that night, and left her to rest. He would call for her at ten o'clock the following morning.

★　★　★

'Patricia? Can you hear me? Yes, I'm here at Maréchal-les-Deux-Chapeaux, thanks to your delightful friend in Paris . . . so kind. I'm a bit tired, but can't wait till tomorrow . . . No! I don't think I like him very much. He's sort of overwhelming. Perhaps it's just because I'm tired and nervous, but I felt he didn't really approve of me. Isn't that silly? . . . Patricia? Are you still there? I'm always afraid with these foreign phones I'll cut you off. Although I must say you're very clear . . . Yes. I'm to go to his house in the morning and then I think and hope I'll see Marion.

'I know I won't sleep a wink tonight. There's so much left unexplained . . . I know and I will try. But you, my dear. I've been so selfish. I let you take on all the arrangements and gave little thought to how you must be feeling. I owe you so much . . . No. It's not nonsense and you know that's the truth. A lesser person would have been more selfish and I might never . . .

'All right! I won't go on about it. I'll hang up now and call you again tomorrow when I know more. Thank you again, my dear. Bless you. Love to Fliss. Bye-bye.'

Despite her fatigue after a day of travelling Shirley lay awake for long hours. She thought of the coming meeting with her daughter. Would she have changed very much? It had been six years. Would Marion find her mother so much older? Grief had put many more white hairs into the rich brown Marion would remember. How had she survived without news of Felicity for so long? Had these people

285

with whom she lived turned her against her own family? The endless questions went round and round. Finally sheer exhaustion took over and she slept.

Her rest was disturbed by strange dreams, where Marion ran away from her. Shirley called and called and tried to catch up, but the harder she ran the faster Marion moved away, until finally Shirley woke with tears on her cheeks. Shakily she rose and washed her face, and told herself it was only a silly dream, but the feeling of impending loss remained. She had pinned so much on this meeting. Was she being foolish to think that after six years they could take up again where they'd left off when Marion and Mark went on holiday? They'd always been close. Was this dream trying to tell her all that was over; that she was wasting her time coming all this way; chasing a rainbow?

Her hands shook as she brushed her hair and applied a light make-up to hide the ravages of the night. She could at least try and give the appearance of the mother Marion remembered.

★ ★ ★

At ten o'clock she was ready for Father Anselm who, thankfully, was on time. He drove her the short distance to his house and bade her take a seat in his study.

Carefully he perused the documents and photographs she offered him. 'There can be no doubt, Madame, that the young woman in these photographs is the same person we have known as the cousin of the Dubuis family.'

Shirley gulped to hold back her tears. To allow herself to believe Patricia's reasoning was one thing; to hear Father Anselm categorically state Marion was alive was quite another.

'Where is she? When can I see her?' she asked tremulously.

'Alas, it isn't quite that simple.'

'What do you mean? Stop torturing me. Where's my daughter? You have no right to keep her from me!'

'Calm yourself, Madame Brookes, I beg of you. The fact is your daughter may not recognise you. You must prepare yourself for this possibility. For six years she has been living as the adopted cousin of the Dubuis family. They are the good people who took her in on the night of what we now know to have been the sad accident, which befell her and her husband. However, she knows nothing of all this. Her memory was wiped clean by her injuries — a severe blow to the head and various cuts and bruises.'

'You mean she didn't know who she was?'

'Exactly.'

'Then why didn't these people contact the police — report her presence?'

Father Anselm related the tale.

'But surely as soon as Marion opened her mouth, they would know she wasn't French!'

'Had she spoken English then, yes, Madame. It would have been simple, but Marie-Anne spoke in French, and moreover in the patois of the region.'

'I don't understand,' cried Shirley, shaking her head in distress. 'She was always good at languages at school and she'd been talking French on their holiday, but I'm sure she wouldn't have tried to fool anyone she was French. That's not like her. And why? So many questions! So few answers!'

'The enquiries as to her identity were made soon after a time of great upheaval. The weather had been appalling. Practically a tornado, I am told, though it was before my time here. They produced no results. Years later, when she started to remember, and learned some facts of which she had been unaware, Marie-Anne, a young woman of great courage, resolved to find the truth, however unpleasant it may be. So you see, Madame Brookes, she has been searching for her family while Madame Rawlings has

288

searched for her. And yet we can only thank coincidence or, I prefer to call it, the intervention of le bon Dieu that the various people involved came together at all. If Father Dominic had not dropped the photograph? If Father Benedict hadn't written to him? Indeed if the little one had left the church in Solesmes ten minutes earlier or later that fateful day after Easter?'

Shirley gave a shudder as she realised just how easily all the priest's scenarios could have happened. 'But those things didn't happen and now I want to see my daughter.'

'So you shall, Madame Brookes. Have you thought how to approach her?'

'Of course not! I didn't know until a few minutes ago she has no memory. Does she remember nothing at all?'

'She remembers you, I believe. At least she has dreamed of someone we believe to be her mother. Had you a swing and apple trees in your garden when she was a child?'

'No, not then. But now, where I live, it's just like that. Mark put the swing up for Fliss.'

'Fliss?'

'My grand-daughter. Marion's child.'

'Marion? Your daughter's name is Marion?'

'Yes. Why?'

'That at least is correct. Although she is

known here as Marie-Anne. And are you a Catholic family?'

'No. We've always been staunch Church of England, right back. My Marion wouldn't have a clue how to go on in a Catholic church.'

Father Anselm smiled wryly. 'Believe me, Madame, your daughter not only knows how to 'go on' as you put it, she follows the Mass, takes Communion and is a regular at Confession.'

Shirley could not have been aware of the expression, almost of horror, which crossed her face at his words. 'Well I don't know where she got that from,' she said indignantly. 'It certainly never came from our family.'

'I believe the good Marie-Thérèse to be the culprit here,' pronounced Father Anselm benignly. 'Apparently, she was so shocked that memory loss could encompass even the religion learnt as a child, she instructed Marie-Anne in her Catéchisme while she convalesced. The Catechism is what every Catholic child learns before they take their First Communion,' he explained. 'As it happens, she did Marie-Anne a service. She would have felt very left out if she didn't know what to do or expect in church. The Dubuis are a devout family and I have always been happy to see Marie-Anne in church with them. She is a delightful young woman.'

'Yes. She always was,' responded Shirley, somewhat tartly. Who did this man, this foreign priest, think he was talking to? Fancy telling her, Marion's mother, how delightful she was. As if she didn't know!

'So, Madame Brookes, what do you wish to do? I have sent for Marie-Anne to come here at noon. She has, as yet, no idea why. When she arrives, do you wish for me to remain with you, or to leave you two alone together?'

Shirley thought a moment.

'I believe I should prefer it if you left us, Father Anselm. If she doesn't recognise me on sight, I shall show her the photographs and hope they do the trick. If not, we must think again. Much will depend on how she reacts and what she wants to do. I'll do anything to help her,' she declared passionately. 'I'm quite prepared to stay here as long as necessary to restore my girl to herself again.'

'Thank you, Madame Brookes,' the priest bowed his head. 'You have removed my last doubt. I am sure you have thought me harsh and unfeeling towards your natural distress. Please realise, all I have done has been to protect the little one. When I replied to Father Benedict, I had not heard the story of the accident or how zealously your son-in-law searched for his wife. We thought her abandoned, perhaps even abused, by those whose task it should have been to care for her.

'See, she is coming across the square. In a few moments, Madame Brookes, your daughter will be restored to you, at least in body.'

Shirley looked through the window he indicated. She saw a young woman with her back to the sun. What held Shirley's attention was the fair-haired little boy, about six years old, who swung her hand in his. He put up his face for a kiss at the gate before he ran off.

'The child, Father. The little boy?'

'Ah! Young Claude. They are devoted. There's the bell. I shall simply tell Marie-Anne there is someone who would like to see her. The rest, Madame, is up to you.' He left the room and Shirley heard voices in the hall. Her head was in a whirl. Marion had had the baby! She had a grandson and Mark had a son he knew nothing about. The son he had always wanted! Fliss had a little brother! How delighted she would be. Shirley wiped away a tear as she thought what joy this child would bring. This must come right. She would do everything she could to restore Marion's memory and give Mark his wife and son.

Marie-Anne stepped into the priest's study. 'Bonjour, Madame. Father Anselm said you wished to see me,' she began in the accent of the region.

Shirley looked at the young woman before her. Bare feet were thrust into comfortable sandals; a pretty cotton frock caught at the trim waist by a light belt; honey-brown hair fell softly in a fringe on her forehead and peeped beneath the hem of a gay kerchief on her head; her skin was a warm golden brown. She looked well.

'I'm afraid you'll have to speak English, Marion,' she said. 'My French isn't good enough to understand everything.'

At the sound of her voice a frown creased Marie-Anne's forehead. She stepped farther into the room and looked more closely at the older woman. 'You . . . you were in my dream. I saw you,' she began. Her heart started to thump heavily. She let her eyes explore the stranger. Sensible light shoes for travelling, a crisp linen skirt and toning collared blouse were matched with a smart blazer. Pearl studs were at her ears to complement the single strand around her neck.

Marie-Anne stepped forward as one in a trance, hand outstretched. She touched the smooth lustre of the pearls as they lay warm against Shirley's skin. 'Mummy,' she mur-mured.

Shirley gulped back tears. 'Ever since you were a baby you've always loved to stroke my pearls,' she said softly.

Marie-Anne raised her eyes and knew her mother's face.

After several minutes locked in a fierce, silent embrace, the two sat down on the shiny horsehair settee, hands clasped.

'Where do we begin?' asked Shirley with a shaky laugh. That Marion recognised her, knew who she was there could be no doubt, but what else did she recall? Shirley determined to go as slowly as was necessary.

'Have you still got the apple trees? I saw them in my dream. And the swing. Is that real, too?'

'Quite real. Although we lost one of the trees in a gale. It blew down and we've used the wood for the fire. Apple wood smells so lovely.'

'Yes, I know.'

Shirley's heart leapt.

'We use it at home on the farm when a tree blows down or grows too old to fruit well.'

Shirley felt her hopes sink again. 'What do you remember now, darling?'

'My school uniform. And Barbara. She lived next door didn't she? She was my best friend. Where's Daddy?'

*   *   *

Time went by. Father Anselm's housekeeper brought them coffee and rolls. Question and answer followed each other in quick succession. It became apparent to Shirley that Marion had gained almost total recall of her childhood, her schooldays, even going to College, but after that, her memory came up against a brick wall. She didn't remember the death of her father ten years earlier. Shirley didn't push her; she just let her bring out the memories as they came. She confirmed and embellished when asked. In the hall a clock chimed four times.

'My goodness. Is that the time?' Marie-Anne jumped to her feet. 'Thérèse will be wondering what has become of me. I must see Father and telephone her.' She left the room.

Shirley felt the exhaustion of too much high-powered emotion wash over her. She sank back on the seat. What next?

Father Anselm appeared in the doorway. 'Are you all right, Madame? Even joy can be tiring. You look exhausted. Marie-Anne is arranging for you to go and stay at the farm. I have suggested she go on ahead to prepare your room and I will escort you and your baggage in the car in an hour or so. I felt you

295

might require a quiet time alone.'

'Thank you. You're very kind . . . and perceptive.'

'It goes with the job,' smiled the priest.

'Can I ask your advice? You must be used to dealing with people's problems, I suppose?'

'True, but thank goodness ones like this are rare!'

Shirley explained the limitations of Marion's recall.

Father Anselm thought for a moment. 'She hasn't mentioned the little girl?'

'No. I don't think she remembers her at all. Yet it was Fliss she saw in her dream. It must have been. We only moved to the house with the swing and apple trees after Marion was grown up and at college. The child she saw me pushing on the swing was Fliss. Marion would sit under the trees and watch us. It was a regular thing, every time they visited.'

'So whatever holds back her memory concerns her adult life. The injury to her brain is healed. Did she get on well with your husband, her father?'

'Absolutely. They were very close. She was our only child you see. They did everything together.'

'And her husband. Were they unhappy?'

'Heavens, no! They adored each other.

Sometimes I was quite frightened at the intensity of their love. Foolishly I wondered how one would ever cope if something happened to the other, as it did. And it was as bad as I'd feared. If it weren't for Fliss I don't think Mark would have survived the loss.'

'So it's not fear of her husband that keeps her imprisoned in the past. And yet, I feel it is a fear of some kind. Madame Brookes, what has she lost — apart from her memory? In her remembering dream of the accident she crawls away from the river on hands and knees. She searches desperately for something. What could it be?'

'If she were alone in her dream she'd be searching for Mark! They were never apart if they could help it. He must have been there, perhaps unconscious, but she didn't know. She couldn't see him or find him! I'm sure that's it. She was looking for Mark, her husband!'

'Then if they were so close why doesn't she remember him?'

'I don't know.' Shirley shook her head in frustration. 'Father Anselm you say I'm to stay at the farm? Is that all right? What are these people like? You say you love her. Will they hate me for coming to find her? Will they try and keep her from coming home?'

'Madame Brookes, you have touched on a

delicate point. For the last six years this has been Marie-Anne's home. There is the possibility she may not wish to return with you.'

'But she must! What about Fliss? What about Mark?'

'We cannot force her to do anything. She is of age and, sadly, it is true that over the years, through her experiences, her affections may have changed. She is at the moment engaged to be married to a neighbouring farmer, Maurice Boucher, an excellent young man who loves her deeply.'

Shirley was shocked. First Patricia with a broken heart, now this unknown young fellow. Was there no end to the suffering? And yet it was unthinkable that Marion would not come back to England with her.

★　★　★

Three quarters of the company assembled around the kitchen table at La Lavendière were ill at ease. Conversation was stilted as Shirley tried out her halting French. Only Marie-Anne was happy. Flushed with excitement she gaily interpreted for both sides as they laboured to appear natural.

'It is very good of you to accommodate me, Madame Dubuis,' said Shirley.

'Not at all, Madame Brookes,' responded Marie-Thérèse with a gracious inclination of her head. 'Where else would the mother of our Marie-Anne stay when she comes to the Sarthe?'

Shirley was immediately suspicious. Surely that sounded as if Marie-Thérèse thought this was simply a visit, of short duration perhaps? Did she really believe Shirley would go tamely away without the daughter she had mourned for six long years?

'The countryside is very pretty around here.'

'Yes. Marie-Anne should show you the gardens while Jean-Yves helps me to clear the table.'

Jean-Yves's face was a picture! Never in all the years of their marriage had Thérèse suggested such a thing. He opened his mouth to say as much and received such a dig of her nails in his arm. Her eyes sent him dagger looks above the smile fixed on her lips. He closed his mouth and prepared to assist her.

'Come on, Mummy,' said Marie-Anne happily.

With linked arms the two crossed the courtyard to reach the herb garden. Shirley was given little time to linger and drink in the fragrances in the old milking parlour. Once seated on the wooden bench, she duly admired and exclaimed as she listened to her daughter describe life on the farm, how 'we' do this and 'we' do the other. Her heart sank. Marion seemed so much a part of all this alien existence, and so happy.

On their return to the kitchen Marie-Thérèse would have led the way into the salon for coffee and cognac, but Marie-Anne laughingly stopped her. 'Don't be silly, Thérèse. You know we only use the salon for visitors. My mother is part of the family. We'll stay in the kitchen, as usual. It's so cosy. Jean-Yves is there any Calvados left? You must really try some in your coffee, Mummy. It's apple brandy and very good.'

Mesmerised, Shirley watched and listened. She tried to follow the rapid accented French and treasured every word Marion uttered. She couldn't take her eyes from this daughter of hers, so happy, so vital — so alive! She accepted in her black coffee a slug of the brandy from a curious bottle fashioned like a small tree branch. Over the delicate coffee cups, carried through from the salon display cupboard in the visitor's honour, they all managed to relax a little. Thérèse looked at the clock. 'Marie-Anne you will need to bring in the laundry before it takes up the dew. Jean-Yves will help you.'

Marie-Anne rose without demur. Accompanied by a speechless Jean-Yves she left the kitchen. The two older women faced each other across the table.

'I regret, Madame Brookes, I cannot speak your tongue,' said Marie-Thérèse slowly and carefully.

Shirley nodded.

'I think it would be wise for us to discuss this strange situation together, alone, without the little one.'

Again Shirley nodded.

'I shall send her to the village for messages in the morning and we can sort things out.'

'Yes, Madame Dubuis. I think that would be a very good idea.' So, thought Shirley, battle lines are to be drawn in private. I'm ready to take on the whole French nation, if necessary. So look out, Madame! She smiled and nodded to Thérèse as they heard voices outside. 'But where is the little boy?'

'Claude? The little rascal! It's surprising he's not around, but he doesn't live here any more. He's with his father at Les Rosiers.'

Shirley was still trying to make sense of this remark when the other two entered the kitchen. Perhaps she had misunderstood what Marie-Thérèse had said. The Sarthois accent was strange to her ears and at the best of times her French was somewhat limited, of the schoolgirl variety.

Soon afterwards it was time for bed. Shirley lay between sweetly scented sheets and tried to sort out all she'd heard. Little Claude looked about the right age, but he could have been younger. Did Marion have two children here in France? And if so where was the other. Why did Claude live with his father and no longer with Marion, his mother?

She had found some answers in Maréchal, but also more questions.

Her exhausting day took its toll. The relaxing, sleep-promoting properties of the lavender did their work and she drifted off to spend a dreamless, restorative night between the soft linen sheets her daughter had washed and ironed so often.

*　*　*

Next morning, with Marie-Anne safely out of the way running messages in the village, Thérèse placed a folded sheet of paper on the table in front of Shirley. 'Please, Madame Brookes, read what I have asked the Father to write out in English for you. Record your questions and when you have finished I will answer everything I can.'

As Shirley unfolded the paper, Thérèse busied herself with her usual chores. The silence was only broken by the sounds of her work as Shirley read the account related to the priest of how her Marion had come to La Lavendière, her illness, and the unceasing care given to her. As she read of the loss of the child a frown of puzzlement crossed her face, a tear was gently wiped from her eye. She learned of the nation-wide quest for Marion's identity, and Grandmère's fears for the safety of the vulnerable young stranger. Marion's life, with these good people, her plans for a cottage industry and her eventual engagement to Maurice were revealed. She was indignant at the viciousness of Madame La Salle, and sympathetic with Marie-Anne's efforts to find her true identity and the fears she had to overcome to do so. At last, she laid the paper down and accepted a bowl of coffee from Thérèse who seated herself. Shirley sighed, 'I have to thank you, Madame, for all your care of my child,' she said sincerely. 'It is apparent to me that without it she would have died. Tell me, if the first baby died, then when was Claude born?'

'We could do nothing to save Marie-Anne's baby, Madame Brookes. It caused us much grief that he died; the tiny boy was so perfect.' At the memory, Thérèse dabbed her eyes with the corner of her apron. 'You ask about Claude. He is a sweet child, and Marie-Anne adores him.'

'I've seen that. When was he born? Who is his father?'

'He is the child of Marie-Anne's fiancé, Maurice Boucher. His wife died just after giving birth.'

Shirley winced as she realised there was no child for Marion to take home with them.

'Marie-Anne already treats him as her son. Claude is so excited that the marriage will make her his proper mother.'

'But they cannot marry, Madame! Marion already has a husband and child in England.'

Marie-Thérèse was dumbfounded. 'How can this be, Madame Brookes? Why did he not look for her?'

Once again the story had to be haltingly told. Marie-Thérèse shook her head. 'What a muddle! If only someone had recognised her picture.'

'It's no good saying 'if only'. I learned that long ago.'

'Yes, indeed,' said Thérèse. 'This husband — and a child, you say?'

'Yes. Felicity — she brought them such joy — is nine now, though we still call her by her baby name, Fliss. She was just three years old when Marion and Mark came to France. She has a picture of her mother beside her bed and we speak of her often. I think most of her memories are implanted, rather than actual. Mark always kept his love for Marion fresh, but at last he had come to terms with the fact that she was gone. I saw the change in him when he came back from Solesmes. It was as though he had made peace with his heart and conscience — he always blamed himself, you know. He was driving. He, too, has made plans to remarry — a lovely girl. If it weren't for her we wouldn't have found Marion again. I can never repay her.'

'This changes everything. I confess I had hoped that, once Marie-Anne had been re-united with her family, she would marry Maurice and remain among us. With you and any brothers and sisters visiting often, of course, Madame Brookes,' Thérèse insisted. 'But now!' She heaved a sigh. 'Does Marie-Anne remember her husband?'

'Apparently not. I can't understand it. They were devoted. She remembers everything up to the time just before she met him, just after she'd left college. Then — nothing until she woke up here.'

'Strange. She doesn't even recognise his picture?'

'I haven't shown it to her yet.'

'Well that must be our next step. Here she comes!'

'You two look very solemn,' said Marie-Anne gaily as she dumped two heavy shopping bags on the table. 'Poof! It's hot out there.'

'Why don't you take your mother into the garden with a cold drink while I sort these things? I'm sure you have plenty to talk about.'

'Good idea. I shall fix us some of Thérèse's famous home-made lemonade, Mummy.'

While Marie-Anne organised the ice-cold drinks, Shirley slipped upstairs to her room to retrieve the bundle of photographs she had brought. Carefully, Marie-Anne balanced the brimming glasses as she led the way to the garden seat in the shelter of the lichen-covered wall, and sat close to her mother.

'Did you sleep well, darling? Have you remembered anything more?'

'I slept like a baby. And no, I don't think I've remembered anything new. My head feels lovely and light. Up till yesterday I was always conscious of a sort of heaviness in my skull, as though the unknown was a weight pressing on my brain, trying to come in.' She laughed, 'My goodness, how dramatic that sounds. I've never put it into words before, but it was just like that.'

'I've got some more photographs for you to see, if you'd like to?'

'Yes, please,' answered Marie-Anne eagerly. She examined each picture as Shirley slowly handed them to her, and exclaimed over remembered houses, cars, pets and friends. Then came the photograph Patricia had given to Father Benedict. Here she paused frowning. 'That's me now,' she exclaimed.

'Not quite now,' corrected Shirley, evenly. 'It was taken not long before your accident.'

'Who's the man?' queried Marie-Anne. She rubbed her head. There was a dull throb under her skull.

'Don't you recognise him?'

Marie-Anne shook her head. 'Should I?' she said, frowning. She looked more closely. 'There is something, but . . . have you got any more of him?' Shirley passed over two or three more of Mark, sometimes alone, sometimes with Marion. 'I feel as if I should know him. There's something there, but I can't put my finger on it.'

She sighed in exasperation. 'It's no good. You'll have to tell me. Who is he?'

'Mark. Your husband,' said Shirley quietly.

Marie-Anne felt a leap of her heart. A door in her mind partly opened, then, quite firmly, she felt it close again. 'My husband? I had a husband? Did he die in the accident when I was hurt?'

'No.'

'Then . . . he's still alive?' Marie-Anne's eyes were huge in her suddenly white face.

'Yes. And loves you dearly still, even though he believes you to be dead.'

'Where is he? You mean he doesn't want to know you've found me?'

'No! No! He would, he will, want to know — very much. So much that, until I could be sure it was really you, I haven't dared to raise what might prove to be false hopes. I don't think he could cope with losing you twice.' Once again the story of the accident and Mark's subsequent actions was related to a new audience. Marie-Anne listened in silence.

'And all this time he grieved for me?'

'Yes, sincerely. It's only in the last year he's tried to build a new life.'

'You know I'm engaged to be married?'

'Yes. Madame Dubuis told me.'

'Well I can't now. Can I?'

'Not without first getting a divorce. Is that what you want? Have you no memory of Mark?'

Marie-Anne shook her head. She looked down at the photograph in her hand and sighed. 'There was a moment when I heard his name, but then — nothing. It's such a mess. I suppose I shall have to meet him before we can decide what's to be done. How can I live with a man I don't know? I've known Maurice for years. He is so loveable, solid and dependable. I was really looking forward to being Madame Boucher. Then there's my little Claude. He so wants me for his new mother.'

Shirley handed her a photograph of herself with a laughing little girl leaning against her, arms wrapped round her waist.

'I haven't seen that one before. Don't we look happy? When was it taken? I must be about seven or eight there.'

'It was taken last summer,' said Shirley quietly.

'Last summer?' Marie-Anne frowned. 'But . . .'

'That's Felicity. Your daughter.'

For long moments Marie-Anne was silent. Then the tears came; painful tears as she gently stroked the picture of her little girl. The child she had subconsciously longed for and yet whose face, even now, she couldn't recognise!

'Why?' She sobbed. 'Why don't I know her? My own child! I've missed her. Ask Thérèse. I've always felt there was something lacking. My body remembered the weight of a child on my heart, the feel of suckling a baby. I did feed her myself, didn't I? After I learned about the lost baby I thought that he was why I felt that way, but I never saw him, never even held him, so how could that be? Now I know it wasn't him, but this little love. She looks so happy. Has she missed me?'

'It was six years ago, Marion. She was only three when it happened. At first she asked when you were coming home, but children are so resilient and adaptable. She has a picture of you by her bed. She kisses you 'goodnight', and she's always demanding stories of 'when Mummy was a little girl'. I'm sure when you meet her it will all come back to you.'

'I hope so. How could I forget my own child?'

★ ★ ★

That evening Shirley telephoned Patricia from the privacy of the hall. Marie-Thérèse and Jean-Yves, who didn't understand English, were in the kitchen. Marie-Anne had gone to Les Rosiers.

'Patricia? Can you hear me all right? . . . Yes and No. That is she's remembered me and it was marvellous, but she has no recollection of Mark . . . or Fliss! . . . I know. That's upsetting her even more than not remembering Mark. I've been thinking. She didn't really remember me until we met. She just thought the woman in her dream must be her mother. Do you know the Shaws? . . . Yes, that's right. He's a Professor or something . . . No. Not Canadian. They're American. He's doing some work in London.

'For a long time Mark's London home was empty. He couldn't bear to go near it. Then he rented it out to them, fully furnished. I thought if I could take Marion there, maybe she'd remember. All the furniture they chose together is still there and the pictures, some of her own work, knick-knacks, bits and pieces, all the sort of things which make up daily life . . . Yes. I know it's a long shot, but we must try everything . . .

'Could you possibly be an angel and contact them for me. If they were willing we could go there, just to wander round and see if it would jog her memory. The trouble is I haven't quite worked out the logistics of it all . . .

'You what? . . . No. We couldn't. You've done enough . . . Yes, I realise it would solve my problems, but I'm not sure I should let you . . . Well, yes. If you put it that way. I suppose this suspense is just as bad for you . . . No. I'll phone you again tomorrow and see how you've got on.

'How's Fliss? . . . Give her my love. I feel

so mean not telling her what's happened, but I think it would be traumatic for her if she realised her mother didn't recognise or remember her. She might not understand . . . All right. Till tomorrow then. Goodnight.'

★ ★ ★

At Les Rosiers Maurice gazed at Marie-Anne in despair. On arrival she had gone straight into his arms. 'Hold me, Maurice. Hold me tight.'

He sensed the urgency in her voice, and felt the death-grip of her arms. 'What's wrong, ma mie? What is distressing you?'

'My mother is here.'

'What? You mean you've found your people? After all this time? Where have they been? What part do they come from? Are they nice? If not, you don't have to know them. Once we're married you'll have a new family. You won't need them. After all you've been quite happy without them so far, haven't you?'

'Hush, Maurice. It's not that simple. My mother is here. My father is dead. But . . . ' She couldn't go on and gently withdrew herself from his embrace. 'Maurice, I'm English!'

'English? Nonsense! You're as French as I

312

am. What craziness is this? An English woman comes here and you believe her when she tells you this. It's madness.' A sense of unreality crept over him. He wanted to wake up from this nightmare. Marie-Anne obviously believed this story. If she was truly English would she want him to go and live in that cold wet country? 'And your name. Whoever heard of an Englishwoman being called Marie-Anne. I tell you it's as French as I am.'

She smiled. 'But it's not Marie-Anne. That was Thérèse. It's just Marion. I remember when I was ill a woman took my hand and called me over and over. 'Marie', she said 'Marie'. At last it irritated me so much I found the strength to put her right. 'Marion', I said and she just put the two together. So I've been Marie-Anne ever since.'

'Now your so-called mother's here, what happens next? Will she come to the wedding? Does she want to live with us?'

Marie-Anne swallowed. 'Maurice, there can't be a wedding . . . at least not yet, perhaps never.'

'Why? You don't need her permission.'

'No. I know. Apparently I already have a husband . . . and a child, in England.'

The man was stunned. He shook his head.

No! He didn't want to believe he'd heard those words.

'I'm not surprised you look so shocked. I can hardly believe it myself, but I've seen the photographs. Maurice, I don't remember him, or my child,' she said in anguish, her hands twisted together at her breast. 'What kind of a mother am I, to forget my own child?'

His attention had been caught by an earlier fact. 'You don't remember him?'

'No. I look at the photographs and it's just looking at a stranger. They mean nothing to me.'

'Well, is he demanding you go back to him? And where is he? If he loves you, why isn't he here? You can't go and live with a stranger, just because you once married him.'

'I know. I don't know. I don't think he knows I'm still alive. There've been so many questions to ask and answer I'm getting confused with who knows what!'

'I want to meet this woman who claims you. And I want some answers. I have the right, Marie-Anne.'

'I know you do. And I want you to meet her, too. She is my mother, Maurice. I remember her and all my childhood. I remember going to college and studying art. We've been talking all day. I remember where

314

we used to live and all my old friends. It's just when I grew up I can't remember yet. Surely it will come, don't you think?'

'I don't know enough about it. What made you remember her?'

'Her pearls. She nearly always wears them. I used to love the feel of them. I stroked them and then I knew her, really knew her. It was amazing.'

They talked for another hour, but there was nothing new. They went over and over possibilities; it always came back to the fact that Marie-Anne was legally married and somewhere her child was without her mother. Until her memory returned or she obtained a divorce there could be no question of marriage with Maurice or anyone. Painfully he accepted the fact Marie-Anne could never be his wife. Divorce was not recognised in the Catholic Church. Even if he could bring himself to go against everything he had ever known and believed in, there would still be the child. He knew Marie-Anne too well to think she would ever give it up. Presumably the father would feel the same way.

Maurice would go to La Lavendière in the morning, but only to reassure himself this family who had come to claim Marie-Anne would treat her well. He felt he had already known what would happen. As she learned more details of her past he had seen the change in her. It seemed lack of memory had kept her young and untouched, the childlike quality he loved. With knowledge had come a maturity, a sense of responsibility, the realisation her life touched others beyond the confines of the valley she loved. In his mind he had already let her go — only his heart refused to stop loving her.

19

Marion and Shirley stood on the London pavement and looked up at Mark's house. In her hands Shirley held the keys that had been left with the porter at Patricia's apartment block. Shirley and Marion had spent last night in Patricia's flat, let in by the same porter with her spare keys.

'Take your time, darling. There's no rush,' said Shirley quietly.

Marion stood examining the façade. She looked at each window in turn. She wasn't trying to remember, just observing. She had already learned if she tried to force memories her head ached and she achieved nothing. So she stood and looked.

'Give me the key, Mummy.'

She put the key in the Yale lock and paused, eyes closed, one palm flat on the white-painted wood. 'There's a door on the left, which goes into the sitting room.'

She waited, relaxed. 'Behind that is the study . . . and then five steps down to the kitchen.'

She stopped. Her body shook, but she kept the images in her head. 'Behind the kitchen is the scullery ... no! It was made into a conservatory.' She took a deep breath and turned the key.

They stood in the hall. On their left was a door. Marion pushed it open and, like a sleepwalker, wandered round the sitting room beyond. She touched small ornaments, stroked the curtains and trailed her fingers along the back of the settee.

She returned to the hall and looked up the stairs. 'If you go straight on, you'll come to a small bedroom. Next to that there's a bathroom. If you turn to the left at the top of the stairs there used to be a door, but that room was made into an en suite bathroom with a dressing room beyond.' The tears rolled down her cheeks as she spoke. 'I loved this house. It was my refuge. Nothing bad could ever happen here.'

She turned to Shirley. 'I remember the house, Mummy, but that's all. I can't 'see' anybody here. I know that little room was Fliss's bedroom. When I think of her name I see the photo you showed me, but it doesn't mean anything! What's the matter with me? Why can't I remember?'

'Don't worry, darling. Just take your time. I'll stay here. You just wander round and soak it in. Feel your house again. Take your time.'

Marion went through the house. All was as

it used to be, except her studio. Here the strong north light still streamed through the big skylights, but there were low settees, occasional tables, and plants everywhere. It was a sophisticated and relaxing room for entertaining. She stood and gazed up at the clouds floating through the sky above. She wished she could as easily float away from her problems.

She heard the door open behind her, then footsteps, muffled by the thick pile of the carpet, new since her day. Hands gently held her shoulders. She closed her eyes and took a deep breath. Her swelling heart threatened to burst through her rib cage. Her knees felt weak. She took one of the hands at her shoulder and brought it to her nose, snuffling like a hound dog. Then she turned it, felt its texture with her lips, and traced the long sensitive fingers with her own. At last, she cradled the palm against her cheek, caught her breath on a sob and turned. 'Mark! I thought you were dead!'

★   ★   ★

Sometime after, when pulses had returned to normal and they had rejoined an anxious Shirley downstairs, questions and answers flew back and forth. 'What I can't understand

319

is why you didn't remember me . . . and Fliss,' Mark puzzled.

'I don't know,' answered Marion piteously. 'It's not that I don't love you both, heaven knows.'

'I've been asking around and managed to do a bit of reading on the subject,' put in Shirley. 'I wanted to know all about it. I think Marion remembered her childhood, because it caused her no pain. After the accident she couldn't find Mark; when she came to he wasn't there, so she believed him dead and couldn't cope with the fact. Remembering him was too painful; her brain blotted out the memory so she wouldn't have to deal with the loss.'

'That would be right, without Mark I wouldn't have wanted to live. I suppose my bodily ailments weren't life threatening so I survived — physically at least. But Fliss!' she said, sitting on the settee in the safety and comfort of Mark's arms. 'Surely I'd remember my own child?'

'The father comes before the child. If your mind rejected memories of Mark then, logically, Fliss couldn't exist in your memory either. And she wasn't with you in France.'

'That makes sense,' said Mark. 'Look we can't stop here all day. Where are you booked in?'

'We stayed at Patricia's last night,' said Marion.

Shock and consternation held Mark silent. He looked at Shirley.

'Yes. Bless her. My friend Patricia is looking after Fliss while I'm away and insisted we make use of her flat while we're in Town.'

She tried to convey to Mark it had been Patricia's idea and also that Marion knew nothing as yet of his relationship with the other woman. Time enough for that later.

He blinked. 'How kind of her. Shall we go back there then? Do you think it's a good idea?' he quizzed Shirley.

'Where have you been staying?' she countered.

'With Geoffrey Brand. In fact he's going off to Strasbourg for a week so I'll be there on my own from tomorrow.'

'Well, I suggest you come back to Patricia's while we sort things out. Then you can spend the night at Geoffrey's and perhaps tomorrow we'll be ready to go up to Settle.'

As she saw the look, which passed between Marion and Mark she felt the last six years had been a dream. 'Let's not go rushing ahead, but take things slowly. We've got a lot of catching up to do; a lot of explanations; a lot of gaps to fill. We can't pretend the last six years haven't happened. There are too many other people involved.'

'Mummy's right,' Marion thought of Maurice, Claude, Marie-Thérèse and Jean-Yves.

'I know,' said Mark. He thought of Patricia. 'A lot of water has passed under our bridges.'

'Don't talk of water,' Marion shivered. 'It makes me remember that awful river; the time when I couldn't find you. I thought you were dead.'

'Yes, darling. I know. But Shirley told you I was alive. Couldn't you believe her?'

'I wanted to. Logic said it was true, but I couldn't feel it. Whatever way it works my feeling memory wouldn't let me accept that truth, and I went on shutting down my real memory of you and Fliss. That's the only way I can explain it.'

'What changed your mind?'

'Your smell.'

'My what!'

'Your smell. You came up behind me. I had my eyes closed, but I could smell your hands. It was printer's ink, and new paper. It was just you. And then I was back with you. I remembered. It was just like it used to be. But how did you come to be here?'

'That can wait,' said Shirley. 'We have to lock up here and post the key through the letterbox. It's the Shaw's spare. Come on, I'm not sure what time they'll get home.'

★　★　★

Back at Patricia's flat the explanations went on.

'How did you get from the river to the farm, darling?' asked Shirley. 'Everyone I've spoken to said it was impossible you could have walked. Who took you?'

'I have no idea. I remember crawling upwards, away from the water. I think it was rising. The next thing I remember was Thérèse calling me Marie. That niggled me. She went on and on, so eventually I tried to tell her my name was Marion. She heard the Anne bit, tacked it on to Marie and that was that.'

'What I can't understand,' said Mark. 'is why they thought you were French!'

'I've had time to work that one out. At first I was so ill I was barely conscious, but obviously I heard them talking. Then, when I regained consciousness, I was so frightened. I didn't know who I was. I couldn't remember my name and I couldn't understand every-thing they said to me. I could have been on the moon or in darkest Africa. It was terrifying. But all the time I felt as if I should understand. They obviously expected me to and I caught the sense of things, even then.

'You know I'd been doing all the talking on our holiday and I've always had a pretty good ear. Of course, they were speaking French, but with their own accent. And you don't realise you think in English, do you? You just do it. So I kept quiet and tried to figure things out. Gradually I began to make sense of their patois.

'He's so lazy,' she said to Shirley. 'He's perfectly capable, but lets me do all the work. So I'd been practising my French, but this was different. It was all in the regional accent with colloquialisms thrown in for good measure. Anyway, as I said, I began to understand and finally I plucked up the courage to ask Grandmère who I was. Poor darling, she was speechless. She'd waited for me to give her the answers to all the questions my arrival had posed and I asked her who I was! I must say she was marvellous.'

'I don't think I met her, did I,' asked Shirley.

'No. She died three years ago.' Marion's eyes filled with the tears, which came too easily these days. 'I loved her dearly. She was so good to me. One morning she just didn't wake up. I never even said goodbye, and she was only eighty-five.' She bit her lip. The loss of the old woman who had taken her in and shielded her was still a source of distress.

Mark held her close. He hated to see her suffer.

'You see there were only three people in my life whom I trusted, or four, I suppose if you count Maurice, but he came later. When she died it was as though my horizons shrank; my life came in on me.'

'Who's Maurice?' asked Mark.

Shirley and Marion exchanged glances. Marion took Mark's hand in both of hers. 'Maurice is the man I was, hopefully, to have married after the Harvest this year,' she said quietly, looking into his eyes. 'We had to establish an identity for me before it could happen, but everyone was on our side. Father Anselm was handling it. He was confident it could be done in time.'

A stab of jealously shot through Mark. He stiffened, but as he looked up, his eyes found Shirley's. She looked steadily at him. He squeezed Marion's hand. 'It's strange how, even though we were apart, our lives ran parallel. I, too, was going to marry in September.'

Marion's eyes widened. How ridiculous to feel this angry reaction to Mark's news. She gave a shaky laugh. 'My goodness, two people had a lucky escape, because there's no way I could've stayed with Maurice, once I'd recovered my memory. It wouldn't have mattered how long we might've been married. I'd have come to get you back. There could never be anyone but you, my darling.'

Mark's arm tightened round her shoulders. 'Me, too.'

Marion laughed, a proper laugh this time. 'Just as romantic as ever, I see,' she teased. 'You never told me. How did you come to be at the house just at that moment?'

'That's down to your Mum, bless her,' he answered with a smile at Shirley. 'When you'd gone to sleep last night she phoned me and filled me in on what had happened. Thank God I had the whole night to try and take it in. I wanted to rush to you at once, but she persuaded me to do it her way. Now, I'm glad she did.'

'I was sorry to make you wait, but I've watched the way Marion remembers things and I hoped so much the house would do the trick. In the end it was just your smelly hands,' Shirley laughed.

'I'll always be glad you told me not to come first thing. I'd been doing some work at the print shop, trying to make the time go faster, so I was certainly good and smelly. I didn't stop for a shower.'

Marion picked up his hands and buried her nose in them breathing in her favourite aroma. 'If I didn't know it would come back again, I'd tell you never to wash it off. It's one of the things that stayed with me. I told Father Anselm I loved to sniff new books. I felt ridiculous when I said it, but he seemed to understand.'

'What'll happen to this chap, Maurice, now?' asked Mark uninterested in an unknown priest, but very concerned about any other man in Marion's life.

'Thérèse had arranged for Françoise Lepâtre to be housekeeper at Les Rosiers, Maurice's farm. They went to school together,' she explained. 'Françoise is very good with children so she'll take care of Claude.'

'Claude?'

'There's so much to explain,' sighed Marion. 'It'll take for ever to give you all the details.' She told Mark about the little boy she loved so much. 'I shall miss him,' she said simply. 'But, darling, there's something else . . .' she hesitated not quite knowing how Mark would take her revelation. 'I lost our own little boy. Thérèse said he was perfect, but so tiny, he couldn't possibly have survived.' She swallowed the lump in her throat.

Mark felt a new spasm of grief for the lost child he had mourned so long. He held her tightly. 'We'll have another,' he promised. 'Not to take his place — we won't forget him, but a brother for Fliss, maybe several!'

Marion laughed, which was his intention. 'Hey, mister. One at a time, if you please. And what about your fiancée? Is it anyone I know or knew?'

'No. I met Patricia about three years ago. She's divorced from her rotter of a husband. She's a lovely person — of course! Otherwise I wouldn't have wanted to marry her. She loves Fliss, and Shirley, and I'm sorry she must be unhappy now. She's a very generous person . . .'

'All right,' said Marion, a little jealous of the praises her husband heaped on this unknown woman. 'I'll take it as read she's perfect, but she can't have you.' She held his arms more securely around herself.

'You don't understand, darling. We owe her so much. If it hadn't been for Patricia, we wouldn't be here today.'

He explained how Patricia had seen Marion in Solesmes and her part in tracking down his wife's whereabouts. Marion sat silent for a moment as he finished the story.

'She must be someone very special,' she began slowly. 'I'm not sure I could have been so honest. I don't think I could possibly have given you up like that, no matter who might have had a claim on you. Poor Patricia! I'd like to meet her one day and thank her, but I suppose I'm the last person she'd want to see at the moment. Mummy, did you say she's looking after Fliss? Is it the same Patricia?'

'Yes, pet. I didn't want to say anything until Mark had told you about her, so it seemed easier to call her my friend. Which she is! The best friend anyone could have. She brought you back to me.' Shirley sniffed loudly and blew her nose on a tissue. 'I promised myself I wouldn't cry again. All this emotion is exhausting. Anyway, I'm so happy; I've no reason to cry. One thing I would like to know, though, is how the accident happened. Mark, you couldn't talk about it when you came back from France and later there seemed no point in dragging it all up again.'

'Yes, do tell. I only remember the storm. There was a huge light and I saw the Abbey. I was falling, then crawling along. Then — nothing. I woke up in bed. What happened?'

'We were on the road from Sablé in that hired car. The weather was atrocious. The rain was so solid the wipers could barely cope. We came round a corner. There was a crash of thunder right overhead and, at the same time, a flash of lightning, which blinded me. I couldn't see the road straighten and the car went over the verge and bounced down the bank to the river. I must have been thrown out as we crashed. When they found me my legs were under water, but they think the level had risen after the crash.

'I was very groggy when I first came to. By the time I could think straight there were police and firemen all over the place. I kept asking for you, but nobody paid any attention. When I finally got through to them, they'd already started heaving the car out. They found your sandal and bits and pieces from your bag, and the suitcase was still in the boot, but no sign of you. I think I went mad. I know they were holding me down and then I felt a jab in my arm and I woke up in hospital. Apparently I had pneumonia, but that was all, apart from a few cuts and bruises. They were good chaps. All the while I was ill the Inspector kept me informed on what was being done. They dragged part of the river and posted notices.' He tightened his grip on Marion, remembering his frantic despair and total helplessness during those dark days.

'Just as I was pronounced fit enough to travel they asked me to identify a body. Fortunately, when we got to the mortuary, a

330

relative of the poor soul turned up and I was spared. They found a piece of your skirt a few miles downstream caught on a weir so, of course, they were convinced you'd been carried away. No one ever dreamed you might have got out under your own steam. How did you manage it? The river was in spate.'

'I don't think I ever actually went into the water. Remember I'd taken off my seatbelt to reach the map, so there was nothing to hold me in the car. I was probably thrown out before we reached the bottom. Perhaps my skirt tore on the door as it was flung open. When I came to, it was pitch black. The rain was lashing down and I was frozen. There were stabbing pains in my head and I hurt everywhere.

'When I tried to stand up I felt so sick I couldn't do it. It's probably just as well,' she considered. 'I might have fallen into the water. I managed to get to my hands and knees and I tried to open my eyes, but it was too much effort. Anyway there was nothing to see. I called to you, but there was so much noise with the wind and the rain, I thought I'd better just try and get help. Rocks stuck up out of the grass everywhere. They cut my hands and knees as I crawled upwards. At last I got to the top and felt the tarmac. I think I must have passed out again then. I remember lying on the road shivering. I knew I had to get to shelter and help. I got up to my feet somehow — and that's all I remember!'

'How frustrating!' cried Shirley. 'We still don't know how you got to the farm. Could you have walked?'

'Mummy! It's over ten kilometres and uphill a good part of the way. I couldn't possibly have done it. Someone took me there. In a car we think, but who and why we have no idea.'

'Well, I'd just like to say thank you, that's all. He saved your life.'

'Maybe so,' put in Mark. 'but if he could see the state she was in why didn't he take her to the hospital or at least stay and see her safely into the farmhouse? If he'd stayed and explained, we would have known where she came from and found out who she was, even if she couldn't remember. Just to dump her on the doorstep and run away is a bit strange to say the least.'

'That's what Grandmère said. She thought he might have been wanted by the Police or something.'

'Yes. That's a possibility. I suppose we'll never know.'

'At least you're home, darling. That's all I care about,' said Shirley comfortably. 'But why was that old woman so horrid to you?'

'Madame La Salle? Who told you about her?'

'Because Madame Dubuis's English was not good, she got Father Anselm to write down everything that had happened so I could read it. It was an excellent idea and helped me so much. He was very thorough. He mentioned her.'

'She thought I was no better than I should be. She knew about the baby and there was no husband.'

'But where was your wedding ring?'

'I wasn't wearing it that day. My hands and ankles had swollen up with fluid retention, because of the heat and the pregnancy. I didn't want to get to the stage where I'd have to have my ring cut, so I took it off until the swelling went down. Do you remember, darling?'

'Yes, I do. And I have it safe at Ravenscourt. Fortunately it was zipped up in your wash-bag in the case, so we didn't lose it. When we get home I'll put it on again.'

'You know what I'd like?'

'Name it.'

'I'd like us to go to St. Alkelda's. Just you and me, and Mummy and Fliss, and I'd like you to put it on again there, in the same place you did it the first time.'

'I think that's a good idea. We'll do it.'

'Yes. That's a lovely idea, darling and Fliss will be so thrilled. But didn't they see the mark? After all you'd been wearing it for over five years. Rings always leave a mark.'

'They probably did look. But they'd have been looking on the wrong finger. In France, the wedding band goes on the right hand. Any faint mark I might have on my left ring finger would probably be disguised by my sun tan or perhaps bruising that night. Apparently my hands were in a dreadful state.' For a while no one spoke; each contemplated their own version of 'what if?'

Then Marion broke the silence. 'You know I have one big regret about coming home, apart from leaving my dear ones in France I mean.'

'What's that, pet?' asked Shirley with a stabbing unreasonable jealousy of the love Marion so obviously felt for her French family. I must stop this and just be thankful to them, she thought.

'My work with the herbs. I loved the whole thing, picking, drying, mixing. The smell of the old milking parlour just before I sent a batch off to Paris was intoxicating. There's no one to carry it on now,' she said regretfully. 'It was never Thérèse's thing. Her daughter Angélique was supposed to take over from Grandmère, but she died in her teens. When I came along it seemed as if I'd been sent. I know that's how Thérèse felt. And the income was useful to the farm as well. I wonder?'

'What?' said two voices together.

'Nothing! I'm home now and the next thing is to see Fliss.'

'I've been thinking, darling,' said Shirley slowly. 'How would it be if I went home to Ravenscourt tomorrow alone?'

Marion frowned.

'I could explain things to Fliss and it would give Patricia a chance to hear the outcome of her good works without having to face you two. It'd also give you a couple of days on your own. I think that would be the best way to go about this?'

Marion and Mark exchanged looks. Much as she longed to see Fliss, Marion felt her mother was right. She and Mark did need some time alone together. Six years of absence had to be bridged. They would feel their way carefully. It would be too easy to allow jealousies and misunderstandings to spoil their reunion. Each would have expectations of the other. They would need patience and sensitivity to come to terms with all that had happened during their separation. Two days wasn't nearly long enough, but they could make a start.

Mark's thoughts moved along the same lines. Although he felt like a coward, he didn't want to see Patricia at this moment when he was so happy. He wanted to shut out her distress. And there was so much to learn of Marion's life in France. He wanted to know it all; to be able to share it; to recognise names when she referred to them. He felt left out, the French people obviously meant a great deal to her. He'd have to cope with his envy of the time she'd spent with them. He nodded agreement.

'All right, Mummy. I'll go to Geoffrey's with Mark. You go home by yourself. Tell Fliss we love her to pieces and we'll come home as soon as we can. Geoffrey's flat will be more private than an hotel. I'll feed him up. He's lost weight,' she teased.

'That's fine. I'll phone Patricia this evening; go home tomorrow and we'll have a couple of days together with Fliss. I don't want Patricia to feel we've pushed her out now we've got you back, darling. If it hadn't been for her . . . ' Quickly Shirley pushed the dark thoughts away. Now Marion was restored to them, her heart would always be full of thankfulness.

20

Marion leaned over her mother's bowl of pot-pourri, closed her eyes and sniffed with nostalgia. This was such a weird existence. She was thankful to be reunited with Mark and Shirley and it was wonderful to cuddle Fliss close in her arms, but she felt useless. She knew she had to rest and recover from the emotional upheaval of recent weeks. Sometimes her head hurt, especially when she tried too hard to remember gaps in her past, but the Harley Street neurologist Mark had insisted she consult, had given her a clean bill of health.

Although she still suffered from occasional headaches, the shaking up she had received had done her brain no lasting damage. Latterly, after the bruising had healed, her amnesia had almost definitely had an emotional cause. She must take time to recover, but she was so unused to having idle hands, she felt almost guilty. She would have preferred to be as busy as in her former life.

There were times when she felt overwhelmed by homesickness for the big old kitchen and sunny fields of France. What would Marie-Thérèse and Jean-Yves be doing now? Soon it would be Harvest Time again. Maurice and Claude, and the other neighbours would go over to La Lavendière to help. It seemed incredible to think that only twelve short months ago she was totally involved in it all, never dreaming Mark, Fliss and Mummy were here at Ravenscourt.

She sat down in the cushioned armchair by the window, leaned her head back on the rest and willed herself to relax. She breathed slowly and deeply, her eyes closed to the scene around her, with the scent of the lavender close by she could almost be back in France. The tears, which rose too easily these days, slid down from beneath her eyelids. What was the matter with her? She should be overjoyed, and she was. She was grateful for the reunion with her original family, but her heart ached for the touch and sound of her French family who had been so good to her. They were a part of her and she felt torn in two.

Letters were little comfort. She could pour out her feelings on paper, but she had to be careful not to give the impression of unhappiness. She had made that mistake once. The reply from Thérèse had come winging back by return, full of concern and exhorting Marie-Anne to return to those who truly loved her and missed her with all their hearts. Marion had to use all her diplomacy and reassurance to calm her old friend's fears.

Letters were lovely, but brought renewed nostalgia and left out so much detail. As each one arrived Marion saw the picture of Thérèse sitting at the kitchen table. First she would have made sure the table was well scrubbed and dried, and washed her hands. Then, with care bordering on reverence, Thérèse would take from the drawer, pristine sheets of good quality paper, an envelope to match, the bottle of ink, her pen and the old-fashioned rocking blotter. With painstaking precision she would form the copperplate letters taught her by the nuns so long ago. At the end she always signed her full name; like most of her generation and background, Thérèse had enormous respect for learning and paperwork of any kind. Each of her letters was a document of importance, containing news, truths and love, so not to be treated casually. She could no more sign a letter simply with her Christian name than she would go bareheaded to Mass.

Marion smiled at the picture she had conjured, but she knew what pains Thérèse took and how long she must spend of her busy day to reply to all the questions Marion crammed into her own letters. It was all very unsatisfactory. She gave a great sigh of frustration.

'My goodness! Be careful, or all Shirley's pot-pourri will get blown away.' Mark quirked a questioning eyebrow across the room as he came in with his hands full of letters. 'The post has arrived. Will that cure your sighs? Or is it something worse? Can I help?'

Marion opened her eyes, smiled and reached out her hand to draw him nearer. Mark hadn't got off scot-free either. He had told her of the nightmares, which had plagued him ever since the accident. They hadn't gone away after her return, so she'd insisted he see a psychiatrist. In Mark's dream he couldn't find Marion and his hands were covered in blood. When he woke up that's what he remembered. The psychiatrist said it was a guilt manifestation. Although Marion had returned, Mark still felt responsible for the accident. It had taken a few sessions to rid him of these horrors, but at last he was free. They should both be content.

'Here you go.' Mark bent to kiss her and dropped a fat envelope on her lap. 'News from France. That should cheer you up.' He smiled as her eyes shone. 'I thought that would do the trick. I'm off to the village. Do you want anything?'

She shook her head. 'Not really, thank you, but can you wait a minute? Come and sit down. I like to be able to touch you while I'm talking.'

'Budge up then,' Mark came to share the big armchair. 'That's an invitation I can't refuse. What can I do for you?'

'It's just that. An invitation. Don't get me wrong, darling, when you hear what I want. I am so happy to be back with you and Fliss and Mummy again, but I do miss Marie-Thérèse and Jean-Yves.'

'I know. And Maurice and Claude, too, I suppose?'

Mark had no idea how his wry expression gave away his otherwise-concealed resentment of Marion's former fiancé.

She smiled. 'You're not going to catch me out that way. You know I miss my little Claude very much, and I miss Maurice as I would any friend far away, so there. But I fret for news of Thérèse, because I know how hard they work and they're not getting any younger. They must miss my help, little though that was.

'I wondered; do you think Mummy would mind if we invited them to come for Christmas? I'm not even sure if they will. I don't know if they've ever left the Sarthe, but would you mind? I know it's the first

Christmas we're together again, but I really want to see them and there's no way I'm going to leave you now to pay them a visit.'

Her forehead was creased with frowns. Mark smoothed them away with his thumb and leaned forward to kiss the top of her head. 'I think that's a brilliant idea. Let's put it to Shirley right away.'

'Of course they must come, if they will,' said Shirley. 'Write today and invite them, darling. I expect they'll have lots of arrangements to make. You can't just go and leave a farm like an ordinary house, can you?'

★　★　★

She repressed the twinge of jealousy, which had twisted her heart when she realised her beloved daughter wanted to share their first reunited Christmas with 'the opposition'. It was stupid and unworthy, she knew, but she couldn't rid herself of the deep-rooted feeling these French people were a challenge to her position in Marion's life. In vain she reminded herself how grateful she should be: without the Dubuis family, Marion might have died. They had nursed her, cared for her and kept her safe, but now they threatened Shirley's happiness.

She didn't really believe Marion would go

back to them. She'd never leave Mark and Fliss again, but just the fact Marion could, if she wanted to, gave Shirley a feeling of insecurity, which was unusual for her. She pushed the thought from her mind and made coffee.

★ ★ ★

Fliss was at school. Her status had shot up overnight when she told her friends how her Mummy had been found in a foreign country. It hadn't been easy for the little girl to adjust to a real Mummy of flesh and blood. In her head was the one who existed in the photograph beside her bed and in the stories Nana told. There had been many cuddles, kisses and promises not to go away again. When Marion's artistic talents transformed Fliss's bedroom into a little girl's magical dream world, their new relationship took a further step forward.

Best of all, from Marion's point of view, was the interest Fliss had in all things to do with the farm and Marion's French life. She could tell her daughter stories by the hour, of how things were done in that other country, the farm, the animals and the people, but most of all Claude. Fliss needed plenty of reassurance that she came first with Marion, but she was nonetheless fascinated to hear all about the small French boy. When she heard of the clogs with mice dancing on them she became very thoughtful. 'But I had them first, didn't I, Mummy? On my cot when I was little?'

With a smile, Marion reassured her and, on seeing her expression, an idea was born.

★ ★ ★

'Hey! I've got a letter from France as well,' said Mark.

The other two looked up and they all wondered aloud who could be writing to him. 'One way to find out,' he laughed and slit open the envelope. Quickly he scanned the lines. 'It's from that retired policeman in Sablé. You didn't ever meet him, did you, darling? In fact he says as much here. Apparently in rural France people move in tight circles of their own home, work, friends and acquaintances and it's not really so surprising he never heard of you.'

'But why is he writing to you?'

Mark smiled. A slight flush stained his cheeks.

'When we got home, I wrote to thank him and the others who had been helpful in finding you. I'd built up a relationship with

Grosmenil when the accident happened. He, of all people, knew how desperate I was to find you. When he retired, the new guy wasn't interested in hopeless causes. As far as he was concerned the storm had claimed the life of a foreign tourist. Very sad, but case closed, unless a body was recovered downstream at some future date.'

Marion shivered. She was still reluctant to think about the river and her traumatic experience on its banks.

'There was no way he would make a connection between that and a young French woman who had lost her memory,' went on Mark. 'In between the two happenings he had taken over a whole new division and had, no doubt, many other cases to consider.'

'But why is the old policeman writing to you now? Is anything wrong?' Marion's immediate concern was for the Dubuis family.

'No, not at all. I sent a donation for him to give out as he saw fit, either to the church or a local charity, in gratitude for your return, that's all. He was just acknowledging it and saying how pleased he was you are fit and well.'

'Thank you, darling,' smiled Marion.

'Yes. Well done, Mark,' added Shirley.

Mark felt he had received too much

undeserved praise for a natural action. No gift could ever express his thanks and joy at the return of his wife. He needed to diffuse the situation.

'So! What's your news from France today then?'

Quickly Marion skimmed through the sheets. She would read them again, often, more slowly, treasuring every word. 'They had a good harvest . . . the news of my identity, and all that, has died down now. Other things have happened to interest the village . . . Several people asked after me at the Harvest Home.' She raised her head from the letter, the easy tears in her eyes. 'Isn't that nice? They still like me and remember me.'

'You've only been gone a few weeks, though it seems much longer, because so much has happened. And why shouldn't they still like you?' queried Shirley indignantly.

'They might think I fooled them, because I'm not really French.'

'Rubbish. Go on with your letter.'

'My little Claude is finding it hard to forgive me for abandoning him,' Marion sniffed back a sob. 'I hope he'll understand as he gets older . . . Françoise Lepâtre, she's the girl Thérèse arranged to be housekeeper for Maurice, is doing a great job . . . Claude is fond of her . . . Oh dear! That's not too good.

Her parents are very strict. While Maurice was engaged to me they were happy for her to work for him, but now they are concerned for her good name. I hope they can sort it out. Maurice would never do anything to hurt her, but people gossip so . . . that's about it really. The rest is just about village matters, which would be boring for you, and news of my herbs. I'll re-read it and then reply and ask them for Christmas. I do hope they'll come. It would be so lovely.'

Her eyes were shining as she left the room. Mark went over to Shirley and gave her a hug. 'Don't fret. You are her one and only mother. You haven't lost her. She's got enough love in her heart for everyone.'

'I know,' she fished her handkerchief from her pocket and blew her nose, sniffed, then squared her shoulders. 'I'm just being silly. I feel jealous,' she confessed to Mark.

'Well don't feel too bad about it. It's natural. At least I hope it is, because I feel it, too.'

'You do? But that's silly, Marion adores you.'

'I know. So I'm just as silly as you are, aren't I?'

Shirley smiled and agreed. Mark's admission had made her feel better. She started making plans for the happiest, and most bountiful, Christmas the old house had ever witnessed. She would be on her mettle to show her French visitors the English knew how to feed their loved ones well.

★ ★ ★

It was nearly three weeks later when Marion received the reply she had awaited so eagerly. She hurried to her favourite seat by the window and slit open the envelope.

★ ★ ★

Maréchal, 10 Novembre

Marie-Anne, chérie,

I trust you and your family are well. All moves along here as usual. New gossip has relegated our exciting happenings to the back seat. But, Maurice, in particular, comes regularly for news of you. He told me you wrote him a most moving and affectionate letter, for which he was grateful. I'm sure he'll treasure it always. Claude still misses you. He finds it hard to forgive you for going away, but he will come round as he grows older and has a better understanding of the circumstances.

We have news also. You may remember Jean-Yves's cousin, Alphonse, in Nantes, who

348

died three years ago leaving a widow, Annique, and a son, Thierry? Now it appears the mother is to marry again and go to live in the South. Thierry, who has trained to be a mechanic, doesn't wish to go with them — perhaps he doesn't get on with his stepfather? Although he seems to be a nice enough sort of chap from what we hear. Perhaps the young man feels it's time to spread his wings and leave the nest. Anyway! Thierry has decided to come and live with us. Yes! He has always wanted to farm — he says. Let him get up in the dark on a cold winter's morning to see to the beasts, eh! Marie-Anne? We shall see how it goes. His knowledge of machinery would be useful. We may send him to complete his training at Agricultural College. Time will tell.

Françoise Lepâtre does well at Les Rosiers. Claude is very fond of her, but comes often to speak of you and collect his gingerbread men. No one will ever take the place of his Marie-Anne, but she's a good girl and I hope she'll stay. I am still concerned about her parents. You know how strict and devout they are. Now Maurice is no longer to be married, they might feel she shouldn't live in. That would make it impossible for her to care for Claude. Maurice has to leave the farm early and sometimes go to a sick beast through the night. He wouldn't like to leave Claude in that big house all alone until she arrived for breakfast. We'll see how it goes.

Your invitation has given us much food for thought and discussion. At first I believed it to be impossible, unthinkable even. However, Father Anselm, who sends his regards by the way, said we should think about it seriously. Maurice agreed. So the answer is, yes. If you really mean it, we shall come to you for Christmas. My head whirls just to think about it. Jean-Yves has been to Belgium and Spain in his youth, but I've never been out of France, and never on an aeroplane! You must write me a list of what to pack and what you wish me to bring for you. Can you get good cheese in England? I shall bring you some of our own. And the ham is particularly fine this year. You remember big Clothilde? She made excellent bacon. I gave some to Maurice, as he is to help supervise Thierry while we are away. I shan't forget to bring you the sabots for Fliss. The foot pattern you sent will be quite sufficient for Monsieur Blanche to pick out her size. Do you mean to decorate them like Claude's?

Merciful Heavens! Here is Jean-Yves back already. He sends his love. I, too, my dearest Marie-Anne.

Marie-Thérèse Dubuis.

★ ★ ★

Marion chuckled, folded the sheets in her hand and went in search of Mark and Shirley. They were together in the kitchen. 'Do listen. I must read you Thérèse's letter. You'll love it. Here goes.'

They listened in silence until she came to the part about her letter to Maurice. Then she looked up at her listeners. 'I felt I owed it to him to explain everything, carefully, on paper. At the time it happened, everything was so confusing, I hardly understood it myself.' Her eyes pleaded for understanding.

'It's all right, darling. You did the right thing, as usual,' Mark smiled.

Marion read on. When she came to the end she smiled at her listeners. 'Isn't that priceless?'

'Wherever does she think we live?' Shirley was put out. 'We don't need her food parcels!'

'Don't be like that, Mummy,' begged Marion. 'Thérèse has never been far from her home. She's nervous. She doesn't know what to expect and she wants to bring me something of home, something she knows I enjoy. Please understand.'

Shirley forced a smile. How it hurt her each time she heard Marion speak of the farm as her home. 'Don't take any notice. I'm just being silly. I'm sure it will be very interesting to compare her cheese with all the lovely cheese we have here. But I don't quite understand; is she bringing this Clothilde person? The one who makes the bacon?'

Marion nearly choked with laughter.

'Clothilde is the bacon. She was one of our pigs, Mummy, and she'll taste delicious, you'll see. I wonder if you're allowed to bring bacon into this country? I'll have to find out and warn Thérèse.'

'I shall look forward to tasting Big Clothilde,' laughed Mark.

Fliss was in a fever of excitement when she heard about the Christmas guests; she only wished they were bringing Claude with them. She plunged into the business of making Christmas decorations and helping Shirley with her preparations. There must be a cake, a pudding and all the other essential goodies to show their visitors the richness of the English cuisine.

21

Before the French guests arrived, Shirley received a parcel from Canada. Quickly she hid the contents — two dolls. One was a Mountie, and one an Eskimo. Shirley knew Fliss would be delighted with them on Christmas morning and would add them to her growing collection. Patricia had not forgotten her promise and had already sent the little girl a cowboy and a Sioux Indian from America.

Shirley settled down in her room to read the latest news from her friend. She would never forget, and could never repay, the sacrifice the younger woman had made so Shirley could be reunited with her daughter. With all her heart, she hoped Patricia would one day find the happiness she so richly deserved.

The younger woman had been doing some advisory work on a period film in America. She had moved on to Canada, doing much the same thing, and fallen in love with Vancouver and its way of life. Her present film was set in Canada and the French Riviera, so there would be more travelling.

She had been invited for a truly traditional French-Canadian Christmas with the family of a member of the filming team called Gilles Belvoir, and she was looking forward to the experience.

Shirley was happy Patricia would not be alone or moping in some hotel during the festivities. For herself, she was on her mettle and prepared to show her visitors just how happy and settled Marion was in her own, real, home.

★ ★ ★

The Christmas visit was a joy, success and revelation all rolled into one. Once Marion realised, not only her mother, but also Thérèse, had felt this tension of competition for her love, she soon put them right. Seated round the kitchen table she carefully and finally explained to the two women how essential they both were to her happiness. Confessions were made, some tears shed and the last constraints disappeared. Before the holiday, Shirley had, with Marion's help, brushed up on her French so she could talk to her guests. Despite his laziness, Mark was quite capable of understanding and holding a conversation. Fliss was the only one who felt left out. Her dismay was comical when she realised her torrent of questions about Claude would go unanswered.

As the end of the visit drew near, Marion's spirits drooped. It was clear to Mark and Shirley that something must be arranged for her to keep in closer touch with the Dubuis.

'How would it be if you and Fliss spent the whole of the summer holidays at the farm?' Mark suggested. 'I usually spend most of my time in London during those months. I could pop over each weekend and I'll make sure I come for at least a fortnight.'

His reward was the joy blazing in Marion's face, the delighted whoop from Fliss and the tear wiped surreptitiously from Thérèse's eye.

'You, too, Madame Shirley, would be most welcome,' said Jean-Yves. 'I should enjoy taking a cup of Calvados coffee with you again.' His eyes twinkled at her from their network of wrinkles, reassuring her of his genuine invitation.

'That would be brilliant, darling,' cried Marion 'and it would mean I could follow up the idea I had, ages ago, when we first came back.'

Everyone looked at her for enlightenment.

'When I first came home, apart from leaving the people I loved, my greatest regret was to leave my work with the herbs and flowers. If we were to spend the whole summer at La Lavendière I could be there for the harvest and organise the drying. I know you haven't got time, Thérèse, and it was never your interest. I wonder if Françoise would be interested? She could keep things going in my absence. It's rather a long time from one summer to the next.'

'You may be able to visit more often than that,' put in Mark. 'The Shaws are returning to the States next year, which means we can have our house back. If we wanted to spend a few weeks there during term time or the holidays, you could drive through the Chunnel quite easily and spend a few days at the farm.'

Marion jumped to her feet and threw her arms around his neck. 'That's the best Christmas present ever. Thank you, thank you.'

Then she had to hug Marie-Thérèse and Jean-Yves. Shirley and Fliss couldn't be left out, so there was a general round of embraces and the rest of the day was filled with plans for the future.

★ ★ ★

Once the Dubuis had returned to Maréchal, Fliss was back at school, and Mark once again immersed in his work, the flat feeling of reaction pervaded Ravenscourt. The weather was dreary, cold and wet with lowering skies and a mean wind that penetrated the thickest clothes and the most tightly-closed windows. Marion thought with longing of the warm sun of France, but the summer seemed far in the future.

Felicity was even more excited about the forthcoming visit. Because of the accident, Mark had never taken his little girl away. Most of her friends spent holidays abroad and returned with tales of sunshine and sand, or skiing and skating among towering peaks glistening with frost and snow. Fliss had listened with envy. Now she could boast of her Mummy's farm and the new French family. Because Marion had told her the Dubuis had, in a sense, adopted her as one of their own, Fliss felt quite justified in accepting a relationship with these new 'cousins'.

★ ★ ★

At the end of term Mark and Marion visited Catteral Hall to talk to Felicity's teachers. They were generally pleased with the comments on her progress. They had always encouraged her to read and to do her homework properly. She was a well-mannered little girl and the staff enjoyed teaching her. But when they arrived at the French teacher's desk, they could hardly contain their laughter at her amazement. French had been one of Felicity's weakest subjects. Recently, it appeared, she had applied herself so well she was top of the class. She had been so mortified that she couldn't gabble away to Thérèse and Jean-Yves she was afraid she would seem stupid to Claude in the holidays. Apart from working really hard in class, she had insisted the family speak in French for at least one hour every day. Her efforts had paid off. The only things that puzzled her teacher were her occasional lapses into the patois of the Sarthe and some unfamiliar colloquialisms. Marion promised to try and take more care in their conversations and to correct her daughter's mistakes. She and Mark congratulated the teacher on her skill and their daughter's progress. Fliss was rewarded with an ice cream on the way home, and her choice of a new book from her favourite Archway shop at the weekend.

★ ★ ★

At the English weather improved so did Marion's spirits. In May she was delighted to hear from France that Maurice and Françoise were to marry. Maurice was a wonderful father and would also be a loving and kind husband to Françoise. Thérèse assured Marion it was not simply a marriage of convenience to silence gossip. It seemed that once Françoise's parents had summoned her home for the sake of her reputation, Maurice had realised just how fond of her he had become. Everyone was happy for the couple and Claude was to have a new Maman. Until the wedding he would stay at La Lavendière with the motherly Thérèse.

Marion received regular reports of the work of the farm. Thierry had settled in satisfactorily. His young presence around the place filled some of the void left by Marion's departure, though his liking for loud pop music was not so well received. When she read of the death of Madame La Salle, Marion said a prayer for the woman's soul, but she could not feel any grief. She could admit the old woman's opposition to her marriage with Maurice had resulted in eventual happiness. It would have been dreadful if Mark had found her married to someone else. But the old woman's unpleasant attitude, her spite, and the unfair treatment of Maurice made it impossible for Marion to regret her demise. It was no use starting along the road of 'what if's?' Father

Anselm would simply say, le bon Dieu had arranged all as it should be. Marion could only agree. If Madame La Salle had been His instrument, who was she to argue?

★ ★ ★

Another doll arrived from Canada for Fliss's birthday. By now both Mark and Marion felt secure enough in their new happiness to want to know how Patricia was getting on. Shirley shared the news she received at regular intervals. The frequency with which the name Gilles Belvoir appeared in Patricia's letters made them all hope that this good friendship may develop, in time, into something deeper. With thankful hearts they all wished for Patricia's happiness.

★ ★ ★

As the time drew closer for their departure for France, Marion bubbled with excitement. She could barely wait to show Mark and Fliss the farm she loved and introduce them to all her friends in the Sarthe. It would be such fun to watch Fliss and Claude get to know each other. There may be some little jealousies at first, but now Claude had a new mother, Marion was confident the two

360

children would enjoy each other's company. Mark had promised to stay for a full month, barring emergencies, and Marion's brain was humming with plans for setting up the aromatherapy business. If Françoise would really like to get involved it could be a happy sideline for her. The necessary frequent visits to La Lavendière would bring Claude more often to the farm and give great delight to Thérèse and Jean-Yves. It could be a satisfactory solution for all concerned.

While Marion talked of her plans to Mark, Fliss listened avidly. She declared her intention of taking over the aromatherapy business herself when she left school. 'Because you'll be too old then, won't you Mummy? You can retire to a non-executive role.'

Mark and Marion listened with mingled amusement, indignation and amazement at her grasp of the correct terminology. When Fliss withdrew every book she could find on the subject from the library they might have begun to worry, but they were well aware of her habit of diving head first into any new subject until the next new fad came along. But, if her interest continued, it would be a joy and privilege for Marion to retrace the lessons Grandmère had given to a troubled young woman who had arrived on the farmhouse doorstep all that time ago.

We do hope that you have enjoyed reading this large print book.

Did you know that all of our titles are available for purchase?

We publish a wide range of high quality large print books including:
Romances, Mysteries, Classics
General Fiction
Non Fiction and Westerns

Special interest titles available in large print are:
The Little Oxford Dictionary
Music Book
Song Book
Hymn Book
Service Book

Also available from us courtesy of Oxford University Press:
Young Readers' Dictionary
(large print edition)
Young Readers' Thesaurus
(large print edition)

For further information or a free brochure, please contact us at:
Ulverscroft Large Print Books Ltd.,
The Green, Bradgate Road, Anstey,
Leicester, LE7 7FU, England.
Tel: (00 44) 0116 236 4325
Fax: (00 44) 0116 234 0205

Other titles published by
The House of Ulverscroft:

THE SCENT OF WATER

Alison Hoblyn

History repeats itself, so they say. Perhaps it has to because no-one listens? Ellie, an artist in her middle age, needs to live her life in a new way after the death of her husband. She enrols on a garden course in Tuscany one spring. Here she begins relationships with fellow students Nerine, an eccentric character in her seventies, and the younger Max. Through the teaching of Salvatore — the owner of an ancient palazzo — who runs the course, Ellie finds that the universal truths, expressed in the Renaissance painting *Primavera* and the philosophy of Marsilo Ficino, are still potently relevant.

HIDDEN RAINBOWS

Maxine Barry

When Persis Canfield-Hope finds her grandmother's diaries dating from 1938, she decides to follow in her footsteps and cross Australia from coast to coast by train. On board, she meets the charming Dane Culver who has a hidden motive in befriending her — involving a fabulous and purloined jewel! Also on board is Rayne Fletcher, an insurance investigator, who is out to nail fraudster Avery McLeod — so falling in love with him was not on the agenda. Unfortunately, however, the real criminal has an agent on board — who is determined that neither Rayne nor Avery will live to see the journey's end . . .

LOOKING GLASS

C. W. Reed

In the north-east town of Margrove, eighteen-year-old Alice Glass is reunited with former schoolmate Elsbeth Hobbs: shy, pretty, and from a privileged social background. Alice is rescued from her life in a small terraced house when she and Elsbeth assist in the wartime evacuation of schoolchildren to the Yorkshire Dales. Here she is caught up in the mystery of foreigner Gus Rielke's nefarious connection with farmer Bob Symmonds. Her admirer, Davy Brown, a labourer on a nearby estate, helps her in her investigation. But it is the truth about Alice's unacknowledged feelings for Elsbeth that brings about the most startling consequences . . .

RED FOR DANGER

Heather Graves

Leaving behind a career in an American soap opera, Foxie Marlowe returns to Melbourne to comfort her recently widowed mother and take over her father's racing stables. However, she learns that during her father's illness, Daniel Morgan — the son of a family friend and the man with whom she once had an affair — rescued the business. Foxie believes that Daniel has taken advantage and stolen her inheritance, until he convinces her to join him as a business partner. Ignoring her lawyer's advice, she invests both her money and emotions in Daniel. But can she really trust him?

EMILY'S WEDDING

Patricia Fawcett

With her wedding date fixed and her mother powering ahead with the preparations, Emily puts aside her niggling doubts about Simon and his refusal to talk about his past. Corinne is making the wedding dress, but she is a woman with problems of her own, not least her troubled relationship with her son Daniel, who hides a terrible secret . . . It is Emily in whom he eventually confides as the two find themselves drawn inexorably together. Pulled in all directions, she is faced with a dilemma — and her wedding day is fast approaching . . .

CINNABAR SUMMER

Danielle Shaw

Rosemary Fielding is delighted when impresario Oliver Duncan suggests turning her novel into a mini-series. However, less delightful is the prospect of meeting Oliver's leading man, the actor Stephen Walker. His rudeness and arrogance cause Rosemary to retaliate, so in an effort to settle their differences, author and actor spend a weekend together in the Norfolk countryside. Rosemary likens their blossoming relationship to the scarlet and black cinnabar moths that abound. But the colours of the cinnabar also herald danger. Increasingly concerned by a predator close to home, are the couple destined to share only one summer together?